Brian McNeill

...In A China Shop

Copyright

Colin Watson, in memoriam

To whom a vast debt of demonic laughter will always be owed
for
Broomsticks Over Flaxborough

Thanks to:

Larry Rone, late of Houston, Texas, for keeping the gear going,
Hugh & Julie Crabtree for a quiet space to get on with it,
Robert Pattison for police and crime advice,
Dinkey the donkey, late of Mount Hooley,
and Jacqueline France.

My friend Brian says that, given the story you're about to read is about me, it really should be me who writes the introduction.

I confess I tried to wriggle out of it—I mean, as if I didn't have enough to do, with the agency and everything—but he's off in the van writing a song somewhere, and you know what he's like when that starts. He gets stuck on a rhyme and ends up driving a hundred miles in the wrong direction. So, in the name of getting the job done...

How did we meet? Just chance, really.

A filthy night in Newcastle-Upon-Tyne, wet and windy. The MG had been playing up—distributor cap—so my old friend Tabitha and I got on a bus. There was this odd-looking chap sitting across from us, dripping all over the seats and wiping his glasses. Once he'd made them marginally less opaque, he started watching me clean my fur.

Very intensely. And with a really puzzled look on his face.

At first I thought he was just weird—lots of strange people about these days—but then I decided he might be worth talking to. Before she went off to flight test her new broomstick, Tabitha agreed.

So I invaded his dreams.

It seemed the easiest way...

Sammy

1

"PRI-VATE-DE-TEC-TIVE. Hmmm..."

Distaste, snobbery and condescension, measured out neatly per syllable. The lingering harrumph at the end was an optional extra.

I smiled sweetly; blue rinse, hatchet face, sixty if she was a day. She was holding her nose at the correct angle for looking down at me—which was also the right angle for looking up from my end, and from the state of her nostrils, heaven help her if she was ever caught in a bush fire. Her name tag told anyone who cared that she was Miss Eliza Dempster, Sales Supervisor, but it said nothing about her girdle being on too tight. It had to be that, or flat feet or corns, I decided—but whatever was giving her grief, she felt obliged to pass it on. She put my application for an instore credit card down on the counter and stepped back in case it gave her rabies.

"Madam's occupation is not, I'm afraid, on our approved list."

There was a pregnant pause, filled by the din of the season of mists and mellow fruitfulness rattling the ancient Victorian windows. Less than a fortnight to Halloween and I had a million things to do. Enough was enough. Carefully, I put the figurine down beside the form.

"Samantha Knox," I said, slowly, letting my smile take on a feral edge. "Miss or Ms, take your pick, I've never been a madam. Twenty-eight years old, no previous convictions. Yes, I'm a private detective. I run my own agency—and as you can see from this form, it probably brings in about six times your salary every month. So what exactly is the problem here?"

Authoritative, firm, take-no-nonsense... I felt quite pleased with all that—until my stomach undercut me with a subterranean rumble.

"There's no need to adopt that tone, young lady."

I pointed at the figurine. "His name's not Tone, it's Juan, it says so on the ticket on his backside, and I don't want to adopt him, I want to *buy* him. With a piece of plastic which I want you to organise for me. Are we clear on that—or don't you understand joiny-up writing?"

She stood there, simmering. A dying breed, the blue rinse battleaxe, but tenacious...

"A pri-vate-de-tec-tive," she began again, "is simply not—"

I leaned across the counter. "Just get-the-man-a-ger."

She marched away stiffly, her feet awkward in their too-tight shoes. Corns, I decided. As soon as she was gone I let seethe subside into sigh. How far could I carry the bluff? And how had I convinced myself this was a good idea in the first place? And most important of all, when was I going to get some lunch? I was two floors above the food hall, the best delicatessen west of London, and I was ready to whimper—venison pâté, taramasalata, hummus, game pie. Game pie! Again, my innards sounded the war cry. I turned my venom on the object of the tussle.

Juan.

Or rather, if the strict orthography of the label was to be followed—*Juan!*

He was a pink porcelain matador, about nine inches high. He was holding a shapeless squidge of pink porcelain clay that masqueraded as a cape, and the strained shape of his pink porcelain smile indicated that he was probably having trouble with his pink porcelain piles. Few objects in my very long life have inspired such intense loathing in me, but I was determined to have him.

Why, I'll explain in due course—but how was much more pressing. Because, I confess it, I'd lied about my income—about my age, too, but that's another matter. (And I'd been a madam, once, come to think of it...) But the monthly take was the biggest fib, for the awkward truth was that S. Knox Investigations was going through a bit of a lean patch. In fact—I could admit it to myself if no one else—the Knox Detective Agency was well and truly broke. The credit card was close to meltdown, the bank manager was sharpening his fangs, and only the most blatant hint of sexual favours, to a besotted and bespotted youth in the local computer shop, was keeping my ailing laptop from the electronic funeral pyre.

Which was why I was applying for this damn card. Outside, to match my mood, the downpour had reached the stage where the street wildlife had to be looking round for Noah. I frowned. Where was the old reprobate these days, anyway? Ages since I'd seen him... The thought drowned in the sight of a sprightly pair of rats, running unnoticed along the far wainscoting. Sprightly and big. Hmm... Not what it used to be, this place, hardly the best recipe for keeping custom, rodents...

But where had the damn woman gone? I had visions of her, feet up in the boiler room, having a quick fag while consigning my application to the furnace. No, she wouldn't dare, would she? But if she did bring the manager with her when she came back...

Yes, that would be my best hope. I walked across to the mirror by the lift and checked myself out.

36-24-36, smoky smile, shoulder-length brown hair with perfect wave in place, blue Ted Baker suit, Kurt Geiger heels, Longchamp shoulder bag... No way of telling that the clothes were all second-hand or that my once expensive knickers were held up with a safety pin. Allure Factor 9.5, I decided; if he was male, he was nailed.

Or maybe not, I thought, catching a passing reflection behind me—if I was such hot stuff, why had these two skinny Blues Brothers clones ignored me? I turned, watched them march away in step, briefcases in hand. No loss, I decided; skinny and sinister with it—shades indoors on an October afternoon, indeed...

Of course, I reflected, turning back to the mirror to apply lipstick, it could have been different if my charge, Miss Elizabeth Martin, had been here as promised. Where was she? This was the second time today she'd stood me up, we'd been supposed to meet for coffee this morning. Not surprising it had happened again, though—she was going through this secretive *I-Have-Business-Elsewhere-That-Concerns-The-Planet* stage, which meant she was always late. It was all tied up with some new best pal. She'd change again soon enough, I was sure—but in the meantime she was driving me and everyone else around her bats. And today it was doubly annoying, because if she'd arrived as promised we'd undoubtedly have charmed old Blue Rinse Betty. We might even have got a discount... Once again I eyed the china statuette.

Thirty-five smackers. The Longchamp bag held an almost empty bottle of Je Reviens and a Gucci purse containing exactly eighty-five pence... Once again, the game pie wafted.

Even just a sliver...

I summoned iron resolve, banished all thoughts of money and grub, and lifted the figurine. It was fitting he was a Juan— I'd known a few Juans in my time and they'd all been trouble. I turned and re-entered the prison from which he was about to be liberated.

The holy of holies between hairdressing and household appliances, the crystal cave where the Doulton could be as Royal as it liked, where the Derby wore its Crown with total impunity.

The china boutique of Turl & Turl's department store.

A mezzanine mausoleum of aircraft hangar proportions, filled, By Appointment To Her Majesty, with Crocks Of Distinction.

You know the kind of stuff; the two hundred piece dinner service the government brings out for the diplomatic bean feast, the pint pot and decanter set every household in the land has to buy or be given at least once, on the just-in-case principle. (I mean, what if one of the Royals is passing at the cocktail hour? You could hardly dole out a belt of gin in a tooth mug, could you?) Impressed despite myself, I measured as I sauntered; four aisles, each about two cricket pitches long, groaning with Sauce Boats Of State and Tumblers Of The Gods—along with tea cups, coffee cups, breakfast cups, saucers, side plates, dinner plates, wine glasses, beer steins, cruets, milk jugs, sugar bowls (with and without lids) and terracotta wine coolers. The word overkill sprang to mind—or should that be *overkiln?* I smiled, pleased with the joke, feeble though it was—and in the next aisle a buxom tweed-coated matron saw me and pursed her lips in disapproval. Such impropriety! Among the Balloon-Sized Brandy Snifters! Beside the His 'n' Hers Mediaeval Mead Goblets! Another figure appeared from behind her, rake-thin and even more lugubrious. She adjusted her Coke-bottle-lensed glasses and let her mouth echo the sentiment. I paused, bemused.

Synchronised scowling—the next Olympic sport?

As their disapproval swept off towards the elevators I turned back and surveyed the ceramic desert.

How much was it all worth? Forty grand an aisle? Fifty? I walked across to a soup tureen the size of a small jacuzzi and inspected the price tag. Eight hundred quid! Eight of the large folding before you even got to the Brown Windsor! As my innards rumbled again in protest, my eyes found the display's centrepiece, a massive red and black Toby jug, five feet wide and the same again in height, perched on a white marble plinth. Its self-satisfied grin said *don't worry, love, you'll never be able to afford me...* I peered at the thing. There was something vaguely familiar about its smugness, but I couldn't work out what.

But if I was iffy about the actual china, at the end of the first aisle I came to the stuff I really couldn't stand—the attendant ceramic coterie that lined the room's walls, the glistening horde of cringe-inducing 'collectibles'.

The good old days, grim, gaudy and glazed, coming to an inglenook near you...

Naughty nymphs and simpering shepherds, maudlin minstrels serenading merry milkmaids, convivial Cole Porters tinkling on purple pianos, laughing labourers, simpering pierrots, jazz musicians welded to their trumpets and hearty butchers with axe murderer smiles... Hordes of them, positive armies of the buggers! They lived in windmills, Bavarian castles, willow pattern Chinese temples and thatched cottages. And the fun they were having! When the demure damsels weren't clutching their crinolines, they were putting up their parasols. When the Scottish terriers weren't tugging at Edwardian hems or begging for Victorian sweets, they were strangling each other with tartan bows. When Ye Olde Englishe Yeomene weren't doffing the cap to John Bull or leading shire horses past country pubs, they were driving antique racing car musical boxes past bendy lamp posts or cavorting round maypoles which looked like primitive surgical aids. My eyes wandered, punch-drunk, along the array. There wasn't a male figure that didn't look as if it was on dope, there wasn't a female one that didn't need a bonnetectomy. It made you wonder about the nation's sanity.

So who bought this stuff, apart from poor suckers like me? Was there a guild of interior decorators with ulterior motives? I found my scowling matron again, the Tyrolean feather in her tweed hat shaking as her hairy-moled mouth pursed over a major decision. Elvis ashtray or Alvis cigar lighter? A middle class penny pincher, I decided, the type who clipped coupons in the privacy of her own bedroom. So why was she ready to shell out—I gave the price tags a surreptitious peek—over seventy quid? For a bit of tat which would give me neuralgia every time I looked at it? Finally sanity prevailed. I watched her put both horrors down and sweep away, followed by her skinny shadow. They stopped at the Toby jug. The older woman reached up and stroked its glaze with a wet-mouthed admiration which could have been mistaken for lust, and from where I was standing I could have sworn she was actually whispering to the thing.

A medical condition, I decided. Advanced ornamentitis. First diagnosed, Doctor S. Knox. No known cure. Addictive. Symptoms; first flush of fever usually followed by rapid weight loss of the wallet...

But then, I thought, who was I to talk? If it was lingerie...

Suddenly, I was prey to doubt. I walked back over to the shelf where I'd found *Juan!* This particular bunch of gargoyles was called Flamenco Fantasy; a toreador (*Enrique!*) with pelvic dysfunction, a guitar player (*Carlos!*) whose hand was inside the sound hole of his instrument, and a pair of dancers (*Juanitas!*) with hair like ice cream sundaes. Frowning, my eyes came to the bull, called, oddly enough, *Olé!*

Chubby and bucolic, hardly looked as if he could stand up, poor thing, never mind get horny with Juan's cape. I compared the two figures. Should I buy *Olé!* as well? I mean, what use is a matador without a bull? But another seventeen quid... Still, in for a peseta, and it might swing the solution to my problem. If—

A sound interrupted my train of thought. Long, low...

...and animal.

It was surreal. I stared at the china bull. Had *Olé!* really just mooed? And then snorted? And how did they get that authentic farmyard smell? There must be a gizmo, I decided, underneath—either that or I was hallucinating with hunger. As I was about to pick it up and look, the next noise came.

From behind me. A thump.

A loud thump, one I felt as much as heard. Something had come down on the floor, hard. Very hard. I watched the rattle zig-zag along the shelves. With a growing sense of foreboding, I turned.

The body of the animal standing about ten yards away was brown, but his face had a definite greenish tinge. Strange... There was no doubt he was a bull, though—I could tell by the knuckle-duster-sized ring through his nose. But that was where any similarity with *Olé* ended. Why did his horns curve upwards like that? He stamped his hoof again. It occurred to me that he might not like being stared at—and then a camera flash went off—some idiot was taking pictures! One, two, three flashes! In response, the beef took a step forward. His head came down. He stamped again, harder.

A pair of Portmeirion pots teetered. The ensuing crash triggered more yelling. People started to run. His tail lashed out.

A Dartington decanter and half a dozen glasses—*didn't real crystal sound nice when*—

One more pace forward. As the panic grew he snorted again. More flashes! He shook his head in annoyance; Villeroy with the left horn! Boch with the right!

Another pace; Lladro bridesmaids, a Waterford jug!

And another; Art Deco teapots, an Edinburgh Crystal vase!!

And yet another; fake Ming!!!

He began to trot, horns sweeping the shelves—and then a stack of reproduction Sèvres toilet roll holders landed in front of him. His hooves pulverised them. The cloud of dust stopped him. He sneezed, shook his head—and when he looked forward again I remembered I was standing in front of a counter with a red tablecloth.

Red rag.

Bull.

Stopping to wonder if it was an old wives' tale didn't seem sensible. Kurt Geigers off, up on the top—and jump!

By the time he'd reduced the counter to matchwood and rammed into the wall behind, I was hanging from the chandelier. As it swung I watched him turn. I hung on grimly while the fitting spun, giving me a panoramic view of the chaos—people running everywhere, shouting, falling over themselves to get to the stairs. I caught a brief glimpse of a raincoated and hatted figure with a camera, crouched by the stairwell. For a split second I wondered who he was, then self-preservation took over. Was there a safer place? Only one of the high window ledges, but how was I to get up there? From all around I heard screaming, but it was receding down the stairs—and it dawned on me that I was now the china department's sole human presence. Beneath my trapeze act, *Olé's* big brother began to move again.

And this time he meant it. He turned, locked horns with the top shelf of the first aisle.

Up... Tilt... A slow keeling over... A rattling slide...

Shazam!

My jaw dropped. So did at least fifty grand's worth of up-market crockery, with a crash to gladden a waitress's heart. Bellowing his rage, he turned—and now he had enough room for a proper charge.

Kapow!

All the Bohemian crystal—and the tinkling enraged him further. He began dancing over the debris, bucking his heels, rodeo-style. Aisle two! Then left, right, random across the floor, bellowing his rage at the far wall. Horns down! Horns up! Aisle four! Tail going like a helicopter's rotor he speeded up. Aisle three! Display stands disintegrating! Figurines exploding! Shards flying!

The entire room started to shake—and within seconds there wasn't two per cent of Turl & Turl's china department left standing.

And then he stopped. And just stood, turning from side to side. I could have sworn he was looking for something else to smash. The only thing left was the huge Toby on its plinth. Miraculously, he ignored it. Instead, he threw back his head and lowed plaintively—then put his horns down and swept along the floor. I closed my eyes. When I opened them again, I saw one of my precious Kurt Geiger slingbacks dangling from his right horn. His eye couldn't escape it—and it was maddening him all over again. Trumpeting, he stamped, tossed his head. The shoe flew. As it sailed past, the impoverished fashionista in me lunged, trying to grab it.

It was the last straw for the chandelier. With a tearing sound, it gave—and my backside landed unceremoniously on what was left of the counter.

The cloud of plaster dust saved me—the second of invisibility gave me just enough time to slide down behind the remains of the desk top. I could still hear his bellowing. Was he coming? Again the floor shook as he went into his somebody's-for-it-now stamping routine.

No time to lose. I tore off my clothes. There was just enough space to assume The Position.

Upright squat on the balls of the feet, hands as in prayer.

Perfectly still, eyes closed. Concentrate.

The Image came, the Power with it, and then the big shudder.

The Change.

—And I was *cat!*

My senses trebled. Fear-born adrenaline electrified my black fur and shot me off through the wreckage, miaaouwing with fright. Which way was the window ledge? I made it into the shelter of a splintered display stand and paused, whiskers trembling.

He hadn't moved. One of his massive hind hooves was about a yard away. If he kicked out... He gave another bellow—and then came an unmistakable sound.

A shot.

I flinched. *They wouldn't have, surely...*

I heard the bull give a surprised snort, then low again, more plaintively than ever.

The crash was thunderous. My refuge came down around my head, the plywood pinning me, the floor going up and down like a trampoline. Once it had stopped moving, I pushed up with my shoulders and looked. Through the debris, all I could see was brown.

I understood. The beef was no longer on the hoof, it was on its side. But why?

Finally, I saw the dart's purple feathered end sticking out of the beast's shoulder.

Tranquillised...

And then something else came into view.

9

A shoe.

A man's shoe, a scuffed black brogue. Big, a size ten at least...

I only saw it for a second, and then another crash shook the floor. I pushed up through the wood.

Not a human being in sight. The bull was still very much alive, I could see him breathing. The second crash had been the plinth. It lay beside the animal, snapped neatly in two, the Toby jug a few yards away, lying on its side, rocking, still whole. I was impressed—they made 'em tough in Ye Olden Days...

But what now? As I picked my way through the wreckage, the hubbub began to swell—people realising the danger was over. Could I get back to my clothes and stay hidden long enough to change back, become human again? No, I decided. I ducked under the remains of the counter top, let the voices pass. There was a crunching of china as they made their way through the debris to gather round the sleeping bull, the oohs and aahs quickly mounting to a roar of speculation. Good. I waited until the whole crowd was straining over each other's shoulders, then threaded my way carefully round the room's edge, heading for the staircase and a nice anonymous exit—but as I passed the lift, the button pinged. The doors opened.

Libby.

My Libby, Miss Elizabeth Martin. Seventeen years old and dazzling.

And carrying, of all things, a wooden broom. Puzzled, she took a step forward and surveyed the wreckage—and then she looked down and saw me.

"Tiddles! *Tiddles?* What on earth are you doing here?"

I winced. Much though I love her, every time she calls me that I could strangle her. I jumped up into her arms. I was ready to start purring when a loud voice intervened.

"Young lady! Don't you know it's forbidden to bring animals into this establishment?"

Blue Rinse Betty.

Shock, I decided, looking at her ashen face—shock exploiting natural sourness. She stood, radiating indignation—and then the sheer idiocy of what she'd said hit her. It hit everyone else in the place as well. One by one, the crowd turned to stare. As if to underline the irony, the sleeping bull started to snore.

She flushed bright red—and then her eyes lit on something in the debris at her feet. She reached down and picked it up.

The sole surviving ornament in Turl & Turl's china department was a witch, complete with broomstick and black cat.

Laughing mentally, I scrambled up on to Libby's shoulder, just to complete the picture. Betty did a malevolent double-take from the figurine to the two of us.

If only she knew...

A warm feeling reached me. I understood. Libby was feeling sorry for her. A humming sound came from the floor—and then the old battleaxe was staring down at her feet. Before she could speak, a bald middle-aged pin-striped type with humongous RAF-style moustaches arrived. He seemed completely unfazed by all the destruction. After a slow scan of the room—and with a definite pause to measure Libby's curves—he turned to his underling.

"You mentioned a private detective, Miss Dempster."

Her eyes came up. She gave him a smile of ineffable sweetness, a young girl's smile that took years off her. Not knowing her corns had just been cured, he looked puzzled. When that brought no response, he resorted to being managerial.

"It's been a terrible shock, I know, Miss Dempster, but do try to pull yourself together. We must—"

The mad peal of laughter would have stopped a saint in his tracks, never mind a floor walker. Libby and I turned.

A man was standing beside the supine bull. A cadaverously thin man who looked ancient. He was easily six and a half feet tall. His straggly silver hair was tucked under the remains of a pork pie hat, his coat was repaired with electrical tape, and his baggy trousers were held up with green plastic string. As suddenly as it had started, his laughter died. He threw his arms into the air and gestured theatrically at the bull.

"He made a desert!" he shouted. "And called it..."

Again he laughed, an immense joyful cackle. He whirled round, pointing at the destruction. He could hardly get the last word out for mirth.

"...pieces!"

Still laughing uproariously, he plonked himself down on the floor and leaned back against the bull's brown hide. The laughter was so infectious that people began to join in.

Libby started to giggle—and then Battleaxe Betty did as well, doing a little soft shoe shuffle. Within seconds, the whole room was splitting its sides—even the two rats, back from reserving their seats on the Ark, seemed to be having a good guffaw. Only the managerial type managed to resist. I heard his whisper.

"Find this detective woman's card application, Miss Dempster, and bring me the phone number."

Phone number. At the words, I snuggled up against Libby's neck.

And then I started to purr.

No doubt about it, business was looking up.

2

ALL RIGHT, YOU'VE GUESSED it—Libby's a witch.

It's simple enough, really—except it isn't, because Libby doesn't *know* she's a witch.

She knows she's got a black cat, though, and she knows how to treat her right, always has done. Outside, the downpour had become a full forty-days-and-forty-nights job, but I didn't care—Halloween and its responsibilities, the pile of unpaid bills on my desk, even my Kurt Geigers, I just didn't care.

Libby, my Libby, was stroking me under the chin. I sat demurely on the polished wood of the Angel's Arms four ale bar counter, paws together, tail curled round them, letting it happen, remembering.

An August bank holiday, fourteen years ago, the sea front at Bournemouth. I'd come from an encounter with a bit of Manx rough under the pier (all cock and no tail, interesting) and I was taking my post-coital swagger along the beach wall.

And there she was. A serious three-year-old in a silly sun hat, earnestly building sandcastles. Exactly like a hundred other kids.

Except that the wind blew the rest away while hers survived.

As soon as I'd noticed it, the tingling had started. Just good luck? Just wetter sand? By the time I'd watched for ten seconds, I knew it wasn't—it was because little Libby Martin, sandy-bummed and snotty-nosed, her mouth and chin ice lolly orange, her flyaway blonde hair chocolate-fringed, was the answer to my prayers.

She was an Adept.

A human being with the power to control her environment—and the minute she saw me, she put down her bucket and spade and started to chortle with delight. Within seconds she was sitting beside me on the wall, calling me Tiddles and stroking me.

Just like she was doing now. I allowed myself the luxury of a deep purr.

When Libby and her father Mike left the beach that day to come back to Cadisham, they didn't know I was in the boot of

13

their Morris Minor—and they certainly didn't know I'd be part of their lives forever. Since then I've done my job, kept watch over her, kept the right forces near and the wrong ones (never slow to gather, especially at this time of year) well away. All while masquerading as a family pet called (my martyrdom) Tiddles. I've watched her powers grow, helped nurture them and guide them. It's been easy enough, because she's got a lovely nature, and she's never been tempted by skulduggery or revenge—except for Sally Stroud's eleventh birthday party, of course, Johnny Bewick and his air gun, the little terror! I wonder if he still has the warts?

But she's still miles away from the full picture. I've got as far as making her understand she can affect peoples' lives for the better, but that's it. She could cure Johnny's warts easily now, just like she cured old Betty's corns, but how was I to get her to the formalised ritual that would let her begin—

"What the bejasus is that black beast o' Belial doin' sittin' on my best bar top, Elizabeth Martin?"

The brogue was pure Belfast, the tray-laden figure at the door, ridiculously small for such volume. I skipped away along the counter, placed myself out of reach in the tiny arched window at the bar's end (the pub used to be a church, of all things) and regarded the source of the interruption.

Rita McArdle. Some things, it occurred to me, are just too complicated to cure.

"Oh, hi, Mrs McArdle," Libby said, smiling.

Immediately, she began fingering the ornate brass key she'd taken to wearing as a pendant, the one her dad had given her for her birthday along with the new bike. It was a pretty thing, shaped like a sword, and somehow it spoke to me. Why, I had no idea, but it set off my charge's neck nicely—one of these objects which doesn't start as jewellery, but looks dead right when the right person wears it. She kept playing with it. That was usually a sign of nerves.

"Actually, I was looking for Sammy."

Why, I wondered. A problem? Or was it makeup? For weeks now, she'd been dropping hints about the new lip gloss which was fast becoming beyond my means. I could sense excitement, though, and a strong undercurrent of confusion along with it.

With Libby, that cocktail usually meant anxiety wasn't far behind. More serious than lip gloss, perhaps...?

"Do you know when she'll be back?"

"Do I know the Pope's phone number? Do I know who'll win the lottery? Do I know why my husband's a big soft Scotch eejit? You've tried upstairs?"

Libby nodded, still fingering the key. I'd make time tonight, I decided, walk the dog with her. Rita started shovelling hot pies into the glass case on the counter.

"Beethoven's movements are less mysterious than that woman's, my girl. Spawn of the divvle—" She glowered in my direction. "—like your feline friend there. Could you not let it loose in our cellar to do something about the visitors, make the beast earn its keep? It's bad enough havin' one free lodger above without a legion of them below, squeakin' away all hours, damn the dirty things!"

Earn my keep! Free lodger! The cheek of the woman! But despite the unfairness, I went on purring—the smell of those pies might not be up to strokeatherapy standards, but it wasn't far behind. Suddenly Rita softened. She took a fork, broke off a piece of crust, then delved in to find a chunk of filling. She put it on a saucer, blew on it to cool it, came over and laid it at my feet. A peace offering.

"Would you like a lemonade, Elizabeth?"

"No thanks, Mrs McArdle. Sorry about Tiddles on your nice counter."

Why were they so formal with each other, these two? Why wasn't it Libby and Rita? I knew they liked each other. Humans are strange... As they shared a smile I compared the two faces.

Pink-cheeked, blooming and generous; the girl to whom I was bound for a lifetime of care.

Red-haired, green-eyed and ferocious, the heart of gold well hidden; the woman I'd plotted to buy off with a pink china matador.

A man came through the door and joined them—a bear of a man, broken-nosed and cauliflower-eared. As the landlord of the Angels' Arms put his huge paw round his wife's shoulder, his face changed slightly. It might have been a smile.

"Rita thinks Sammy's after my body," he announced in deep Glaswegian.

If it was a joke, nobody was laughing. I looked at George McArdle's ex-boxer's face, ring-battered to inscrutability, and wondered.

Would it have worked, the bribe? Our secret plot, the unexpected birthday present for her figurine collection, the matador she'd always wanted? A month's leeway, that's what George had reckoned it would buy me, six weeks, tops, before she tightened the purse strings to eviction level. And then there was the domestic bliss spinoff for him because she'd be in such a good mood... Finally Libby managed a nervous laugh. Rita's voice cut through it like the crack of doom.

"Your body, is it? If the hussy pays the eight hundred she owes us in back rent, George McArdle, she can have it!"

Damn.

*

Pushing forty down Cadisham's picture postcard High Street an hour later, the taste of the pie filling was still driving me crazy. Eighty-five pence... I traded off hunger and finance and came to the conclusion that if I didn't eat something, I'd go feral. The question was, what to do about it?

Cadisham, you see, has one major disadvantage; the dreaded double yellow line. Invented by the mindless, enforced by the soulless.

Should I chance it? On the fortune favours the bold principle, I decided to. With a grinding of neglected brake pads I pulled in at Otley's takeaway. By the time I emerged again, cheeks bulging with baked monosodium glutamate bliss, a small man with a red nose and a black-and-yellow striped hat was already there.

"Mwnwshhorry!" I shouted through half a Cornish pasty. "Mwwwnnahurry!"

He shook his head. "Just who do you think you are, miss?"

He looked like a leg man. I gave him lots of it as I got back into the car, with a jaunty wave for afters—and then I gunned off, ticket-free, with the wind in my hair and a smile full of minced beef.

Who did I think I was, indeed!

You see, I know exactly who I am—or rather, what I am.

Familiar Class Two, special responsibility, talented Adepts, finding and training of.

Human/cat metamorphosis licence granted.

Age optional.

Profit motive n/a, basic living/operating expenses approved, FPGS Grade 3b.

Angel status reapplication, hundred year review.

That's what the forms say, honest to You Know Who. In triplicate, five centuries ago—I've still got the carbon somewhere. Gabriel's got the top copy in his filing cabinet, and The Headmaster (Jehovah, Our Father, whatever you want to call Him) has the last one, although it's a pound to a penny He has no idea where He's put it. (He's definitely getting worse, something's going to have to be done, soon...)

Anyway, all it means, if you strip away the awful officialese—all the finding and training of gobbledygook—is that I can change between woman and cat, that I'm over five hundred years old but choose to stay twenty-eight, that I'm here to nurture my chosen witch's powers and help her cast spells, and that I'm not allowed to make any real money out of it. FPGS (Familiars, Poltergeists, General Supernaturals) is about as tight as it gets, but if you want to stay with the good guys, that's the price you pay. The rewards are much better on any of the other teams, especially The Bad Lad's, but that's another story.

Oh, and of course, the last line of my CV tells you I was originally a trainee angel. That's what Familiars are, you see, failed angels. I won't get into why I failed, but if I keep my whiskers clean (Yes dear, pat on the head from The Headmaster, pat on the bum from Gabriel) they'll think about letting me back in.

Once a century, they'll think about it.

Big of them, eh?

The only other things you need to know about me are that I'm always hungry, that I eat like a herd of horses and never put on weight, and that my charge, Libby, has no idea about any of this. She knows Sammy Knox, the good looking green-eyed private investigator (not as stunning as she is, but heads do turn, though I say so myself) and she knows Tiddles, the drop dead gorgeous green-eyed black cat. Some day, she's going to have to know they're one and the same, and the how, when and why of that is my biggest problem.

But anyway, as far as heaven's concerned, I've not the slightest intention of going back, not while Gabe's still in charge—although my friends up there (Big Mickey, Rafe, that lot) tell me he's a been more bearable recently. When I got the boot he was going through his Adjutant Of The Armies Of The Lord phase, all Bashing The Bad Lad Wherever We Find Him and a Double Smite On Sundays. Even the Headmaster thought it was a bit ridiculous—I mean, an Archangel in armour? These days? He was forever losing the spanner and having to borrow a thunderbolt from Jove's lot on the next cloud to get his codpiece off. Did nothing for his temper.

But it's always like that with the vain ones, isn't it? The minute the pose gets laughed at it's all lower lip a-trembling and stamp the little foot. I mean, just look at Napoleon—the stories Josephine used to tell me! Forever trying to look statesmanlike—but the minute anybody asked him why his tit was itchy, the toys were out of the pram. She used to say it was because he was a shortarse, inferiority complex and all that, but I don't buy it. Some men, darlings that they are, just have vanity etched into their genes. Along with a pathological desire to give orders.

Which brought me firmly back to the present. I looked at my watch, then gunned the MG (my wonderful black second skin chrome bumper 1967 MG Midget which Gabe keeps trying to replace with a flaming *Lada!*) towards the emporium which had Served Cadisham With Distinction For Over One Hundred And Twenty Years. The posh voice on my answering machine had asked me—ordered me, in fact—to be there at two. Two *prompt*, Ms Knox.

Yes, I was pretty certain I was on my way to meet another Napoleon.

Just taller.

*

I was right. As I stood in front of the desk in Turl & Turl's oak panelled office in my second-best business rig (Karl Lagerfeld clone, Anglican Church Bring & Buy), I knew it. Obviously the secretary (blonde bun, horn rim specs, high heels) was used to it. As she fussed about, arranging a trio of Hobnobs round his coffee cup, I watched Wing Commander (Retd) J.D. Stoneyhurst's back and read the signs.

Hands clasped behind him. Total silence. We'll Fight Them On The Beaches scowl out of the window at the market place below.

Yes, it was The Captain Of Commerce At Bay.

When the secretary left he deigned to turn. He gave me the same unsmiling *you'd do* once over he'd given Libby that morning, which gave me time to appreciate his long skinny nose and watery eyes. Still, maybe he was nice to his mum. When he sat, the enormous whiskers undulated.

"What exactly do you know about Turl & Turl's, Miss Knox?"

In the interests of landing the job I killed the frown. What happened to 'Please sit down?' or 'Fancy a Hobnob?' If I was classy enough to ogle, then I was classy enough for coffee. Rudeness, I hate it! Remedial action would have to be taken to establish the correct pecking order. I walked over to the club armchair in the corner and plonked myself down on the worn leather.

"Founded 1902," I began. "Capitalised on younger son Bertie Turl's profits from the Chinese opium trade. Once a byword for cachet, one of the few provincial stores in England rivalling Liberty or Harrods. Always family owned, which is the cross you've had to bear, because the family's long suit in every generation has been either the nuthouse—late religious conversion a speciality—or the whorehouse. Usually the latter, with all the attendant razzamatazz—which means bookies, showgirls and pub landladies the world over toast you twice a week. The public, on the other hand, thinks you're too posh for the high street—locally they call your stiff upper lip number the Turl Curl—and not quite posh enough for the Sunday supplements."

19

I watched the purple rise in his cheeks and smiled. I was beginning to enjoy this.

"You should have gone public when you had the chance, ten years ago," I went on, "but, oddly enough for an organisation with a long history of in-house boozing, you didn't have the bottle, so now you're all shabby gentility, peeling wallpaper and threadbare carpets. You've got accountants stalking the aisles, two empty warehouses, a bargain basement you don't know how to run, and—I feel I have to share this with you—a rat problem. And you should never have got rid of Ernie."

He sat there, moustaches quivering, the rise of apoplexy temporarily checked. "Who," he said finally, "is Ernie?"

"Your commissionaire. Little fat chap in a big blue greatcoat, gilded lavvy brush epaulettes. Town loved him."

I waited for him to ask what a lavvy brush was. He didn't. I was disappointed. I reached into my bag and brought out my notebook.

"So how did you get in? Marry one? A Turl?"

"And what business is that of yours?"

I shook my head. "Temper, temper. Don't take it out on me, I didn't knacker your knicknacks. In a case like this, everything's my business."

He tried to recover his gravitas. "The infestation problem is being addressed, an exterminator has been hired—and I'll remind you that you, so far, have not. This is a job which calls for the utmost discretion, and frankly, given your attitude—"

I rose, went over to the desk and put both fists down on it. "Listen, Biggles," I said, "I saw what happened down there. You were expecting it, weren't you?"

His pause was barely discernible, but I was right and we both knew it. "How do you deduce that?"

"The only two profitable bits of this dump are the food hall and the china palace. The latter gets flattened and the manager doesn't turn a hair? Nothing left but one Toby jug and you've still got time to check out passing seventeen-year-olds? I was there, remember, I saw you. Now either hire me and start explaining or stop wasting my time. Half a minute."

We were eyeball to eyeball across the desk. A nanosecond

before the deadline, he cracked.

"No publicity. We just want the harassment to stop. Your rates?"

"Two hundred and fifty a day plus expenses. The tall skinny one with the pork pie hat—you know him. He's family, isn't he? A Turl."

"Mister Jonathan. Is there a retainer involved?"

I bought out a pen and wrote on his desk blotter—I knew it would annoy him. When I was done I spun it round. He read, frowning.

"Ted Baker suit, four hundred and twenty-five pounds? Kurt Geiger slingback shoes, three hundred and thirty? Is this some kind of joke?"

"The clothes I was wearing when the animal attacked are ruined. That's what they'll cost to replace."

To replace new, of course... Most of them had come from the posh second-hand stalls in Covent Garden, but I was damned if I was going to tell him that, the way he'd treated me. And then, as he lapsed into silence, worry stabbed at me. Had I blown it? Pushed him too far, with a fat cheque within reach? Brass it out, I decided. I forced even more toughness into my voice.

"Add five hundred for working expenses," I said. "Of course, if you'd rather I sued..."

He held up a hand in defeat.

"Right," I said, reaching for my note pad to hide my relief. "Now talk."

He brought out a key and unlocked his desk drawer. "The animal's name," he said gloomily, "is Calgacus."

I was mystified. Nice ring to it, though—and I hadn't really had *Olé's* big brother down as a Buttercup... Stoneyhurst put a cellophane packet down on the desk. It contained an opened A4 envelope, addressed to *The Manager, If He Can Still Call Himself That, Turl & Turl's*. I teased the contents out by a corner. One sheet. Cut-out newspaper/magazine capitals.

YOUR PLANS CANNOT SUCCEED!
MEND YOUR ESTABLISHMENT'S EVIL WAYS!
NOW!

I turned it over in my hands. Prints? Paper analysis? As I examined it, Ms Horn Rims And High Heels breezed in. Without knocking, I noted. Though she seemed to notice nothing, Stonyhurst made a surreptitious motion telling me to hide the paper. I palmed the sheet into my bag. As she cleared away his cup, I considered grabbing one of the unclaimed Hobnobs—the pasty was wearing off—but I didn't quite have the nerve. Instead I looked down beneath the desk.

And found myself staring at his feet.

Big feet. Size tens, at least.

And beside the black slip-ons he was wearing...

...stood a pair of elegantly scuffed black brogues.

When she was gone the Wing Commander looked up again from the list on the blotter. "Two handbags?" he said, miserably. "Louis Vuitton *and* Moschino?"

I found my cover-all smile. "Put it down to emotional distress," I said, "and while you're at it, I'll need an immediate advance. Part in kind. I want a slice of game pie. Right now."

3

BACK AT THE SCENE of the morning's Armageddon, but this time with a halfway full belly and a cheque in my pocket, I pulled the clipboard I'd filched off the Wingco's shelf out of the carrier bag I'd grabbed from the lingerie department, pasted a professional frown on my face and pushed my way past the crime scene tape.

And then stood, taking it in.

Seen cold, the destruction was even more awesome. The bull was gone. In his place were clusters of coppers wearing white plastic overalls, crunching solemnly through the debris with evidence bags full of (literally) bullshit. They were totally absorbed in their routine, and my clipboard/snotty look combination obviously conveyed the right status. No one seemed inclined to pay any official-looking dogsbody the slightest attention.

Which was fine by Yours Truly, because there was one detail I had to take care of before things went any further.

My clothes; awkward if they were found.

I headed for the remains of the counter under which my metamorphosis had taken place. Good, nothing seemed to have been shifted. Where was my stuff? A pink fragment caught my eye. I lifted it. Poor old *Juan!* Legless and capeless. Where was *Olé?* Gone? Pulverised? I saw the left Kurt Geiger under the remains of a display case, but before I could reach down, an ominous crunching came from behind me.

"To what do we owe the pleasure?"

I kicked the shoe out of sight as I turned. The figure facing me was smaller than the bull, but not by much—and at least the animal hadn't been wearing that sickening nineteen-seventies bathroom shade of avocado green. The sandwich in her hand smelled wonderful, though. My mouth began to water.

"Hello Beth."

I held up the accreditation card the Wingco had given me.

"Ah," Detective Inspector Beth Walmsley intoned, removing a stray prawn from her chin, "public sector and private come together in one thrusting, symbiotic whole. Don't bother telling me how much you don't know, Sammy, I like to save the best lies for the pub, they go down easier on a G&T."

"Symbiotic," I replied. "I'm impressed. New promotion, new wardrobe, new vocabulary." I took a step forward and wiped a smear of mayonnaise from the green lapel. "Now tell me about the stain remover budget."

For a heartbeat we stood, regarding each other with polite suspicion, friends on opposite sides of the professional fence—and then we both smiled.

"Lunch at Angelo's next week," I said, making a quick mental cheque clearance calculation. "Power lunch, even, two classy operators like us—if you'll consent to helping a poor private investigator save some legwork."

We both knew I could get the information anyway. She pretended to consider.

"Power lunch my arse," she said. "Pie and chips at Mavis's on Tuesday." She turned away, scratching her extensive backside. "Animal's very rare—Fortingall Longhorn bull, only a couple in the country. Bit of a genetic oddity. Head and chest turn green when it's angry."

"I noticed."

She ignored me. "It was ferried in to Turl's loading bay in an unmarked lorry, then brought up in the freight elevator—none of which could have happened without inside help."

"Any idea where it came from?"

"Briggs Rare Breeds Farm, ID number tattooed on its ear. Briggs Rare Breeds is owned by one Jonathan Turl, currently helping us with our enquiries, but I doubt if we can hold him, even though he wants us to. Your turn."

No mention of photographers or tranquilliser darts... There was only one thing I could tell her.

"The bull's name is Calgacus."

"Cal *what?*"

Before I could reply, a new voice interjected. "Calgacus. *They made a desert and called it peace.*"

I knew that voice. The modified reprise of the morning's valediction turned me—and within seconds, the combination of aftershave and pheromones was turning me on.

RSPCA Inspector Glenn Barnes. Six and a bit feet of well-muscled male, broad sheepish grin in place beneath curly corn-coloured hair.

And gorgeous—despite being clothed in a sartorially challenging white lab coat. Anyone else wearing it would have looked like a high street chemist's assistant, but he looked like Doctor Rugged the brain surgeon. *Hand me the scalpel, Nurse Moist...* I gave him my coolest smile. I'd been about to hand him considerably more than that not so long ago, all lace-edged and lipsticked trimmings included, the full seduction number, but someone else had got there first. With a two carat ring, the brazen red-haired bitch. However, that's another story. But we hadn't met since, and now he was eyeing me nervously, wondering if he'd been forgiven. He had been—but I had, of course, no intention of telling him so.

"Calgacus," he went on, finally, "was a Scottish chieftain. Reputedly made the quote after the Romans gave his lot a black eye. About 65 AD. Tacitus, Roman History."

I turned to Beth. "And we thought the RSPCA just took care of dogs with diarrhoea, eh?"

"Never wasted, a classical education," she replied, in an ostentatiously neutral voice.

Glenn's grin buckled. He camouflaged it by running a hand through his hair. My nipples responded. Beth noticed, he didn't, the bastard. Without warning, he was all business. He turned, surveying the damage.

"Anything left?"

"One Toby jug," I said, crossing my arms. "Black and red. Five feet high, fat and ugly. And half a plinth."

"Better than no plinth at all," he said, giving me the full dazzle smile.

As his eyes went to his watch, his wrist turned. The ring was still there, dammit!

"I have to go," he said. "I've got hides to set up. Cameras. Gin traps turning up on the Widgely estate—poachers, the unscrupulous kind."

Beth and I watched him pick his way through the debris.

When her voice came, it was clumsy with the attempt to comfort.

"Never mind, Sammy. Some day your plinth will come."

I snorted. Yes, I thought—but unless I did something soon, it'd still be over the wrong bloody plintheth.

*

Insurance?

By six-thirty, after two hours in the car, I'd managed to banish all damp-thighed thoughts of the RSPCA. The weather helped by being decidedly unromantic—the season of mists, in fact, was blowing a gale through the MG, and the fabric roof was leaking mellow fruitfulness at the left windscreen corner. I forced my mind back to the job.

Yes, insurance...

Avoiding the drips, I wriggled out of skirt and blouse in the driver's seat, one eye on Turl & Turl's personnel entrance. Yes, it could be that, I thought, plugging the roof hole with a lipstick-covered tissue I found on the floor—a scam someone imagined would fool the wide boy investigators. Except it wouldn't, because I knew a few of these boys, and they were as deep and hard as they were wide, any day. As I pulled on denims and a polo neck, I contemplated the thought of the Wingco trashing his own store, as per the black brogues. I wouldn't have credited him with so much imagination, but then, still waters... And moustaches conceal multitudes, I never trust a man with a hairy top lip. Had he been the photographer? No, too tall.

Battleaxe Betty appeared. She was wearing a truly terrifying pink and grey tartan rain cape and practically skipping across the car park towards the bus stop. A few gaggles of teenage assistants later, Ms Horn Rims And High Heels emerged. I watched her shoehorn herself into an ancient Fiat Cinquecento. That surprised me—hardly her style, an old Italian rust bucket—but then Turl's were renowned for slavery wages...

So where was the Wingco? The light still burned in his office window. A covert sortie? I toyed with the idea, then decided on patience. Sooner or later he'd have to leave, and tailing would be no problem, not in Cadisham. On foot, there's always a half-

26

timbered gable end to slip behind, and with wheels, well, anyone who could keep their eye on a rear mirror for more than ten seconds, given the kamikaze proclivities of the local pedestrians, was bucking for sainthood, and by definition out of my remit.

But what exactly *was* my remit now, given my current suspicions? Could I still take the job? In answer, the sodden roof repair tissue fell pinkly. The drip began again. Damn. How much would a new hood cost? As I frowned, the office light went out. One finger plugging the hole, I scanned the remaining vehicles in the car park; a superannuated Hillman Avenger, a scuzzy Transit van, a sleek red BMW—and a silver Mercedes with a Hertz sticker. Who might that be?

The question was answered immediately. The two Blues Brothers clones appeared, briefcases in hand, marching in step. In fact, everything they did seemed to be in step. I watched them open doors, get in, sit down and fasten seat belts in perfect sync. It was vaguely comical. Who were they? Some kind of Arts Council line dancing duo? Maybe you could get a grant for stuff like that... As they drove off, their heads swivelled towards the MG. I ducked. By the time I'd straightened up they'd gone. I frowned. Somehow they weren't funny any more.

Just as I was noting their registration in lipstick on my last tissue, Biggles emerged, bowler-hatted and Burberried, rolled-up brolly stabbing the tarmac into submission at six foot intervals. The red BMW, no prizes for guessing. As soon as it was out of the car park, I followed.

High Street, Fiddle Lane, then the back road out into open country. Interesting. I tried to think of any upmarket suburban ghettos out this way and couldn't. He headed south at a steady forty, driving the BMW like a learner, even though the road was all but deserted. Through the gas main repairs at Tetchley, then into Noddlesham, then Barclayhurst, Trench Magna—and then he nearly threw me by diving off up a rutted track to the left, just before Little Simpering. I drove past—if I followed him up there he would notice, and a beautiful relationship would definitely be soured. Fifty yards further on I pulled into a lay-by and got out, in time to see his lights come to a stop in a big copse of silver birches on the crest of a hillock. Through the drizzle I could make out a chimney behind the trees.

Foot, I decided. I opened the MG's boot, reminding myself, for the umpteenth time, to get the lock fixed. Various smells reached up to me; oil, mud, and half a chicken tikka sandwich which had seen better days. I rummaged. Eventually I found what I wanted under my spare petrol can.

The wellies were George's, a couple of sizes too big. On the waste not, want not principle, I'd snaffled them when Rita was throwing them out. I felt in the toes of both of them; good, the rolled-up socks were still there. I pulled them on, then my trusty green Barbour jacket, and began my trudge.

It took me about ten damp minutes to reach the red car. It was parked beside a little honey stone *Winnie The Pooh* cottage. I stopped in the copse and took stock of the scents surrounding me. Apart from damp vegetation and wood smoke, there was dog, cat, donkey, goat and rabbit; someone liked animals. I began a circumnavigation.

I quickly found the source of the smells. None of the inhabitants of the pens seemed alarmed to see me. The golden retrievers wagged their tails, the hutched rabbits kept chomping their vetch, and a white billy goat paid me the tribute of a foot-long erection that looked like a pink dowsing rod. Propped up against the cottage wall was a distinctly skew-whiff henhouse on stilts, with a flock of brown chickens milling round it. Round the next corner, though, things got more interesting.

The Cinquecento. It stood, dripping dismally under a wicker lean-to. Behind it was a lit window.

The billy goat's mood hadn't been far off the mark. Ms Horn Rims And High Heels had doffed the glasses and gone horizontal to become Miss Blonde Vamp. Above her, the Wing Commander's moustaches were having a right old waggle as he proved that one bit of him certainly wasn't retired. His mouth was opening and shutting good-o, but I couldn't tell if he was shouting, singing, or just explaining. But there was no doubt the blonde was getting the, er, thrust of his argument. Did the whiskers tickle her ankles, I wondered, or did the stockings help? Lovely stockings, too—Dior—and the rest of her outfit didn't look exactly cheap, either. The stilettos round his ears were Escada, and the teddy, if I wasn't mistaken, was vintage Janet Reger—very nice indeed. Suddenly, tongue hanging out, he gave a great heave which signalled the end of the proceedings. Her response was as fake an orgasm as I've ever seen, all clutching the sheets and open-mouthed oh-you-brute ecstasy. When he rolled off, her face, hidden from him, reverted to a mixture of boredom and distaste.

And no wonder, I thought, catching my first sight of his size tens. He was still wearing his socks. Men, honestly...

The next bit of the *son et lumière* went exactly to plan—a man's plan, straight out of the Aftermath Of Seduction For Mistresses Handbook, circa 1955. Little-Woman-Who-Has-Serviced-Her-Lord-And-Master smile firmly in place, she fussed round him, helping him dress, rubbing herself up against him while she buttoned his shirt, giggling while she straightened his tie. As soon as he was back to tailor's dummy perfection, she got a perfunctory peck on the cheek—and no smile, the bastard. He checked his watch. When he made for the door, I made myself scarce in the trees.

Within seconds, the BMW had lurched away. I watched it go, then turned back to the cottage. The bedroom light had gone out, but another had come on at the building's other end. I went as close as I dared.

It was all change, now—a khaki t-shirt and faded army fatigue trousers. She was standing in front of an oval mirror, the central point of a wall laden with animal art. Her hair was tied back in a pony tail, and she was taking off her makeup. Without it, she looked ten years younger. Suddenly she laughed. Relief? At being shot of Bomber Command with socks on? No, I realised; it was a response, there was someone else there. I circled away through the bushes, giving the house a wide berth until I found a vantage point which let me view the room's other side. Only when I was sure I couldn't be seen did I raise my head again.

To see the skinny prophet of the morning, minus hat, but with the same manic grin plastered across his features, and a bottle of beer in his hand. Still laughing her head off, the blonde lifted her handbag from a coffee table, opened it, and took out two dark woollen balls.

Socks. Rolled-up socks.

I felt my toes wiggle; just like the ones I was wearing in George's wellies... In my mind, things clicked into place. Well, well... What now?

Still laughing, the old boy got up, went to the window and opened it.

What happened next surprised me so much I nearly put my neck out.

From the shrubbery, a cat sprang up on to the sill.

A black-and-white cat with one eye and a badly torn right ear, his head criss-crossed with evil-looking pink scars. I watched his tail as he jumped down into the room. For a split second I lost sight of him, then he reappeared.

In the old man's lap. Immediately, a bony hand started stroking the thinning fur.

I stood, stunned.

I couldn't believe what I was seeing. No cat hated the human race more—and yet there he was, letting himself be petted to the sound of their laughter.

My friend, my confidant, my helper...

My ex-lover.

The cat other cats called the Fighter Of A Thousand Battles, the cat humans called Scrapper.

I stood, water dripping down my neck. What did it mean?

4

AT EIGHT O'CLOCK the next morning I sat, paws tucked up under me, in my favourite corner of Mike Martin's garden, the triangular suntrap/wind shelter between the new greenhouse and the old stone wall. Through the polythene panes I could see my two favourite people having an argument.

A gentle one as yet, but it had potential... Libby was standing, compost-blackened hands on hips, head cocked to one side, frowning in exasperation. I couldn't hear the words, but I could understand why she was at her wits' end with her father. Mike was scouring out plant pots with a brush, speaking with the kind of patronising smirk on his face which meant that, whatever his daughter was saying, it wasn't being taken seriously. Voices began to rise. I heard the syllable *veg*. Yes, veg, definitely.

Something to do with Mike's new market garden venture? I hoped not. He'd had a hard time of it this last few years—a battle with the bottle, single fatherhood, the accident which had killed his musical career and robbed his right hand of two fingers. His interest in computers had saved him mentally, and the market garden, we all hoped, was going to save him financially. The initial prospects had seemed risky, but lately things had been looking up, and now one of the big supermarket chains had expressed interest, so I was praying—everyone who knew Mike Martin was praying—that there would be no problems.

So was this serious? Spats between father and daughter used to be rare, but there'd been more of them recently, and this one wasn't over yet; the awkward silence between them was still charged. I could feel Libby's frustration through the polythene—witch and Familiar, the cord's tighter than umbilical; within range, every emotion she feels reaches me. But she hadn't been like this yesterday, in the pub... No matter how blissed out I'd been under the old strokeatherapy, I'd have picked it up. Excitement, yes, and confusion, but there had been none of this out-and-out frustration. And what had she wanted to see me about? I still didn't know. Finally, Mike shook his head and headed for

31

the far end of the greenhouse. After another five minutes, I felt my charge begin to calm down.

People who love each other get angrier faster, I decided. It was odd, but then love, generally...

I can't feel it, you see. Lust, yes, by the bucketload—the mere thought of Glenn's body sets my whiskers trembling. And obsession. I looked at Libby through the glass, her face smeared with dirt, her arms black to the elbows. My Libby, as happy with John Innes No 3 as I am with Chanel No 5. I wanted to devour her, just being near her was meat and drink to me.

But love...

Especially the romantic kind—that angst-ridden, awkward-yearning, toe-curling thing, all wild joy when it's right, all wasting away pathos when it's wrong...

No. As far as that's concerned, I'm pure cat. Like the rest of my race I've got gentleness, aggression, joy, sadness, satisfaction and frustration—just not all bundled together in one great unwieldy hairball. Who needed that?

The flinging open of the greenhouse door ended my musings. Libby stomped past me, scowling, fists clenched. Mike followed almost immediately, looking rueful as he wiped his hands on a rag. He sighed, then came across and hunkered down in front of me.

"The two words I do not want to hear for the rest of my life, Puss," he said, earnestly, "are 'animal' and 'liberation'. No, make that three, add 'vegetarian'."

He ruffled my fur. I could smell the earth on his hand; nice...

"I love her, I really do, but when she gets this kind of bee in her bonnet..."

He stopped, sensing a new arrival. When he turned, the scarred black-and-white cat at the wall's far end met his gaze calmly. Mike stood up, then gave me an ironic little bow.

"I'll leave you to it, Tiddles, I know when I'm outnumbered."

Neither of us reacted. Once the greenhouse door had closed, my visitor padded across to within a yard of me. His voice was calm.

"A dark night and a good scent, Changeling."

"And enough moon to see the grass whisper, Fighter Of A

Thousand Battles."

We stroked and licked our way through the formalities, then settled the regulation distance away from each other. Politenesses observed, Scrapper spoke again.

"The signal you left for me, the dead Long Tail, that speaks of urgency."

How best to proceed? He sat upright, began a rhythmic licking at the fur of his left forepaw.

"I need information, old friend. About the lives of two Loud Ones."

"Ah, there are Loud Ones better known to me than to one who is half Loud One herself. How curious," he finished, drily. "Why do you need this information?"

How does one cat explain to another the concept of a job? Of work?

"It concerns the security of my lair," I said.

"Your Loud One lair?"

"Yes."

"A Changeling who lives in a Loud One lair needs the help of a poor cat to protect it from other Loud Ones?" The droll tone came back to his voice. "Again, you surprise me."

"But you will help?"

"If I can."

"These Loud Ones, they are friends to you."

"Loud Ones, friends to the Fighter Of A Thousand Battles? Are you crazed, Changeling?"

I recognised what cats call the avoidance of truth. It was time to cut through his rhetoric.

"Last night, old friend, I found myself looking into a Loud One lair. Two of them were inside, coupling."

"What of it?" he said. "they have the right—"

He paused. The sarcasm which was his bulwark against pain found his voice.

"—no matter what strange rituals they bring to it."

"The female's fur was almost white," I said. "The male had big whiskers."

The rhythm of his licking slowed, but he said nothing. I began to get angry.

"And then I saw a strange thing," I went on. "I saw the famed Fighter Of A Thousand Battles lay his head in the lap of an old Loud One. Like a dog. Like a slave submitting to his master."

Scrapper's head whipped up. His back arched. Hissing, he came towards me, his scars livid.

"My respect for your bravery is all that saves you, Changeling. He is no master and I am no slave. What you saw was the embrace of equals—of warriors! He does more for our kind than you ever have! He is the Cage Destroyer, one of us in all but name!"

A noise came from behind us. Mike had come back out of the greenhouse. Libby, face expressionless, appeared from the house door, carrying two mugs of coffee. Her father stopped, unsure what to say—then tried a peace offering.

"If only they could talk, eh?"

"If they could talk, dad, they'd tell you to be a vegetarian. Like they would if they hadn't been conditioned by years of—"

Mike's temper finally broke. "Enough, Libs! Give it a bloody rest! Save it for your pal Blossom down at the drama group!"

She put the mugs down on the wall and flounced back into the kitchen. Mike stared after her, then closed his eyes in frustration. Absent-mindedly, he reached out a hand. Before I could intercept it, he tried to stroke my companion.

"Ouch! Damn you!"

Scrapper stood his ground, fur puffed out, tail whipping, spitting. Mike waited, puzzled, the blood seeping from his finger. Scrapper jumped up on to the wall, then turned to me.

"Oppose the Cage Destroyer or his daughter, Changeling, and you answer to me."

And then he was gone.

*

His daughter...

What kind of father orchestrates his child's seduction, mock or real, by a man almost his own age? Then sits down with her to have a bottle of beer and a good laugh? As I padded through the long grass between the allotments and the railway tracks, careful

34

to keep myself in cover and upwind, the question nagged at me. And then there was the opposite...

What kind of daughter, knowing her father was in the next room...?

However annoyed they got with each other, I couldn't imagine Mike and Libby ever playing such brazen games. But if—

Damn, the wind! The creak of a weathervane told me it had changed direction. I ducked, eyes on my quarry. Had I been fast enough? He had stopped. He was sniffing the air and looking round. Careless. I chided myself—his defences were never down, no fighter ever won a dozen of his kind of battles, never mind a thousand, without eternal vigilance. I held myself as still as I could.

The only scent was the rosebay willowherb. Would it mask me? I moved sideways, slowly, smelling the ripeness of dug earth, the trails of rat and Brother Reynardine. I waited.

A flutter of pigeon wings from one of the allotment's lofts...

A murmur of Cadisham's distant traffic, the impatient crow of a cockerel...

Was I hidden from him? I poked my head up. Scrapper was nowhere to be seen. The bottom end of Acacia Avenue, across the railway tracks, was the only paved street in sight. The weathervane I'd heard, a rusty iron cockerel, poked up from the convoluted roof of the last house. Was that where he'd gone to ground? I began to slink forward. At the tracks I stopped.

Between the rusted iron rails lay two birds. Two crows. Their bodies had been laid nose to tail, in a rough symmetry simple to read.

A signal. From my quarry.

Stay away.

I turned. I'd have to be smarter, much smarter. As I loped back towards Mike's garden, the cockerel crowed again.

*

Back at the cottage, I put on my Familiar's hat. Libby's unease was troubling, it wasn't like her. Investigation was needed. The question was, which version of me was best suited? Cat or hu-

35

man?

Tiddles first, I decided. Let her tell me her troubles, then when Sammy came up, she'd have more information to go on. I went into the kitchen, padded between Mike's legs, ignored his shout of annoyance and bounded up the stairs to her room.

She was sitting in front of her dressing table mirror, utterly dejected. Why? The vegetarian thing? Unlikely, I knew—it was usually just a lightning rod for her emotions, a hardy perennial that let her cloak whatever anger she was feeling. So what was this...? I miaaouwed a greeting—and when she turned, I saw she'd been crying. I hopped up on to her lap, let her arms enfold me, then began nuzzling her face with mine. She lifted me, held me at eye level, then sat me down on the glass top and gave me a brave smile.

"What would you do, Tiddles?" she whispered.

Father and daughter, both talking to a cat as intermediary because they couldn't talk to each other... Not good. She gestured at the bed. A folded-up letter was lying on it.

"Would you show it to him? I'm just so frightened."

Of what?

Mike's voice came from downstairs. "Libs! Teatime!"

"Not hungry!" She shouted, sulkily.

His voice came again, conciliatory, a let's-make-up-it-wasn't-serious voice. Nothing more guaranteed to infuriate.

"Come on, love, it's just cheese on toast. You've got to eat something!"

She burst into tears, then shooed me away and threw on her hoodie. Still crying, she bounded down the stairs and out of the kitchen door.

Troubled, I listened to her running footsteps until they'd disappeared down the lane.

*

My head full of the day's encounters, I rounded the last corner before the pub.

Libby... Until I knew what was in this mysterious letter, I couldn't take it further. All I knew was that it was serious. Tomorrow I'd make time, get her to talk.

And then there was Scrapper. Where was he? I'd tried everywhere, from the dangerous eyrie which was his lair to all his known bolt holes. No trace. His haunts were unvisited, his lovers jealous and sullen at my questioning, his friends clueless. Why was I surprised? When a world class escapologist decides to vanish, it stands to reason that lesser mortals—even lesser immortals—are going to be left scratching their heads. Weary, I scanned the Angel's Arms.

And geared myself up for the day's final problem.

No lights. My watch said eleven-thirty, which meant George would be in bed. He always was, bless him—as soon as the pub closed, an earthquake couldn't wake him. But Rita was another matter. The woman had *antennae*.

Carefully I opened the side door which led directly up to my rooms. I took off my shoes. Avoidance therapy; if I managed to avoid the squeaky steps, then I'd also avoid volume forty-three of The Conversation About The Rent. If she thought I was alone it didn't matter how late it was—and after the events of the last two days I was taking no chances, even though I was technically employed and theoretically within sight of solvency. I reached the first landing in silence; good. Now if I just could keep off the dodgy top step...

I was so intent on making no noise that I was slow to register the smell of coffee from behind my own front door.

Someone was in my domain.

Gently, I tried the handle; still locked. Nobody had a key. I stood there, putting two and two together. It could only be one person—and that was someone I wasn't anxious to meet, given the events of the last forty-eight hours. I turned, ready to tiptoe back down.

"Knox, come back here. I want to talk to you."

Another woman with a megaphone for a voice. Somewhere below me, a pale light registered; Rita... I sighed, accepting the inevitable—and then, just for badness, I stepped on the squeaky step, put my full weight on it and rocked back and forward for a good ten seconds.

The nightingale cacophony was gorgeous. Write that one off

to the rats, I thought. If I was going to miss my beauty sleep, then Rita McArdle could damn well do the same.

*

"What is it with you and stripping off, Knox?"

"Every girl's got to have a fantasy."

"Oh, yeah? Why is it yours always seems to involve getting your kit off at the scene of a crime?"

When your office space used to be a broom cupboard, someone the size of Beth Walmsley thinks carefully about breathing out. She put her set of skeleton keys—the only thin thing about her—down beside the pile of clothes on my desk. Her huge hand went first to the single Kurt Geiger slingback, then to the knickers on the top of the pile, the ones I'd been wearing during the Calgacus episode. Damn, I thought, I knew this would happen. As she smoothed them out, I found myself wondering, not for the first time, about Beth's fantasies. Did they include me? Was she gay? I forced away the thought and made myself concentrate— the one thing I didn't have to wonder about was Beth Walmsley's intelligence; this wasn't the first time she'd come across traces of my double life. I kept my voice deliberately light.

"All right, guv, I'll come quietly," I said, "it was me in a panto cow's outfit, you guessed it. Actually, I had a change of clothing with me, if you must know—I was on my way to a business meeting." I gestured at the pile. "They must have spilled out of my bag. When it happened. The bull, I mean."

She eyed me thoughtfully, then let her hand wander back to the pile on the desk.

"Interesting word, bull," she said. "Don't think I don't know when I'm hearing it, but we'll let that pass. What we won't let pass is you not telling me you were there, hanging from the bloody chandelier, no less! How did you expect to get away with it? Your clothes are found not twenty feet away from the animal, you're on a dozen eyewitness reports. In addition to which, of course, you're a witness yourself—unless you've got something to do with this nonsense, in which case you're an accessory, and I'm not talking about a matching bloody scarf. So start spilling, quick, otherwise it'll be me getting lunch for you down the cells instead of you getting it for me at Mavis's. First of all, what's this about a Toby jug?"

"It was the only thing that survived whole," I replied. "Huge thing, ugly. Black and red. Has to be at least five feet high."

She regarded me with suspicion. "No item of that description has been found."

I frowned. "Maybe it got it in the rush after the animal went down," I said. "There were enough people milling about."

I didn't believe it myself, but I had nothing else to offer. Beth kept up the basilisk stare for another second or two.

"As one investigator to another," she said, "let me share a few observations with you." She held up the knickers. "Item one. La Perla. Very nice if you don't mind lace scratching your bum, but it's definitely seen better days. Elastic gone, held up with a safety pin." She lifted a dark grey stocking. "Item two. Unattractive hold-up, of the variety occasionally bought in the supermarket and often disparaged by someone in this room as a cheap and nasty thigh nipper. Item three." She lifted the slingback. "Expensive ladies' shoe, a week's wages for a poor copper like me, buckle badly repaired with superglue."

"And your deductions, Sherlock?"

"You're broke. Stony." She gestured at the coffee cup in front of her. "Not even a drop of gin in the place to comfort an ageing plod in the twilight of her years. I've searched."

I believed her. She let the pause get pregnant, then delivered.

"You need help, Sammy? Money?"

She was a good friend. I shook my head.

"Thanks, Beth. As you know, I've got a client. And a brief."

"Indulge a nosy Inspector of Her Majesty's Constabulary. Is your brief the nipping-in-the-bud kind or the bringing-to-justice kind?"

"The former. Not the latter—emphatically not the latter."

She nodded, several times. It reminded me of Calgacus. How would Beth look with horns? Finally, she spoke again.

"A lot of the lads down the station think this one's funny. I'm not one of them, rampant bull—" She gave me the full sarcastic stare. "—not being exactly my line." She jerked a thumb at the pile of clothing. "Came from the RSPCA, this lot. A certain friend of yours recognised them, passed them on. Apologised for not finding the second shoe."

She stood up, lifted her keys from the table and replaced them with a grimy page of Cadisham police stationery.

"This address, tomorrow at two. Oh, and I brought this."

She dropped a folder on the desk. I read the name Jonathan Turl upside down.

"Good night, Sammy."

"Good night, Beth."

*

After she'd gone I sat back in the office chair. Feet up on the desk, I went over the next day's task list.

Ollie Babbage at Mavis's, get him to check Turl's share price...

Libby for a heart-to-heart...

Reglue the damn shoe...

And...

As I stared at the damp patch behind the kitchen tap I realised logic had left me. Two distinct feelings had me in their grip.

Satisfaction—I was pleased he could remember the clothes I wore.

And grumpiness—I was bloody annoyed with myself for being pleased.

5

THE NEXT MORNING'S drive was the kind of fun a girl with a black MG can't get enough of, winding through the pristine Cotswolds countryside like Rupert Bear's Scalextric set. I was tempted to take the top down—there was so much gale getting in through the hood that full-on weather confrontation would have been a relief, and anyway, windswept and interesting suits me. But then the sky started to leak properly, so I went for the other option and pulled my muffler tighter. No long Isadora Duncan floaty jobs for me. (We all know how that one turned out, don't we?) As I negotiated a honeysuckle-lined chicane at sixty, I tried to organise my thoughts.

The exact machinations of Jonathan and his daughter might not be clear yet, but I didn't have to be Einstein to work out that they spelled a good bit of anarchic mischief for Turl & Turl's, and I was content to let the details filter through in their own time. But where did Scrapper fit in? If the commission I'd taken from Stoneyhurst crossed some scheme of his, how would I square it? And were we still on speaking terms? Feline disputes are complicated. Perhaps if I got a mediator... Who, though? Old Rune? Sevastopol Sal? Or maybe—damn!

I slammed on the anchors, then reversed back to the lump of granite which had my destination's name expensively gouged into it. I peered past the stone. A gateway, a gravel drive. Made for roaring up in a sports car, so that's exactly what I did.

And at the top of the rise, I switched off the engine and let the MG coast to a halt while I took it all in.

Briggs Rare Breeds Farm.

Nobody does it better than the English—impressing the peasants, I mean. The French and Germans think they do, but there isn't a formal *Château* or a hilltop *Schloss* anywhere that can match the sheer rightness of the right kind of English country house—and this was definitely the right kind. A two-storey Georgian job, elegant and square, modestly clad in off-the-shoulder russet ivy, its windows wearing their long lintels like stern eyebrows. It was flanked by a brace of stable blocks, each of which could have held ten of my Cadisham abode. In front of the main house stood a sundial—because the sun would obviously respond to orders and come out sooner or later—and a fountain, an Art Nouveau water lily, happily gurgling away just to tell the rain it wasn't needed. And somewhere in the grounds, no doubt, there'd be a ha-ha, and maybe an ice house, and probably a folly...

And in case anyone missed the point—dosh in spades—two horse boxes and a muddy Range Rover were strewn around the the semi-circular drive, to remind passing plebs that only the lower ranks bothered cleaning their automotive toys. The whole thing was set in the kind of pristine paddock which looks like it's trimmed daily with nail scissors.

Not an animal in sight, though. Rare breeds? Wherever they were, it wasn't here—or maybe they were too rare to be left out in the rain. My eyes went back to the ivy. Briefly, I fought the feeling, then succumbed and let my rump twitch in pure feline reaction, tailless or not.

Spiders. Mice. What pouncing there would be...

And then concentration returned. Also in spades. Three million? Four? How had the Turl tearaway got his hands on this? One of the wives? The actress? The Nepalese tantric yoga specialist? The boutique chain owner? And which of the six exes was mother to Ms Horn Rims And High Heels?

Only one way to find out. I turned the key, tore up some more gravel and aimed for the empty spot between the horse boxes before the car in my rear view mirror could nab it. They'd have to park somewhere round the back.

Just as well, really, I thought, sniffing—can't have the neighbourhood's tone being brought down by cop cars at the front door.

Police at the portcullis? Unthinkable, my dear!

*

Beth's shade of the day was a pink shocking enough to stampede Calgacus into the next county. I mentally dubbed it *migraine*, but

I doubt if Jonathan Turl even noticed it. As she droned on in officialese about inexplicable security lapses and repeats of this regrettable incident, he stared dreamily out of the drawing room window with his back to her, coffee cup in hand. Finally, she wound it up.

"...which is why I've asked one of Cadisham's leading security consultants, Ms Knox, to talk to you. She's senior partner in a reputable firm and has co-operated with us in the past."

He whirled round. "Expert in chicken snatchers, is she? Some cheeky bugger raided my coop the other night and got my Tuscaloosa Tartans! All ten of them! Cockerel and nine hens, best eggs I've ever tasted! Think she can get them back, Inspector?"

Beth never missed a beat. "Purloined chickens are not what brought your premises to our attention, Mr Turl, but if you'd care to give Ms Knox the details..."

Before she'd finished, he'd turned back to the window. Beth stepped it up a disapproving gear.

"We recommend you consult her about the farm's arrangements, sir. We *strongly* recommend it."

She managed to imbue the words with a fine mixture of sarcasm and threat as she gave me the eye. I understood, of course. A trade off. Beth gave me quasi-official status, I gave her the benefit of whatever phone tapping, surveillance, B&E and general hooliganism I thought necessary—anything the cops couldn't get away with themselves. Senior partner, indeed... It was all illegal, of course, nudge, nudge, wink, wink—but gift horses being the rarest breed of all, I wasn't about to argue. It wasn't the first time Beth and I had come to this unspoken bargain, and if Cadisham's Finest wanted exactly the same as the Waggling Wingco—no circus—who was little Sammy Knox to argue? Especially if access to all these nice cop computers moved me faster in the direction of my fat department store fee. I tried to shoot Beth a smile of complicity, but the implacable pink turned it into a wince, and I got an eyeful of bureaucratic stone face in return as she gathered up her papers and stalked out.

Which left Jonathan and I cosily to it. I was wondering whether the opening shot should be mine when he twirled in my direction and unleashed the anarchy of his smile.

"Best looking security consultant I've seen all day, Ms Knox. Married, are we?"

Flattery lapped at me. Was I being considered for number seven? Pension age or not, he was still attractive enough, the old devil... I crossed my legs and gave him the coolest smile in my repertoire. He laughed in appreciation, then picked up his hat and clamped it on his head.

"Care to view the bull's bollocks?"

*

Calgacus was a field away, beside yet another block of ever-so-tasteful farm buildings. He was happy today—no trace of green about the face. In fact, he was so happy to see the pair of us that he turned his back and deposited a large steaming turd on the sward, well within olfactory range. Then he stumped off to investigate two of his cud chewing groupies by the far fence. The aforementioned bollocks were, it had to be said, impressive—I'd been too busy to notice them at our previous meeting, but I'd no doubt they possessed the capacity to gladden many a bovine maiden's heart. We leaned on the fence and watched their stately dangle in companionable silence.

"Happy to see him again, are we?"

So I'd been recognised... Interesting.

"Where were you?" I asked.

"In the lift. Very fetching, the way you hung from the chandelier. Nearly took my mind off why I was there. Lovely arse you've got."

The cheeky old bugger, I thought.

"You cheeky old bugger," I said.

We both laughed.

"Seriously, though," I said, "What were you up to? The experience must have scared the animal out of its wits."

His smile never wavered. The eyes—a gorgeous blue, really unusual—bored into me. I felt a definite quickening of the pulse. But when the voice came, it was like granite.

"What, exactly, do you know about me?"

I stood for a moment, getting my concentration back, then let fly. "Born 10.4.1940, Turl Hall, Gloucestershire. Got through four nannies by the age of five, one of whom ended up in the local asylum. A committed Trotskyist by the time you reached prep school, you celebrated your fifteenth birthday by impregnating your first chambermaid, opening the doors of Turl Hall to the dispossessed of Cheltenham and declaring all six hundred acres of the Turl Estates a Workers' Soviet. The ensuing permanent revolution lasted a week, until your parents came home from Monte and the Red Guards discovered the wine cellar. You denounced your father as an effete tool of the establishment and claimed the discovery of the cellar keys was the work of revanchist agent provocateur under gardeners. How am I doing so far?"

The smile's dazzle doubled. "I may have been naïve," he said, "the butler had a grievance. He was after the chambermaid too. But carry on."

"Next, a character-building public school in the Australian outback, where it was a toss up whether it was the two pregnant dinner ladies or your attempts to introduce collective bargaining to the school fee system that got you expelled. Then, three years of Oxford's dreaming spires on a scholarship finagled by your ever-patient old man, countless Penelopes and Prudences in the pudding club, no degree, sent down after being found in flagrante with the female—"

The interruption was wistful. "Vice-chancellor. Right on the money with the title, I can tell you."

I ignored him. "Then London, just in time for the Swinging Sixties. After several years of serious dope smoking you became a disciple of Timothy Leary and began succumbing to the only chink in your armour—" I paused. "—a strange weakness for getting married, usually when well and truly stoned. Half a dozen brides in fifty years, in an eclectic—and may I say, charming—array of ceremonies. Apart from that, you spent a fortune on eyeball-searing psychedelic clothes, failed to learn to play guitar, bass or drums, and got a recording contract. By the time the advance was blown you'd discovered—" I allowed myself a gentle chortle. "—witchcraft. The bunch of Lord's Prayer Backwards gabblers wife number three hooked you up with wouldn't have known a black mass from a black pudding, but they had no prob-

45

lem spotting an aristocratic meal ticket—or pandering to his pro-clivities. Sabbaths twice a week, hot and cold running totty. The orgies were laid on with a trowel."

He was laughing now as well, enjoying it. Enjoying me.

"Then it was a commune, then Transcendental Thingummy-bob, then a spot of finding yourself in a monastery, and after that, the environment. Greenpeace recruited you—then dropped you like a shot. Something to do with a plan to harpoon the captains of whaling ships and flense them in public, I understand."

"Socially just, I thought," he said. "I still do."

I blinked. Was he joking? Evidently not.

"You can see their point," I said.

He nodded in rueful agreement. "Perhaps not the best PR."

"Anyway, the family deals with you as they've done with all previous Turl cuckoos, at a long suffering distance. You're a re-mittance man. Regular handouts from the family's bankers in London give you enough rope to fund whatever the latest cause is while they wait for you to stylishly hang yourself, but you haven't, which makes me wonder just how tightly the mad Turl straitjacket fits. For the last ten years, though, you've played by their rules, and you and your daughter are now on nodding terms with three quarters of your relations, which, for a Turl black sheep, is a first. The genteel proviso implied in the financial arrangements—that if you ever came back to Cadisham for more than a funeral, the cash would stop cold—has never had to be even threatened. Until now. Until you became—" I was guessing, here, but not hard. "—an Animal Liberationist."

An urgent lowing from across the field stopped me. We both turned to see Calgacus up on his hind legs in mid-mount. Be-tween his legs a blancmange the size of a drainpipe wobbled menacingly.

"Well, I'll be damned," said Jonathan, in genuine surprise. The pork pie hat turned back to me. "We've been trying to get him to do that for weeks! You must be a good influence on his testosterone, Ms Knox. Fancy having a go at mine?"

The pure cheek of him... Attractive as hell, and he knew it. Thirty years ago—hell, even twenty... Again, the blue eyes nearly captured me; behave, Knox.

"Anything I left out?" I said, coolly. "Of your CV, I mean?"

"Not much, Ms Knox," he said, amiably, his smile undented by the rebuff. "I declare myself impressed. You certainly know all there is to know about me."

I doubted it. I was considering my next move when a noise crossed the meadow from the farm buildings.

A peal of maidenly laughter. Two riding-breeched girls appeared, leading horses. One of them was Jonathan Turl's daughter. The other was...

The connection skewered me, straight through the heart.

...Libby.

Not much doubt about where the good influence on Calgacus had come from now, was there? But yesterday's tears were gone, at least. I turned back to the smile beneath the pork pie hat, the questions forming.

One. Mad, or just crafty?

Two. What was my charge doing here?

Three, and much more important than either of the other two. If I knew all about blue-eyed Jonathan Turl, Esquire...

"Yes, absolutely everything." he repeated.

...how much did Jonathan Turl, Esquire know about me?

*

It didn't bear thinking about, it really didn't. As I prowled the gutters of the farm building's roof, tail swishing in anger, I tried to separate out the problems.

All that hooey from Beth about Senior Partners and Security Consultants and Reputable Firms... Turl would know all about my one-woman pub garret detective agency—his daughter was employed by/went bedspringing with the man who'd just hired me. And my rejected store card application wouldn't have been far away, either... If—

I stopped. The ivy had rustled. My eyes found it—a flurry of brown, a thin tail. I let my claws come out, but denied myself all else.

No twitch of whisker. No breath. No heartbeat.

It travelled diagonally across my path, up towards the roof's apex.

Gently, I got down and laid my forepaws together in advance requiem.

A squeak. How sweet! It didn't even know I was there.

I let the muscles of my haunches tense.

I aimed.

I quivered, and then—

The spring! The hunter's triumph! The closing of talons and jaw, the velvet struggling! As the blood sang in me I bit hard, snapped the neck, and felt the panic cease. Below me, a door slammed. I watched Jonathan Turl stride away, Libby and his daughter in his wake. A snatch of conversation reached me.

"...but once the meat's out of his system, Bloss, do you think he'll change?"

Bloss? Blossom, I realised, it had to be—must have been in Jonathan's hippy phase...

But with my charge happy and my mouth full of mouse, I let contentment hold sway. I leaned down and placed my prize on its bed of ivy, then regarded it. Mmm... Fresh mouse. Nothing quite like it. My left forepaw reached out and turned it in the gutter until it pleased me aesthetically.

Finally, I let myself salivate.

Why on earth would anyone want to be a vegetarian?

*

An interesting question, though, the veggie one... I was still ruminating over it as I gunned the MG, top down, back towards Cadisham.

But the weather had cheered up, and under the accumulated bliss of speed, sunshine, solvency and satiation, I felt my worries begin to melt away. Eventually I succumbed. It was Friday, the weekend beckoned! Enjoy it, Knox! *Carpe Diem!* The mood lasted until I looked in the rear view mirror.

The night before's Hertz Mercedes was a hundred yards behind me. Any lingering doubts about it being the right car were dispelled by the two silhouettes in the front seats.

The Blues Brothers.

Coincidence?

I didn't believe in it—which brought me to one very logical question.

Were these two cartoon cutout gangsters following me?

Sod *Carpe Diem,* I thought. *Carpe Computer;* check the buggers out as soon as possible.

6

"WHAT I NEED, Ollie love, is the real skinny, the inside dope. What is the honourable or otherwise firm of Turl & Turl up to?"

The bald pate in front of me was fringed by greasy brown hair and had a great bullseye boil smack in the middle of it. It bobbed in acknowledgement of the question, but the face below didn't rise from its current business. I did my best to ignore the sound of sausage and mash being hoovered up with industrial efficiency and looked round the gleaming plastic interior of Mavis Brent's caff. More boils! Was it my destiny to be besieged by sulphurous swellings? The two teenage boys who were the only other customers both had faces at the lunar crater stage. I eyed their bulging trousers and bestowed an Older Woman Who Knows It All smile; one should always acknowledge tribute. Behind me a contented sigh and a smacking of lips signalled the end of phase one of my business lunch.

I turned to find the sated beast, Oliver Brimlington Babbage, defrocked financial journalist and now stock tipster to the parish of Cadisham, leering at me.

"And what," he said, scooping up a last smidgen of gravy with a distinctly grubby forefinger as he eyed my tits, "is in it for *moi?*"

"One of Mavis's mum's turnovers."

The leer remained impassive. I mentally calculated my ongoing tab behind the counter. When would the Turl cheque clear?

"And a cream bun," I said. "That's it."

He sighed, theatrically. "It'll do to be going on with."

I smiled. If some movie producer ever needed an urban Bacchus, Ollie was it. Take away the greasy Eton tie and the decade-old Savile Row pinstripe, add the requisite small horns, a lake of Montrachet and a clutch of maidens who didn't mind foreplay being in French and through keyholes... That had been his downfall, the keyholes. If he'd only stuck with the secretaries' lav instead of the female executive washroom... He leaned across the table as far as his paunch would allow.

"I don't suppose you'd fancy upping my Dow Jones a few points, would you, *chérie?*"

I gave him my sweetest slap-it-down smile. "More likely to be a quick FTSE in the balls, old son."

His leer widened enough to show his yellowing front teeth. "One does feel obliged to try."

"Two turnovers, Mavis, love," I sang out to the counter.

Ollie sat back, grinning. He was at least a practical Bacchus; impending food over thwarted fornication any day. Suddenly he was all business.

"Finger on the pulse, as always, eh, young Sammy? Turl & Turl! Trust you to know a rising stock when you see one."

"Rising?"

"As inexorably as the Member for Brimlington South at the sight of your peerless *nichons.*"

"Why?"

The leer returned, with a calculating edge. "Top two buttons of your *chemise.*"

It was my turn to sigh. I undid them. He shivered with delight, his eyes fastening on the extended cleavage like a dying sinner on a priest.

"Nobody's entirely sure," he said, hoarsely, "but rumour, like rejection, is rife."

Cheeky git! But I didn't do up the buttons. Instead I lifted this morning's Clarion from the next table.

CHARGE OF THE HEAVY BRIGADE!

Cadisham's local rag had done Calgacus proud. Beneath the red banner he was caught in full multicoloured profile, one horn complete with dangling slingback. So that's why the camera had been there...

"A takeover?" I said.

"Or a merger. Nobody's head's above the parapet yet."

"This nonsense had no effect?"

"Nary a blip on the graph. One pound fifty-nine a week ago, two twenty-seven this morning. Its progress is as certain as my failure to render you horizontal, and twice as mysterious. Buy all you can get your hands on, then seat your shapely rump on the pile and prepare for riches."

The turnovers arrived, both apple. I pushed one across to Ollie and bit into the other. Orgasmic! I polished it off, quickly—it had been an hour since my *al fresco* starter, and a feline full belly somehow never translated into a human one. I closed my eyes in bliss. When I opened them again I saw that my companion's leer had become tinged with astonishment.

"Where on earth do you put it all, Sammy?"

"About a foot above where you'd like to, you old goat."

We both had a good chortle. I stood up and slung my bag over my shoulder.

"You'll keep me posted when you find out more?"

"Does your flat have a keyhole, *ma petite?*"

I leaned down and whispered in his ear. "Yes, but I usually hang my knickers on the doorknob."

I turned my back on his shudder of lust and bestowed another smile upon the two pimpled youths as I left.

Such a difficult age, thirteen, the days delicately balanced between skateboarding and more solitary exertions. I slid into the MG, still smiling, sure that, for the next few hours at least, I'd decisively tipped those particular scales.

*

The rain had stopped, but rivers were still running down the drainage channels between Mike's polytunnels. He had his back to me. Waste pipes and half-full pails lay in disarray around his feet, and his blue-gloved hand was pumping frenetically at the kitchen sink's plughole. The plunger in his fist looked a sex aid for Calgacus. The dislocated U-bend dangled suggestively.

"Hertz," he said, between mammoth heaves. "Difficult, leave it with me—but Turl's should be easy enough, I can't see the likes of them having any kind of sophisticated firewall." The metal draining board bulged with his exertions, but still nothing shifted. "Mind you, if it's firewalls you're worried about, Libby's the ace these days—we're at the stage where she could even teach me a thing or two. Won't be long before it's her you're after instead of her old man. And if—"

I looked down at Lochinvar the bloodhound. He looked back up at me, confirming my feelings by taking his ears out of his food bowl. The left one was full of gravy. He was the stupidest dog in creation, but even he could hear what I was hearing.

"It just all seems so far-fetched," Mike went on. He was gabbling, now. "This Jonathan character lets a bull loose in Turl's to drop the family biz in it and stop them being attractive to some big buyer. But at the same time he's dependent on Turl dosh! The man must be a nutter! But then, the upper classes always were a bunch of idiots, weren't they? And the Turls—"

"Mike," I said, gently, "why don't you tell me what's wrong?"

His shoulders sagged, and when he turned I saw the pain on his face. He stuck the plunger decisively to the kitchen wall. As it quivered, he looked out over his polytunnelled baby, Cadisham Organics. Then he reached across to the bottom shelf of the dresser and pulled out a sheet of folded paper from under the soup plates. It was the letter I'd seen on Libby's bed. He handed it to me.

"Found it when I was looking for stamps," he said, miserably. "In her desk. It's her job to bring in the mail in the morning." His voice became even more miserable. "She never showed it to me."

I unfolded it; Pelhams, the local estate agents.

Dear Mr Martin... ...instructed by our client, Kirkcaldy Holdings... ...hopes of a speedy transaction... ...we would be prepared to act...

I sat there, puzzled. A Cayman Islands holding company was offering to buy Cadisham Organics, lock, stock and barrel, for four hundred thousand pounds.
Why?

*

"OK," I said. "Letter first. Are you interested?"

He stood there, mouth open, looking like a yokel at a Find The Lady game. "In selling?" His voice filled with outrage. "After the work we've all put in! I'd cut my hand off first!"

"And did you tell Libby that?"

The moment of bravado died. He shrugged.

"And you wonder why you had a bloody great row?" I said. "Don't you see? I'm willing to bet that's exactly what she's terrified of! You taking it into your head to change everything about your life and hers, just for money."

He pumped himself up again. "She should have shown me the letter!"

"Of course she should. But you should have had the sense to tell her you'd never sell. And you didn't."

Mike gave a confused scowl—and then, without the slightest warning, the sink's blocked innards spluttered. There was a putrid eruption of greyish water, then a gloopy sound as sludge landed in the bucket.

"Jesus, what now?"

His blue rubber hand reached into the bucket and brought a lump of the sludge back out.

By its tail.

A very pink tail. Belonging to a very large, very smelly, very dead rat.

He turned back to me. "On the increase, these buggers, no doubt about it. Where's that damn cat when you need it?"

*

Damn cat, indeed!

But he was right. As I sat on the wall which separated the market garden from the vicar's terrifyingly neat shrubbery, I admitted it. A bargain was a bargain, and pest control was what Tiddles got food and board for.

Or rather, food and bored—it had never been a duty I enjoyed.

The first problem is, I've never cared for the flavour of them, no matter how the connoisseurs drool, and even bearing that in mind, this lot undoubtedly tasted off—earthy, oddly so. Their mouths seemed full of dirt, which I'd never encountered before. Was that normal?

And the second problem is that by and large they're just not good sport. I mean, don't get me wrong, you still get the frisson—the tail excites as they scurry, they're fast enough... But there's no finesse, no grace. A mouse's terror is a weaving of adrenaline, a pigeon's panic is fluttering and exquisite, but a rat's fear... It's as focused as the rest of its existence—a straight line for the nearest bolt hole. It's a response which belongs to the group, not the indi-vidual—if you catch me I can be spared, it says, if I die the species will continue. For they do come in packs, these days, more often than not. Had they always? I could remember more placid times, more rural, perhaps, when the odd one would lope with impun-ity across a farmyard.

And pack... Was it the right collective noun? From where I was sitting at the bottom of Mike's garden, a sewerful seemed a better description. I stared at the pipe's mouth. No doubt about it; a steady half dozen every ten minutes or so... It added up to a lot of rats. Why? The market garden? The greenhouses were Grade A secure, I should know, I'd done my concrete shovelling number to help Mike and Libby lay the foundations. I tried to think of any other five-star rodent attractions close by. The pea-nuts in Widow McGinty's bird feeder? Furry brown things the size of small dogs had been known to shin up the drainpipe like crazed Adventure Scouts, until Glenn threatened to prosecute her for the animal equivalent of entrapment. Entirely over the top, I thought—how else was the woman to get her target prac-tice? So what else? The riding stables had shut down six months ago, the straw was long gone... Or was it the abattoir? Wrong side of town, I decided, the all-night bakery too... As I mused, another phalanx of six scuttled out of the round black mouth. There was a sense of purpose here, no question about it. Hmm...

And while I've never been the kind of hunter who's happy to just cut the weakest out of the herd, I wasn't used to the going being this tough, not with rats. I looked back along the line of six corpses, the night's haul so far, then surveyed the scratched mess of my forepaws. They were definitely bigger than usual, this lot, and they knew how to fight when they were cornered. Biting the neck on that last one had taken real effort, I could still feel my jaw muscles. Maybe I was getting—

No, I thought, smiling to myself in the darkness. Whatever

else was happening here, I wasn't getting old.

I'd always been old.

I shook myself out of the reverie. Nothing else for it, I decided, if the clichés were coming this thick and fast—old, indeed—the time for action had arrived. I took a last look at my trophies and put my best paw forward.

*

Slime. Cold and clammy, it oozed between my pads. A hot bath would be necessary at Knox Towers, later. I let my eyes adjust to the light, then moved my whiskers to left and right to establish the width.

Then I began. It was slow going, given the suction powers of the glop I was wading through. How far was it? I passed the junction of another pipe. Phew, even smellier—the vicar's, stood to reason, trust the holier-than-thou to dump a more potent class of crap. I ploughed on. How far to the next branch line? Mike would know, but I'd never be able to ask him. *Mike, I was just wading along your main—*

And then it grabbed me.

A scent, faint but insistent.

I was about a twenty yards in. Up to here the olfactory cocktail had been pretty much what I'd expected, the sewage stink and the rat reek—but this was acrid and nauseous at the same time. And alluring, I had to admit. I found myself picking up speed. What was this new thing? It was alive, that much I knew, but it wasn't any animal I'd ever encountered, I knew that as well. As I padded along it got stronger—and suddenly I was sure that whatever it was, it was a mask for something else. How to get beneath? To the real...

I was going uphill now. There was light, far off, and I could hear a high-pitched noise, a keening. And then, without warning, I was running, skidding and slithering through the muck. Why? What was happening to me? The circle of light got bigger, the noise louder. This was beyond scent, this was—

I burst out into wind and skidded to a halt on some smooth surface. Where was the light? What had happened to the keening? I fought for calm, got myself under control. The clouds parted, let the moon show me my surroundings.

I was almost exactly where I'd lost Scrapper. A low brick wall faced me. I hopped up on to it; the back of a large two-storey detached house, the last one in Acacia Avenue. Its garden was grey in the moonlight. My eyes searched its shadows; pot plants, cracked concrete pathways, sheds, a round brick building, and a wire mesh enclosure. Through the gloom I made out the comic waddle of a phalanx of chickens, odd-looking ones with feathers in a weird geometric pattern. As they observed me, a loud crowing came from behind them, scolding them back into their coop; the cockerel, the one I'd heard earlier. He advanced in that bizarre break-dancing strut they have. Then he stopped and surveyed me, his head jerking from side to side. I stared at him—until I caught the glint from one of the house's second storey windows. Spectacles? Binoculars?

Good reflexes are everything. I was in mid-leap before the words *telescopic sight* had even formed in my mind. The shot pulverised the brick I'd been perched on and another half dozen round it. To frantic squawking, I landed, tumbled, then got my grip and sprinted behind the nearest of the sheds.

In time to feel a rumble beneath me. A rushing sound filled the air, punctuated by squeaking. It was already receding by the time I'd recognised it.

The rats, hundreds of them.

Leaving.

I was sure of it. Where were they? Below me, somewhere. I held myself still and listened. Were they laughing at me? Something was, I could have sworn it.

And I could understand why. I sneezed away the brick dust, shook myself free of earth—and wondered how to shake myself free of stupidity. The cockerel crowed again, loudly adding his contempt to the rats' mirth. I hissed at him.

What was this thing?

This thing I thought I'd been hunting...

...when all the time it had been hunting me.

7

DAYLIGHT DID NOTHING to lessen the affront. The cheek of it! If a cat couldn't go out for an honest night's ratting without some bugger taking a pot shot... But I was more annoyed with myself than anything else—for letting myself be caught by whatever that catastrophic catnip had been, pulling me along the sewer like a dipsomaniac spinster after drink.

And I was worried; seductive lures, hordes of laughing rats, some trigger-happy hooligan having a go—it didn't add up to negligible.

Something was gathering.

I pulled up fifty yards short of the Acacia Avenue house, wound down the Midget's window and sniffed. Whatever the scent was, Mother's Ruin to the power ten, it seemed to be gone. Good. I lifted the clipboard from the passenger seat and got out, resisting the urge to scratch my backside. Why were these uniforms always made out of cheap polyester? I should have worn knickers, hussy that I am, but I had no clean ones—and no prospect of any, not until the Wingco's cheque cleared and Rita restored laundry privileges. So lump it, Knox! I forced my mind back to the job in hand.

Not a soul in sight, but in the name of anonymity I kept the cap low on my head. As I approached I scanned the windows; curtains drawn. At the gate I paused and took in the name.

Nether Kilns House.

On a black ceramic plaque with a motif of red flames behind the letters.

Kilns...

Cadisham had once had potteries, quite a few, and this was roughly where the last one had been, around the Boer War years. Peregrine Prendergast's place, old Praise The Lord Prendergast, Perdition Perry to the locals, a lay preacher with a special line in grisly gloom. Cadisham Lustreware, that was the stuff, Of Superior Strength And Unbreakable Beauty... Rita had a fruit bowl of it on the four ale bar's top shelf, ugly thing, lime green and yellow.

But the kilns... I vaguely remembered them being demolished about ten years back, and the property being sold off. Who owned it now? I marched up to the front door and rang the bell.

No answer. I tried the handle. Unlocked. I pushed it open. Stale air met me.

"Gas 'n' lectricity, my dears," I yelled in my best Gloucestershire, "come to read the meter."

No answer. I closed the door behind me. Abandoned...? I almost scratched my bum in surprise, but I stopped myself; discipline, Knox. I began throwing doors open.

Living room, bedrooms, bathroom, attic. Nothing. All cold as a harlot's heart and empty as a politician's promises. No furniture, no carpets, the cupboards bare, the lampshades gone. I was mindful of booby traps as I searched, but by the time I'd done the first couple of rooms, I knew I was wasting my time. The shot had come from a box room at the back—the only one with a window that opened. No sign of the shooter's presence, though—and then I looked out of the window and stopped.

No sign of the hens, either. Hmm... The chicken coop was still there, but it was empty. I felt my brow crease. Odd, that—anyone doing a runner would hardly be bothered about fresh eggs...

I went back down the stairs, then into the kitchen. A gloomy room, untouched by the morning sun. I reached over for the switch. Sickly light from a fluorescent tube flashed a couple of times, then illuminated bare surfaces. I smiled; first mistake they'd made—empty houses don't still have the lecky on. I went across to what had to be the cellar door—and found a big hefty padlock barring my way.

A big hefty *new* padlock.

I frowned at it, then looked around for anything to help a girl perpetrate a bit of B&E. Nothing—but my eyes did alight on a corner of white paper sticking out below a cupboard door. Carefully, I teased it out.

A receipt. From, of all places, Turl & Turl's china department. Dated October 20th, the day I'd been there.

A receipt for one replica Alvis cigar lighter...

And it was made out to a very old friend of mine—well,

friend was maybe stretching it. I celebrated by finally allowing myself a good scratch at my long-suffering backside, then put the receipt in my top pocket.

Time to go visiting.

*

The garage had all the charm of an up-ended cereal box, but through its plate glass window I could make out a prosperous-looking clutch of BMW and Jaguar bonnets. A quick scout, I decided.

The first thing I found round the side was a bunch of bins with a very identifiable rotten smell to them. I inhaled it like a connoisseur and moved on. And round the back—my, my, what a coincidence—what should I find but a brand new chicken coop, full of the strange checked darlings I'd met the night before. The cockerel came out and treated me to a confrontational stare, then backed off like Michael Jackson doing *Thriller*. Before he could crow, I continued my recce.

The third side was more upmarket; a gleaming beige Range Rover. Again, interesting... My old mate Bertie was coming up in the world—this one at least. I looked round. Nobody about. I took off my lovely Dents gloves, pulled the catch and opened the bonnet. The engine was pristine. I leaned over, made a quick security adjustment and closed it again. Business taken care of and gloves redonned, I sauntered back round to the front and checked out the Olde Worlde lettering of the sign.

CADISHAM CARRIAGES.
VEHICLES OF DISTINCTION.
PROPRIETOR : LIONEL BUBB ESQ.

Lionel! I smiled. Did he use Zebediah? Somehow I doubted it. What had the last operation been called? I trawled the memory banks; Bubb's Bargain Bangers, that was it, down the iffy end of Gasworks Lane. How times change, I thought, not at all wistfully.

Which was just as well, because wistful was already being taken care of. By a portly gent with bad teeth, wire-framed specs

60

and a Beatles haircut modified to hide his bald patch. Had he looked like Paul McCartney forty years ago? He certainly didn't now... Mind you, not even McCartney looks like McCartney any more, does he? (Not that I'd ever fancied him, anyway—rugged over cute, always—Harrison was the one.) But this chap had definitely neither Twisted nor Shouted for many decades—the opening comfy slippers clarinet of When I'm Sixty-Four was what came to mind. The eyes behind the wire frames were misty as he stroked the perfectly restored trim of Cadisham Carriages' Offer Of The Month. He turned at my approach.

"I had one exactly like it," he said, proudly. "Same colour, everything."

Not a car I'd been fond of, the 1966 Hillman Imp—no style, and no way of avoiding the gearstick during more intimate moments. But I had to admit, someone had done a lovely job on this one. The bumpers gleamed, the powder blue bodywork shone, the aerial swayed gently in the breeze. I looked back at the ageing Beatle, trying to pinpoint the nostalgia. First car? I watched my effect on him, saw the lump in his throat relocate to his trousers. No, I decided, first carnal. How nice to see hope springing eternal... I rewarded him with a measured jiggle of my dove grey Hugo Boss backside as I passed (excellent charity shops, Cadisham) and left him deciding whether to drool over chrome or curves.

Inside the glass doors it was cold, and my presence went at first unnoticed. An oleaginous youth in a particularly revolting double-breasted blue suit was draped over the big desk in the corner, pencil in hand. The science fiction-breasted blonde on the other side of it was filing her nails to lethal points and giggling at whatever sweet nothings he was scribbling on her blotter. Neither of them looked old enough to hold a rattle, never mind a job. I coughed. They whirled round. He reacted fastest. By the time he'd scissored himself off the desk, his smile was at full servile wattage. His mouth opened. I pre-empted the spiel with a gloved finger pointed at his feet.

"White socks and brothel creepers with a royal blue suit? A definite no-no. Don't they teach you anything Down There?"

His face crumpled. I patted his arm and smiled sweetly.

"Business. Outside."

As he scampered off I confronted the blonde. "Mr Bubb in?"

I might as well not have spoken. Mouth open with concentration, she spent the next minute studying everything I was wearing as though there was going to be an exam. Her eyes were slightly too close together. I watched them fasten on my shoes.

"They from TK Maxx?"

Only the desk between us saved her. I put my balled fists down on it, leaned over and gave her the full lightning bolt with both eyes. Her nipples shrank in fright.

"Just get him, love."

Eyes still on me, she yelled over her shoulder. "Lionel!"

The door behind her opened a crack. "Kylie, 'ow many times do I 'ave to tell you? No interruptions when I'm—"

The pause in the conversation told me I'd been recognised, the door's slam suggested that Auld Acquaintance had not, indeed, Been Forgot. I heard running feet. I gave Kylie a *What Fun* smile, skipped round her desk, and followed the footsteps to the side door.

Where I came upon a small portly man, as bald as a coot, fruitlessly trying to start the Range Rover. The minute he saw me, a smile of unsurpassed villainy appeared in the five o'clock shadow beneath his snout of a nose.

"Sammy!"

"Bertie!"

Long lost greetings over, I got in beside him. From my pocket I brought out a small metal object.

"That's my bleedin' rotor arm!"

"A for observation, Bertie. And I'll be delighted to give it back to you. Once we've discussed this."

I brought out the receipt I'd found in Nether Kilns House. As he looked at it, his head swivelled from side to side as though it wasn't connected to any neck.

"Nuffink to do with me, Sammy! I never seen—"

The brimstone smell of the bins got stronger. I laughed.

"Oh, you are an old fibber, Bertie, aren't you! Look, it's even got your name on it—Mr B.L.Z. Bubb!"

"More 'n' my job's worth, Sammy, even to you. The information to which you're referrin's extremely commercially sensitive. In the wrong 'ands..."

There was a moment's respite as we both watched the greasy youth shepherd When I'm Sixty-Four round the gleaming Imp for the third time. My companion's head gave another of its rear window nodding dog shakes.

"Pitiful, Sammy, innit? I'd've 'ad that one past the finishin' post long ago. Think they know it all, the young 'uns, the 'ole—"

"Bertie," I broke in, "talking about finishing posts, do you remember the 1908 Derby? The outsider, what was the name? Signorinetta? Came in at a hundred to one?"

The piggy eyes retreated, glittering malevolently. Again, the brimstone smell intensified.

"Nice wedge you got out of that one, didn't you? How exactly did it work—special dispensation from the Boss, was it? No Private Enterprise rule lifted for the day? Or wasn't he in on your role in the proceedings?"

"You wouldn't," he said, furiously.

"In a heartbeat," I replied, smiling my widest smile. "Be a positive pleasure. You bankrupted two of my mates and lost me dinner at the Savoy. So cough now, otherwise..."

I put thumb and pinkie to my ear in telephone dumb show. He sighed in resignation.

"Goes no further?" he said, eventually.

"Of course not!"

He stared out of the window. "Remember 'ow it used to be, Sammy? In the old days? A soul up for grabs, 'e either went up the old apples 'n' pears or down, eh?"

For a second, the pathos in his voice got to me. The lamb...

Or rather, the pig, I thought, coming down to earth. We went on watching the dance round the car. Kylie had joined in now, breasts swelling improbably across the Imp's roof. Bertie's voice came again, resigned now.

"Fact is, things ain't wot they used to be, so the Boss, in the Infinite Wisdom Of 'Is Malevolence, decides to send us out to do a bit of recruitin'. 'Bertie,' 'e says, 'New times need new torments, get your arse up there an' find me summink to sharpen up the old tripods.' 'I live to serve, Your Excrescence,' says I." He jerked a thumb at the group by the car. "An' then, 'e tells me it'll be a trainin' exercise, an' I'm lumbered wiv young Putreficia there, and the new apprentice, Baraquiel. So I—"

I sighed. The only thing more boring than Heaven's protocols was Hell's.

"Get to the point, Bertie. Big bum, mole on her mouth the size of the Albert Hall, dresses like Sherlock Holmes in drag, has a skinny drip half her size trailing after her like a sheepdog. Who is she and why have you got her hens?"

Defiantly he reached inside the jacket's pocket, brought out a huge cigar—and then the Alvis lighter.

"Let's just say Grizelda and 'er companion Olive are friends of mine—and I'll remind you, young Sammy Knox, that beauty is in the eye of the beholder." He lit up and leaned back. "Grizelda and I, two souls no longer in the first flush, 'ave decided to enter into a relationship. She's beginnin' a new phase..."

I stopped listening. The mind boggled—she was three times the size of him! Be like a Pekinese on a Great Dane...

"...as a community activist."

Ah, I thought, that explained the chickens, at least.

"You mean she runs the local coven?"

"You could put it like that," he said, in a hurt voice. "Personally we prefer to call it the local Alternative 'Istorical Society."

I suppressed a giggle. Would the minutes be the same? Bonfires, booze and buttocks? Horny housewives and cavorting carpenters, basted in bantam's blood?

"What happened to old Bertha Pike?"

He shrugged. "Vote o' no confidence. Went rogue, got caught collectin' for the Salvation Army."

"When's the next meeting?"

"Tuesday. Believes in regularity, does Grizelda. Every Tuesday night, seven till nine, Buncle church 'all. Then Morris dancin', ten till two. Light refreshments provided."

Morris dancing! I choked back another giggle.

"Still out by the racecourse?"

He shook his head. "Nah, Sammy." He turned up his piggy little hands in a gesture of resignation. "Not quiet enough these days."

I nodded in sympathy. Cadisham Racecourse had now become one of the south's favourite places for MPs taking backhanders (or backseaters) for services rendered—on any night of the week you'd find a queue of Rolls Royces. Hard to get a bit of ritual on the go when all you can hear is creaking springs...

"So where?"

"Blatherwick Manor. The maze, beside the nature trail."

Nature Trail, indeed...

"Back to the old stamping grounds, eh, Bertie?"

The neck retracted shiftily. But it was a good choice; lots of associations. Old Sir Stanford Blatherwick had had the next best thing to a deflowering factory there in the 1830's. Bertie grinned, a bit too cockily for my liking; time to get down to business.

"So whose idea was the rifle?"

The answer came too fast. "Sammy, 'ow could you think such a thing? You know I've always 'ated gratuitous violence."

"You're not denying it though, are you?" I leaned across to him. "You should have trained her better, she's a terrible shot."

He sighed like an old loco letting off steam. "Just business, Sammy, you know 'ow it is."

"What business, you disgusting carbuncle?"

Suddenly the air around us was freezing. The chickens went quiet. I watched the cigar lighter start to shake in Bertie's hand.

"Sammy," he said, softly, "There's an inspection due later this afternoon. If we was to be caught talkin'..."

"Don't you try and con me, Bertram Bubb!"

But my own antennae were telling me it was true; something very senior and very nasty from the nether regions was on its way. Damn! Grudgingly, I tossed Bertie his rotor arm, then leaned over to him.

"Don't imagine this is over, you pustule."

"Sammy—"

I ignored him, got out and started walking. By the time I was back at the MG, peals of maniacal laughter were coming from behind me. I turned.

"An' now the finance agreement, sir!"

Kylie/Putreficia's breasts seemed to have expanded even further, the would-be Beatle's nose was lost between them. Her taloned hand was gripping his as it held the pen. Bertie—he was a fast mover, I'll give him that—was holding up the clipboard. The greasy youth, Bara-something, was dancing around like he needed to pee. Inside the showroom window's shadow I could just make out a tall figure. I shivered.

Were those horns? Was it the Bad Lad himself? As I watched, the figure dissolved into darkness. I refocused on the action outside.

"There, sir. An' there. An' initials 'ere, an' 'ere' an'—oh, dear, sir, you're bleedin'! Kylie, girl, if I've told you about them nails once, I've told you a dozen times—not to worry, though, sir, you just go on writin' through it, a bit o' blood never spoiled a contract yet, did it?"

I got in the MG. I knew what was coming.

A flash of lightning was followed by a long peal of thunder. The heavens opened.

When I'm Sixty-Four stood there, alone and dripping, the sodden contract in his hand, staring at the worn tires, the cracked windscreen, the rusty, dented body. He looked around him, bewildered, then turned to the garage behind. The peeling facade, shuttered and barred, looked as though no one had been inside for years.

He got into the Hillman Imp he'd just sold his soul for. It started on the fifth attempt. Before it reached the top of the hill, it backfired, twice.

*

As I negotiated Cadisham's one-way system—there's a hell for you, Bertie, I thought—I pondered it.

It's a tricky one, it really is—but you can't interfere, no matter how sorry you feel for them. It's in the rules.

Protocol 43b, sub-section 5: No operative shall interfere in another's operation.

But I'd stuck my nose in often enough before, so why not now? Was I on the turn? Ready to sign up for a life of crime with the Bad Lad? It had happened to plenty of others. There was Solly McGuire, perfectly respectable number as a spider, spinning away in old Mrs Minton's cowshed down in Taunton, free travel on a first class broom, all mod cons—seduced by a Goth granny in Devizes, helpless attraction. Sends nuclear waste to African landfills now. Or little Jeanie McLean. Started off as one of Quasimodo's bats in Notre Dame, couldn't stand the bells, ended up as a parliamentary lobbyist. I shuddered; grim stories. But no, I didn't think it was that... So what?

Finally, it came to me. I felt sorry for him. For Bertie, of all people! The break in his voice, when he'd talked about the old days...

I was amazed at myself—how ridiculous! As I passed Otley's, an errant waft of fresh baking reminded me I'd skipped breakfast. Food—that'd sort this nonsense out; feeling sorry for Beelzebub, the very idea! I screeched to a halt in the taxi rank, got out and went in. As I joined the queue, my mobile pinged. A pair of texts. The first was from Ollie. Five words.

T & T Merger. Banbury Vale Supermarkets.

The second was from an unknown number.

Operation Supermarket Comeuppance.
Banbury Vale, Nobbs Cross.
Forty-five minutes.

I paid, stuffed the pasty into my mouth, then ran for the MG. Within seconds I was heading for the metropolis of Nobbs Cross.

8

BANBURY VALE SUPERMARKET never stood a chance. I hid myself behind a mound of cabbages, watching anarchy unfold in the unlikely shape of Jonathan Turl, raincoat tails flapping like begrimed regimental colours as he crashed open the double glass doors with a trolley.

A trolley with two live lambs in it.

He pushed it in, lifted the animals out and set them down on the floor. They gambolled off gaily, then tried an Everest expedition up a handy pile of potatoes. The spuds rolled everywhere. Chuckles and sporadic applause followed—but the laughter was nervous, edgy; it couldn't have been mistaken for anything other than an opening of hostilities. As my dark glasses feigned interest in kiwi fruit and things which resembled undernourished starfish, other figures appeared. I knew instinctively they belonged to him.

A middle-aged woman in a cast-off psychedelic skirt, her mouth frozen in the perpetual smile of the sixties burnout.

A fat man in a frayed tweed suit which must have looked perfect about forty years ago, his bare feet confronting the world through the open half moons of his boot toecaps.

A couple barely into their teens, with punk hair and pierced noses, their trolley filled with their worldly possessions, a listless spaniel in their wake.

Jonathan Turl gave them all the benefit of his beatific smile as he scanned to right and left. The pork pie hat slipped on the straggly grey locks as he turned, like a periscope which couldn't quite catch up with the submarine's intent. He scooped up a bunch of bananas and darted off. Before he'd reached the end of the aisle the first one was half-peeled and his cheeks were bulging. As the rest of his people scattered, a ripple of alarm shuddered along the line of checkout girls. I saw one teeter in high-heeled panic towards the manager's office. Still beaming, Turl strode on. I followed his coat tails, smiling; zeal's infectious, mischief even more so. As he veered off into the cooked meats, his free hand delved inside the coat and came out with bundles of yellow leaflets. He flung them right and left, thrust them at people. No one refused—they wouldn't have dared, he had that born-to-rule air which clings to aristocratic English madmen. A harassed-looking manager in a grey suit appeared in front of him with a chiller cabinet smile. Turl handed him his banana skin and swept on. I grabbed a leaflet which had landed on a pile of chicken portions and read it on the hoof.

STOP THE OBSCENITY!
INSTEAD OF MURDERING ANIMALS,
SUPERMARKETS SHOULD FEED THE HOMELESS!
EAT THE FOOD NEAREST YOU!
NOW!!!

An unholy row broke out somewhere to my right. I ran. A quick glance down each aisle confirmed that people had taken the Turl tactics to heart. They were throwing each other packets of bacon, running for the exit with armfuls of gin bottles. Overweight security guards were panting after them, shouting into their radios. In the dairy section, the tweed-suited tramp was stuffing Brie into his mouth with a gourmet's gusto. Opposite him, the spaced-out hippie was wolfing down pasta salad, and further down the aisle the two punks were laughing uproariously—or at least as much as they could while ramming Black Forest gateau down each others' throats. From somewhere, a chorus of baaing indicated the rest of the flock's arrival. Turl appeared, doing his maniacal laugh number now, holding the heavy brass snout of a fire hose. I watched a posse of cute lambs use the fat snake of it as a skipping rope while Banbury Vale's customers scattered. He beamed at me across the chaos.

"Ms Knox! How's the security consulting? In a wet t-shirt mood, are we?"

So the second text had come from him... I wagged an admonitory finger, but not even the sound of the approaching sirens could kill my smile. As half a dozen lambs and I headed out through the sliding doors, I wondered where the daughter was—and then my smile died.

69

A very nice Morgan Plus Four was sitting in the nearest parking bay. At the wheel, dressed for the office, sat Ms Horn Rims And High Heels—and beside her, wine bottle in hand, looking as pleased as punch and more than a bit pissed, was Miss Elizabeth Martin.

*

I hopped up on to the Morgan's rear bumper, hoping the waves of contentment I could feel radiating from my charge meant she wouldn't sense my presence. I listened; girlish titters, clinking glasses—and then the sound of a mobile phone. I understood. This wasn't just a girly afternoon with an illicit bottle—this was Operation Supermarket Comeuppance Command Central.

"Yeah, dad, the fuzz are here." I never heard the answer. "The ugly one with the huge arse. The Clarion's here, they're holding the front page, and the local radio and tv people say they're ready. If you turn on the fire hose, they have to take you in. Go on my count."

I jumped down and stationed myself behind the rear wheel.

It was beautifully done. I saw Beth (mauve suit today, you could have seen her from space) striding through the doors with two attendant minions, very stately, very organised, very proceeding-in-a-westerly-direction. The ensuing lull was pleasant, placid, even.

A television crew arrived. The young brunette at the head of them, microphone in hand, squatted down to give her makeup a once-over in a car mirror.

The spaniel came to the sliding doors, gave the outside world a dismissive sniff, then went back inside.

A spotty youth appeared with a Nikon bag over his shoulder. "Three, two, one. Now!"

A highly unrefined fart came from the car above me. *Really, Libs, a lady doesn't...*

As the sound drowned in bawdy laughter, Banbury Vale's alarms went off. I winced at the decibel damage. The supermarket doors clanged open—and then I was treated to the most wonderful sight.

A scurrying of lambs, a scattering of shoppers, a miniature tsunami which washed potatoes, cabbages, and rafts of cereal packets out on to the tarmac.

And then, poetry in motion.

The reversing figure of Detective Inspector Beth Walmsley, murderous in mauve, stuck bum first into a shopping trolley, was propelled out at high speed by a horizontal waterspout. The trolley banged against a lamp post, capsized and left her in a bedraggled heap on the tarmac. The tv camera caught every rung of the laddered tights, the Nikon's motor drive whirred remorselessly as it captured acres of buttock. Bellowing with a fury worthy of Calgacus, Beth finally rendered herself vertical and charged, dripping, back in.

The laughter above me went on for a very long time. If I'd been human, I'd have joined in. (Cats can't, you know—I wonder why?)

It stopped two minutes later. Jonathan Turl Esq., beaming like a Victorian missionary happy to climb into the pot, was led out in handcuffs. He forced a halt in front of the tv camera and addressed the small crowd which had gathered.

"Banbury Vale is an utterly unprincipled enterprise! Its proposed merger with Turl and Turl's—"

Libby's voice came from above me, slurred. "He'll be OK, Bloss, won't he?"

"My dad? In the jug? A bit of pokey's like a holiday to him, don't you worry. And anyway, I'll have him sprung by a week on Sunday."

The Morgan started, a lovely throaty growl. I skipped across to the Mini in the next bay, sneezing at the exhaust.

What was significant about a week on Sunday?

*

By one am, I was knackered.

Doing the Martin household's laundry hadn't been on the day's original agenda, but I'd let myself be conned into it—after all, Mike was spending hours on the computer for me, far more work than I'd originally asked for. So it seemed the decent thing

71

to do.

But how could there be so much? Mike was obviously a do-it-when-there-isn't-a-thing-left-to-wear man, which meant mal-odorous mountains with a nuclear half life of aeons, lurking in corners. And then there was Libby's pile... Who gets through more clothes than a teenage girl? And it all had to be washed just so, and ironed just so, and folded just so. And, come to think of it, wasn't the laundry usually my little witch's job anyway? I let my whiskers indulge themselves in a put-upon twitch.

And then, as I padded round for a last patrol, all sense of grievance vanished.

At the memory of her; the glorious memory of Libby Martin, hilariously happy and hiccupping, pie-eyed and proud of it. I filed away a grin for later, when I was human again. She'd ap-peared at the kitchen door around nine, legs like jelly, eyes on independent suspension, grinning inanely at me. Then she'd turned, still grinning, and stuck her tongue out in the general direction of her father, who, thankfully, had been too engrossed in yet another spreadsheet to notice. After the boozed-up day she'd had it was probably best if she was kept away from any-thing with a spin cycle, so I abandoned the laundry and shep-herded her up the stairs as fast as possible. Was she still snoring like a colony of sea lions? I wondered, but not with too much urgency. But I'd better check, just the same... And afterwards?

Home, I decided—a glass of Muscadet, unwind, review an action-packed day.

Weary, I stopped at the apple tree outside Libby's window, did a slow limb by limb ascent, then wrapped my tail round my forepaws on a swaying branch. Beneath a sliver of moon I watched her, greedily.

Mine, all mine.

She was sleeping in the same position I'd left her in, on her stomach, face to one side. Something was clutched in her left hand.

I looked at the walls around her. It had changed, her room, yet again—I'd been so busy getting her tucked up that I'd barely noticed. The only thing untouched was the hockey stick by her bed. When did this latest incarnation happen? Minimalist, it was an improvement, I liked it.

For a start, all the horse posters and pony club rosettes had vanished. The boy bands were gone too—and even the hunky movie vampires. I remembered having a good giggle at them; what was she going to think when she met a real one? I sat, swaying on the branch, enjoying the wind in my fur. So what was she into now, my lovely Adept? Was a cooling-off period between crazes obligatory?

Suddenly my whiskers were prickling, and it wasn't just the wind. She wasn't sleeping at all, I realised. Her bum was moving. In fact, it was moving in the rhythmic way that could only mean one thing.

One very private thing.

Libby, to quote an old Yellow Pages ad, was letting her fingers do the walking.

Well, every girl's got a right, I thought, watching her lower lip all a-quiver. And you do meet a better class of people, as my old friend Jayne Mansfield used to say. And it's not as though I didn't—I mean, I might have banished Glenn bodily, but he was still handy enough mentally, when the urge became uncontrollable and Changing wasn't an option. (Much easier for cats, by the way—frenzy beats foreplay any day.) So who was Libby's current hunk? I tuned in to her thoughts, searching for images.

The fog around her brain was the result of the booze—she'd pay for that in the morning—but her inhibitions had definitely been lowered. Waves of excitement were rolling through her—and by extension, through me as well. I was getting antsy, out on my branch—the power, the urgency! It kept getting stronger as it climbed its inevitable mountain. Oh, to have a seventeen-year-old witch's libido! And then—

The intensity of it! It exploded in me, rippling through my fur like a sensuous earthquake. And then the fog cleared, and I saw—

I was so surprised I fell off the branch and landed in a mound of leaves. Immediately, I scrabbled up again.

Libby was lying on her back now, the covers thrown off, each blissful snore suspending a stray straggle of damp hair like a miniature pennant of pleasure. Her left hand lay open. I could see what she was holding.

A lock of blonde hair. Her other hand held a crumpled picture to her breast. She must have been lying on it.

Out on the branch, I blinked.

Confirmation, even though I hadn't needed it. A head and shoulders shot; ash blonde hair, horn rimmed glasses, butter wouldn't melt expression.

And there was no doubting the emotions, either—lashings of them, flowing abundantly from Miss Elizabeth Martin, drunken witch of Cadisham parish. Yes, she'd been letting her fingers do the walking—and the walk they'd taken had definitely been right out there on the wild side.

Lust. Yearning. Abandon. All that and more. Much more.

Maybe not all mine after all...

Libby, my Libby, was in love—head over heels in love—with Jonathan Turl's daughter Blossom.

9

I WOKE WITH fifteen minutes to go. Yawning, I wound up my Felix The Cat singing alarm clock, pressed the release and let it ring, watching the key turn as I sang along with the scratchy mechanical voice.

Felix the cat, the wonderful, wonderful cat! Whenever he gets in a fix, he reaches into—

The spring gave a forlorn boing as the clockwork died—just before my favourite line, the one about the bag of tricks. I rewound it, then stared down at my toenails; grubby, chipped and charmless, in need of a good dose of TLC... And then I fell back on the pillow.

Libby.

I sighed. Not at all my thing, women, although enough offers have come my way—but whatever, as they say up in Newcastle, turned a girl's crank... And anyway, it wasn't my witch's choice of gender that was the worry, it was her choice of *partner*. Had an actual move been made? And if so, by whom? Lovestruck Libby or brazen Blossom? Had the lock of hair been stolen or given? And if Blossom was the instigator, was there an ulterior motive?

Like setting Elizabeth Martin up as some kind of fall girl for future chicanery? Not impossible, I decided, given what I'd already seen of Ms Horn Rims And High Heels...

But what to do about it? Again I contemplated my toenails, that row of irreverent piglets. Nail varnish, I decided, catch-all balm for the troubled soul. What had I done with the bottle? As I foraged, I looked at the clock again. Seven minutes. I willed myself back to work.

And it was a right old puzzle, work.

In the continuing saga of Jonathan Turl's machinations, what was the real motive? And more to the point, what was the next move? What I'd overheard being cooked up yesterday in the Morgan? Something to do with a week on Sunday? Was an even deeper scrape in prospect for my sexually ambivalent charge? A fresh lure, laid on by the ever-adaptable Blossom? At the thought of Turl's multi-talented madam, I felt resolve stiffen in me, darkly. One thing was sure; that young lady and I were going to have a no-holds-barred heart-to-heart, and soon—the mayhem she was causing, the trollop... And I'd never forgive her for the Hobnobs.

But first things first, organ grinder before monkey. The pork pie-hatted prophet would have to be approached—and given that he was now incarcerated in Cadisham's cop shop, how could I interrogate him? The list of questions I had was getting longer than the Bad Lad's tail. Would Beth give me an hour with him? In his cell? Maybe if I begged... Or could I bargain? I stared into Felix's rust-rimmed eyes. Not in a month of Sundays, he seemed to be saying—and he was right; this wasn't a plan, this was barrel bottom scraping, pure—

I sat up straight.

Pure wishful thinking, definitely. But what about a spot of the old wishful drinking? Beth's weakness. All girls together, a G&T or ten. Maybe...

And then I sat back—talk about a two-faced bitch! Here I was, plotting to wheedle a favour out of my best mate, while getting ready for... I blushed—I wasn't going to tell anyone, was I? This was an entirely private entertainment, she'd never know.

I banished conscience. What else could I do to further this damn case? My frown deepened. It probably came down to plan F—i.e. poking about till I made enough of a nuisance of myself to provoke some kind of reaction from somebody. Private Eye Bible, *Desperations 1 v. 13; When In Doubt, Kickest Thou The Furniture And Seeest Thou What Crawleth Out Of The Woodwork.* Ah, finally! My fingers found the varnish bottle in the tooth mug. I fished it out and contemplated it. Deep scarlet. I looked down at my feet; toenails, you've been typecast... None of them blushed. I tried the cap. Stuck. As I grunted, trying to undo it, I began a mental list.

Mike to investigate Briggs Rare Breeds.

Ollie for more on the merger.

Pour moi, a scratch about in the basement of Nether Kilns House, which I presumed was chez Gargantua (sorry, Grizelda). The new padlock told me there was something important down there. Something nasty?

And finally, I'd look in on Libby.

I paused, bottle in hand. The sex thing... An actual choice, or a teenage crush? A passing fancy? If it was, then was gentle intervention required, or did it have to run its course? Would I be more than a shoulder to cry on? And what did it mean for my end of things? There was nothing in the rule book to say witches had to swing one way or t'other in matters of what George referred to with Glaswegian gusto as 'rumpy-pumpy'. But if it was a forever job, then a fair few of the rituals would need redesigning. I mean, how did one do a decent fertility rite without—

Felix the cat, the wonderful, wonderful cat! Whenever he gets in a fix—

I dropped the bottle, banged the clock and scrambled for the remote. A minute to the local news! I stabbed at the ancient video recorder—salvaged from a skip on the industrial estate—and slapped it till the red light came on. Just in time. The screen filled up with the brunette anchorwoman.

"...something of a fracas out at Nobbs Cross yesterday. Whatever the Saturday shoppers at Banbury Vale supermarket were expecting..."

Turl's face loomed from the screen, shouting, but they'd left the sound down; somebody's lawyers had moved fast.

"...and the estimated cost of Mr Turl's ten minute visit has been put at over two hundred thousand pounds. Cadisham police responded to the call—" She gave a roguish smile. "—within minutes of the event being reported, although Mr Turl's eventual arrest was hampered by the fact that at least one of them—"

It's coming! *Soon!*

Shot of Beth going in; businesslike, authoritative.

Sooner!

"—found herself unexpectedly in reverse gear during the process."

Soonest!

Slow motion shot of Beth coming out.

Yes!

Mauve mountain wedged into a shopping trolley!

Yes Yes!

Laddered legs flailing! White knicker moon over Cadisham!

Yes Yes Yes!!!!

And then the heave out on to the tarmac, the pantomime rage face!

Oh frabjous day! Oh pure bloody joy!

I flailed about on the bed, beating my fists and screaming with laughter, the tears running down my cheeks. I was laughing so hard, in fact, that I never heard the door open behind me.

Beth.

Hands on hips, she placed herself firmly between me and the screen. Still stifling giggles, I angled my big toe round her and found the off button. For about a minute, she did furious/outraged.

"You can't do pissed off in yellow, Beth. Doesn't work."

She gave a snort of frustration, grabbed my clothes from the chair and flung them at me. A D-cup hit me on the nose. Not funny! My brows creased.

"Manners, Beth Walmsley! Whatever you're after, you don't have to be so bloody rude about it! And you do not—" I heard myself go all Queen Mother. "—interrupt a lady about to adorn her toenails."

Felix the cat, the wonderful, wonderful cat! Whenever he gets in a fix, he reaches into his bag of tricks, Felix—

This time it was Beth who thumped the clock, and not gently either. Her voice was a vengeful hiss.

"Good idea, a bag," she said. "An overnight bag, no tricks necessary." She picked up the nail polish bottle. "Might as well bring this, though." She leaned over towards me. "Lots of adorning time coming up, Sammy. Lots."

"What do you mean?"

"I mean, Samantha Knox, that you're nicked." The smile became pure malice. "And your pretty little car as well."

*

"Won't be long, Sammy me duck. Be down Mavis's caff scoffin' all 'em pasties in no time."

As the door of cell three slammed shut on Sergeant Daisy Driffield's beery breath, I sighed with relief. A kindly soul, Daisy, but I was in no mood for company. In fact I was in no mood for anything except screaming, and that would have done no good at all—two of my fellow inmates were reviling each other at the far end of the corridor, and the high decibel exchange of bodily abuse tips wasn't attracting a blind bit of notice. As the key turned in the lock I looked at my watch.

Two and a half bloody hours! Fingerprints, mugshots, the same questions over and over! And only in the last ten minutes had Beth let me know what it was about. As Daisy's flat-footed waddle receded, punctuated by several none too discreet burps, I subsided on to the bench and kicked off my shoes.

But it wasn't Beth's fault, not really—or at least, not entirely. Grudgingly I had to admit it.

The letter, after all, had been specific.

The can which had brought the petrol had come from the MG's boot.

And my fingerprints were all over it.

And I had no alibi, because Mike had disappeared.

And she'd been dead right about one thing, at least—I was going to have plenty of time.

Toenail time?

I snorted in derision as I contemplated them—*bugger you lot!* I was going to need every minute I could get for the serious stuff.

Like working out who had tried to torch Turl & Turl's number two warehouse on the Evesham Road.

*

Anonymous letters...

Arson...

As I stewed in the cell, I knew there was only one conclusion.

I'd been shafted. Somebody wanted Sammy Knox out of the way. But was the fire part of the frame, or was it an end in itself? That took some thinking about.

Who? The bold Grizelda? She was the one who'd attempted to off me with the rifle, Bertie had all but admitted it—but somehow I didn't like her for this. Wrong feel. Getting me so neatly banged up had been sophisticated, quite subtle, and anyone consorting with Bertie... But was I underestimating her? For the time being I put her on the mental back burner.

So who else had a motive for having Sammy kept on ice? Whose wheel had I put a spoke in recently? A long enough list. As I pondered it, a drunken baritone came from one of the nearby cells.

My love, she has left me, whatever shall I do...

As the answering suggestions came from his neighbours—thick, fast and anatomical—as to exactly what he should do and in which orifice, I wondered how I could get on with what I had to do—stopping mad Jonathan (only a few cells away from me, how bizarre was that?) causing yet more grief for the Waggling Wingco. The thought pulled me up short. Rue slid into the mental gap.

Haven't done much of a job so far, Knox, have you? A supermarket trashed, a warehouse damn near fired...

Fired.

The word enveloped me like a cloak of doom. Would Stoneyhurst fire me?

I thrust away visions of eviction. I wasn't beaten yet. Back to the main question.

Who?

I began tallying up unexplained bits of behaviour. Scrapper? Perhaps... Not impossible, at any rate—there was no doubt he and I were at odds over the Turls. But I couldn't believe he'd let anyone harm me. We were old friends and older lovers, it didn't make sense—or at least I hoped it didn't. But then he wasn't always, I reminded myself, the sanest of creatures...

Turl himself? My current near neighbour in the nick? Or his chameleon daughter? I'd already had my suspicions that the family knew more about me than they should...

Footsteps came from the corridor outside.

Not Daisy's, Beth's.

My rage rekindled itself. I was about to let fly when a sheet of paper slid under the door. I frowned. What now? Remorse? Atonement? All is forgiven, bouquet at the front desk? The footsteps receded. I picked up the note.

Mike's just phoned. He'll be interviewed in the next few hours. If he confirms your story, you're free to go.
You cow.

My anger drowned in remorse; I shouldn't have, really... But it hadn't occurred to me that thick-necked coppers could be so thin-skinned. Down the corridor, the singer began again.
...and we'll change the green laurel for the bonnet of blue.
Blue.
The Blues Brothers.

*

It had to be a possibility. Who exactly were they, this weird pair of *eminence grises*? Or rather *eminence bleus*? I thought back to them goose-stepping through Turl's the first day I'd seen them, their hats at the same angle, their matching shades in see-nothing-that-wasn't-straight-ahead sync. They'd looked official. Consultants? Management? They certainly looked cold enough for the executive suite—cold enough, but not old enough. But then, whizz kids these days...

Why had they followed me back from Briggs Rare Breeds? Did they have any connection with Jonathan? A sudden banging of doors announced more humanity at the end of the corridor. Over the jangling of keys I heard Daisy's voice, the halfway posh one she kept for visitors.

"Cell nine, duck. On the left. Don't look old enough to be his lawyer, if you don't mind me sayin'. Fancy a good-lookin' young thing like you workin' for that old git! D'you want a cup—"

"If you could take me to my client, please."

As Daisy's shuffle died huffily away, followed by a brisk tattoo of heels, I blinked in amazement.

His lawyer!

The last time I'd heard that voice, it had been in a Morgan Plus Four outside Banbury Vale supermarket.

His bloody lawyer!

And then I was grinning. Cell nine. Talk about falling into my lap!

I bent down and checked the ventilation grille beneath the bench. Four screws, same as always. Piece of cake. I reached into the bag and dug out the makeup pouch Daisy hadn't bothered to check. I unzipped it. Good, a selection. I held the thinnest one up to the light.

Handy things, nail files.

As soon as Daisy's afternoon six-pack kicked in, she'd start snoring her head off. And Mike wouldn't be interviewed for a good while yet...

Strip off. Hang my t-shirt over the spy hole in case of passing interest.

Change.

And then, a spot of light eavesdropping.

10

THE VENTILATION DUCT was cold, dank and cramped. My whiskers could touch both sides at once, and they didn't like what they were finding; mould, slime, cobwebs, nameless nastiness. And I was having to be careful with my paws, there were droppings everywhere; mouse, rat—

I stopped in surprise. Guinea pig? Had some kid's pet done a runner? But as I slunk along, I kept the hunter's instinct firmly suppressed—serendipity like this wasn't to be wasted.

But at least nothing had changed since I'd been down here last. When had that been? 95? 96? Nicked for refusing to confirm a client's identity, it all came back to me. I'd had to get out of my cell and find a pay phone to warn her the law was on its way, then get back in again. Had she unloaded the diamonds? For the life of me I couldn't remember—but she'd been a terrible jewel thief, even for an earl's daughter.

There was a dim light ahead. A vacant gaff. I padded past. At the next one I had to do a tight slalom past a couple of empty beer cans. Obviously I wasn't the only one who knew the duct's secrets, but using it for a stash had never occurred to me. Handy... The melodic humming I could hear through the grille told me I'd reached the abode of the corridor's musical director. Still trying on his blue bonnet? No, I thought, he'd gone even more Scottish. I recognised the tune—George was wont to indulge in it after closing, when he'd had, as he called it, 'a few sherbets'. I went on. One more grille, through which the smell of overripe unwashed feet—phew!—wafted, and then I came to a junction. Left, I decided. After five yards a growing jumble of sound told me I'd chosen correctly. A second later, the noises solidified into speech.

"...we'll have to regroup, dad. Blick's in a different league from anything we've met before. Banbury Vale are babes in the wood by comparison."

Blick?

"And we always knew the lab was..."

A cell door slammed. Damn! The reverberations stole the last word. *Was what?* Finally, I reached the gap. Not even a grille. I peeked. Between Turl's disreputable trouser legs I could see the hem of a black skirt and a nice pair of black patent Ferragamos. She was standing with her back to the cell door. Good legs, too, I had to admit. His voice came, tinged with regret.

"No matter how I feel about what it's become, it's a shame to see the old place brought quite so low, I have to say. An empty warehouse... What was the point of trying to torch it?"

"I've no idea."

I found myself believing them both. Another theory gone...

"No one hurt, though?"

"No. It was set for midnight. It blackened a door and popped out a few windows. No night watchman, my ever-so-nice boss sacked him last month."

"You're still, er, seeing him? Stoneyhurst?"

"Three nights a week," she said matter-of-factly, "randy old git can't get enough."

His voice became concerned. "Getting you down, Bloss?"

"No, dad. All for the cause. No problem." Her voice took on an edge of humour. "By the way, whoever rigged the fire set up the Knox woman for it. The cops are holding her, she's in here somewhere."

Closer than you think.

"Should take her down a peg or two, the smug bitch."

You'll pay for that.

"I rather like her."

"No, dad, you rather fancy her. Something rotten. Admit it."

Go on, admit it.

"Well..."

I perked up. They shared a laugh which sounded genuinely affectionate.

"And Sunday week?"

"All set. Early evening, just for a change, they always expect us later. Five minutes gets us through the fence, another twenty to do the business, a good dose of chaos to make it look like an ordinary raid. With any luck they'll never even know we've hit the office."

A raid... *Where?*

"The cat's going? Old Scrapper?"

"I can't tell like you can, dad, but I'd put money on it. Out at the cottage he never leaves my side."

"And your friend? Your special friend?"

"If she passes the tests, yes. One more training session, then I'll decide. I hope she makes it, though—doing the business without her would be tough."

Silence. I heard words being carefully chosen.

"She's just a kid, Bloss. Remember that. What she feels about you might well pass, but it's real enough to her at the minute."

Real enough? How did he know?

She didn't answer him. I sensed something. What? Stubbornness? Worry? Disapproval? Were they at loggerheads over Libby? And who was Blick...? Frustration washed over me; not knowing stuff was unbearable. From outside I heard Daisy's laboured approach.

"'Bye, dad. Chin up."

"'Bye, Bloss."

The cell door clanked open, then slammed shut. I listened to the retreating heels, trying to work it all out.

*

An hour later I hadn't moved. I lay there in the duct, musing, munching on fresh spider. Delicious, piquant... Should I go for a third? No, two was enough, an elegant sufficiency, as my friend Beau Brummel used to say, at least while his waistcoats still fitted him. Once the last morsel was gone I folded my forepaws beneath me, licked my lips and tried to be objective.

Was she right? Did he fancy me?

Old enough to be my father, if I'd ever had such a thing...

Was I just flattered, or was it mutual? I mean, he wasn't exactly Glenn, but I was pretty sure I had a rump reaction building up for the old rascal. Could he still...? At his age...? Maybe I was just curious. Was that dangerous? Curiosity killed the cat... Superstition, I told myself, defiantly—I'd do it if I felt like it, wouldn't I? I closed my eyes and began fantasising.

Once he's asleep, slink into the cell. Change... First thing he

85

knew there'd be hands all over him. Then maybe lips. Then...

I began to feel a creeping warmth about the loins. My glands were approving the scenario.

He'd think he was dreaming, wouldn't he? He'd think—

"Well, well, what have we here?"

I yelped as he pulled me out. Damn, I must have started to purr and given the game away. Despite my struggling, he kept a firm grip of my neck as he sat down again. The blue eyes bored into mine.

"Aren't you the pretty one, eh?"

He began to stroke me. After a few seconds, I began to feel... ...peaceful. Really, really peaceful.

I stopped struggling and felt myself surrender.

To the sensuality, the bliss.

"And how did you get in there, Puss?"

What eyes... How could they be so blue? He settled back and laid me in his lap, still stroking.

"Lovely coat, you've got. Like velvet. Nice and black, too."

Really, there's sex...

"Bet her hair's like that, Puss. Soft as your fur."

...and there's sex.

He chucked me under the chin. "I wonder what the rest of her's like? I bet she's stunning in the buff."

I heard myself miaaouw. Damn right she is!

"Bet she's a tiger between the sheets, too."

I miaaouwed again, then flashed my claws. Of course! He laughed mellifluously.

"And I'll bet she doesn't know that I know—"

His hand went to the never-fail spot, the bridge of the nose. My purring was like a Ferrari in overdrive, now.

"—that she fancies me just as much—" He tilted my head up. "—as I fancy her."

What?

I squirmed out of his grip, jumped to the floor, then shook myself out of the trance and faced him. This time the laugh was different; knowing, superior.

"Just as much as you fancy anything that'd give you a good seeing to, you no-morals baggage."

His brows creased. The patrician voice became thoughtful.

"You know, you're like her, somehow—same aura, or damn near. And there seems to be some connection between both of you and another soul I know. Strange... I wonder what it means?"

I felt the ends of my whiskers tremble, become sensitive. He couldn't know, could he? Our mutual stare seemed to last forever, and then he leaned back against the wall. His smile had changed, now—to an expression which was frankly scary. When he spoke again, it was with a strange authority.

"Yes, Puss, I can read other creatures. Humans, cats, dogs, every beast under the sun."

He paused. When his voice came again it was wistful.

"Lonely though, having a secret like that. You daren't let on—not even Blossom knows. Not even my own daughter, can you imagine? The only reason I can tell you is because you can't understand a word I'm saying. Not a single damn word."

He leaned back, closed the blue eyes. The voice slowed, became something near incantation.

"Every soul I search, I know. Every joy, every sorrow. Every need, every desire."

I hopped up on to the bench beside him, drawn despite myself. The blue eyes snapped open. Any sadness was gone, now, the voice was quick and bright again. He crossed his arms and grinned at me.

"Which means that, even if I can't tell exactly what you're thinking, you wanton black hussy, I can tell exactly what you're feeling. And you can't kid me. What you're feeling now is fear. I wonder why." The grin widened. "But what you were feeling, until ten seconds ago, was pure, unadulterated, gutter-grinding, back-alley legover lust." His face came down to within inches of mine. "And I suspect that, at any given moment in the universe's bottomless tub of time, Puss—" His voice was a whisper, now. "—you're never more than a minute away from being randier than a sackful of stoats."

Fur up, claws out, I hissed at him—and then I jumped down and dived for the duct. As I sprinted along in the cramped darkness I could hear his mad laugh, following me. The shivers which convulsed me were strong enough to be painful.

*

A lucky escape.

Back in my own cell, clothed again but still shivering, I assessed the risk. Could he join up the dots? Specifically, my dots? If he could see the overlap of souls between a bonny black cat, a curvaceous private eye and a confused teenage girl... It was highly dangerous, all of it—and to think I'd been scheming to get an hour alone with him! An hour—he'd have had me sixteen ways to Sunday inside the first ten minutes, the old bugger!

But how had I missed the Turl talent? Sheer bloody complacency! It had never even occurred to me that the old rogue might have powers.

That he might be an Empathetic.

A Soul Seer.

They were the rarest of rare birds, readers of need and emotion. They were also capricious, misunderstood and, in my experience, completely unpredictable. (The last one to cross my path had been Marie Antoinette, if that gives you any idea.) I found myself wondering how much of the mad prophet's success with the ladies could be put down to his gift. I mean, knowing when an advance would be welcome was half the battle, wasn't it?

And then I wrote off the thought.

Jonathan Turl was the genuine business with women, second sight definitely not needed. One look from the old reprobate was enough to induce horizontality, even in as hard-bitten a case as Yours Truly.

The question was, did he scare me more than he attracted me?

11

MANY HOURS LATER, I pushed open the cop shop's revolving door, seeing red.

Blood red—had a certain policewoman been within strangling distance, I would happily have swung for her.

No lift home, I'm afraid, Ms Knox. Inspector's orders.

Beth Walmsley's revenge, as unsubtle as her backside. The duty sergeant's smirk had been the last straw.

Just you wait, Beth.

I stood, fuming, the rain coming at me in freezing sheets. Incarcerated, interrogated, bloody nearly conned into yielding my all (OK, it was a stretch, but tantrums take precedence) to an octogenarian sex maniac! Who could read me like a bloody book! And where was my bloody car?

And then, as I came down the steps, reality dawned—*they'd have impounded it, wouldn't they! If the petrol can had come from it, it was still evidence.* To rub it in, the town hall clock chimed a smug midnight. I bunched my fists, gave a yelp of sheer frustration and stamped my foot—*and it'd be tomorrow morning before they bloody well unimpounded it!* And I hadn't eaten for six hours and I was bloody starving! And I didn't have a snowball in hell's chance of finding a bloody taxi at this time of the bloody night and I didn't have my bloody mobile—

This time, it wasn't a yelp, it was a full-throated howl. Pigeons fluttered in fright from a ledge across the street.

Somebody was going to pay for this!

I waited for my fury to subside, but it didn't. I stood there, simmering. A mile and a half trudge back to Knox Towers! In the pouring rain! I pulled up my collar and began forcing one foot in front of the other.

Just you wait, Beth Walmsley...

A hundred yards behind me, a car came round the corner. I turned; an ancient grey Saab, one wiper working, a headlight out. The bubble of my fury burst. The cavalry! It revved towards me and drew up in a squeal of brakes. I pulled open the passenger door, ready to vent—and then the look on Mike Martin's face shut me up.

"It's Libby," he said, hoarsely. "She's gone."

*

I sat at the kitchen table, fingering the note.

Need to get away for a few days, dad, stuff to sort out. Back soon. Got enough dosh.

L.

"No clue where? Mates from school?" I managed a straight face. "Boyfriends?"

Mike let out a long sigh and shook his head. "I've been out searching all day. I've tried every number I've got, been into her Facebook page, everything."

Some of this was my fault, I realised—I hadn't been around enough—*physically* around. Sammy Knox, glamorous pal-cum-auntie, would need to remedy that; with a teenager you couldn't take your eye off the ball, not for a minute. But what was my little witch playing at? Was this the logical outcome of the rows, or could it be to do with what I'd heard the Turls discussing in the nick? Mike stared morosely at me.

"I know the two of us haven't been getting on, but it's so out of character, Sammy. Oh, she was a bit moody yesterday, but I put it down to..."

As the explanation petered out, my mind wandered. Late teens; time I stopped thinking of her as my *little* witch...

"Mike," I began gently, "couldn't you trust her? To do what she's said she's going to? Take a few days, then come back? She might just need a bit of space. She is seventeen now, after all."

All I got was a dejected stare. I felt a stab of anger at Libby; her father didn't deserve this. I forced myself on.

"Anyway, you were in the middle of telling me something. What conclusion did you come to?"

It took a while for the words to come. "I thought perhaps she'd had some kind of tiff," he said, finally, reddening. "With,

90

you know, Blossom..."

So he knew about her feelings. Or suspected, at least. I saw his face achieve full blush; he knew. He tried to give me a defiant stare, but it drowned in an embarrassed shrug. He fished in his jacket pocket and put a mobile phone on the table.

Libby's.

"Never known her leave home without it," he said, quietly. "That's what scares me most." He paused. "But she has taken her laptop."

The phone I understood—*leave me alone*, but the laptop...? It didn't add up. I let the pause hang a minute longer.

"You want me to find her, don't you?"

He said nothing, his eyes on the steam rising from the mug. When he finally spoke, his voice was still miserable, but it had found an edge of determination.

"If she's ok, leave her to do her thing. Make sure she's got whatever she needs." He looked at me. "Ask her to ring me, Sammy. Tell her I'm not angry, I never have been. I'm just worried."

I nodded, then finished my soup and leaned in to warm my hands at the fire. It was pretty much what I'd planned to do anyway.

The day job—the for profit job, the Turls, Bertie, my fee, all the skulduggery—would have to go on hold.

The forever job came first.

*

I stood in the middle of her room. She wasn't anywhere near, I'd have known—which meant I'd better find some clues. And fast.

It was the same as usual, the obligatory teen chaos; barely corralled piles of clothes, a litter of soft drink cans, post-its all over the old desktop and the TV. I read them all; *must phone J, do eyebrows, update F page.* Nothing out of the ordinary. I knocked over her hockey stick as I made for the bikkie stash behind the hard drive, then put it back by the bed. With a mouthful of chocolate digestive, I began in earnest.

Paperbacks. I riffled through them, then checked the shelf beneath. Nothing but dust. I went through her CDs. More dust, still nothing, ditto her soft toys and her framed prints of Bacall and Monroe. Dresser drawers, nothing out of the ordinary, or at least nothing I could see.

Rugs. After I'd rolled them up and put them back down, I did the computer desk's drawers; the usual reefs of pencils and rubbers, sticky tape, odd bits of Christmas gift wrap I recognised from two years ago. I started on the bedding, upending the mattress, checking out the pillows.

Still absolutely nothing.

And one possibly significant nothing.

No lock of Blossom's hair. Hmm... Good sign or bad?

Binned?

Or possibly boxed?

I bent down, reached under the bed and pulled out her treasure chest—Mike's battered old sax flight case.

Photo albums, swimming medals, the ballet prize she got when she was nine, Spice Girls hair clasps, the braces from her teeth, star-shaped pink sunglasses, the baseball cap she used to wear with her pony tail stuck through the back, the gymkhana rosettes she'd taken off the walls.

And then, underneath it all, I found the black satin heart. I smiled. The first spell she and I had cooked up together, to stop Mike drinking. She hadn't understood its meaning then, would she now? No matter, I thought, putting it back, I was just pleased she'd kept it—ridiculously pleased. I flipped open the top photo album; a new one, I hadn't seen it before.

Her and her school pals, crammed together in a photo booth, tongues sticking out at the camera.

Her and her hockey team, laughing, hands up at brows in mock salute, sticks shouldered like rifles.

Her when she was about seven, dressed as a Christmas elf, holding Tiddles. I ran my finger over the excited sweetness of her smile; good times...

I kept flipping.

Mike and her in the Saab.

Her, frowning in concentration, tongue sticking out of the side of her mouth, drawing with crayons at the kitchen table.

Her in her first school blazer.

92

The last one was the two of them and me in wellies, each with a foot up on a spade, the day we'd started on the market garden. Who'd taken it? I couldn't remember. I closed the album, then pulled out the one at the bottom of the pile. The movement uncovered a glint of gold. I reached down.

A locket.

I frowned. This, I'd never seen before. I pressed the catch.

Baby Libs, the obligatory happy gurgling infant.

I closed it and turned it over. No inscription. I put it in my pocket; I'd ask Mike. I went back to the album which had dislodged it; a musty smell, this one hadn't been opened in long enough.

Mike in proud dad mode, looking ridiculously young, holding Libby upright as she took her first steps.

Mike again, a publicity shot of him in his long-haired rock band days, sax held high, eyes closed in ecstasy.

Then Mike and her and...

...her mother.

Her awful, greedy, self-obsessed mother, the complete bitch who'd upped and walked out without a word. On a three-year-old and a husband who'd just lost his living after a backstage fire had robbed him of two of his fingers.

Belle.

Just remembering her name had me tasting bile. A chameleon; the sweetest of smiles and the sourest of dispositions, a vindictive, revenge-ridden harpie who could turn milk with a two-second scowl.

Libby wouldn't have, would she?

I stood up and scanned the room, troubled. What else? And then I realised I'd ignored lesson one of the Private Eye Bible. *Procedures 1 V1. Searcheth Thou The Waste Paper Bin.* I reached under the computer desk, dragged it out and emptied it on the floor.

Tissues, pencil stubs, wads of chewing gum... And enough discarded paper to rewrite *War And Peace*. I unfurled every crumpled page; first drafts of essays, to-do lists, flyers from rock clubs she was supposed to be too young to go to, doodles of Tiddles, some of them really good. And then, a result.

An unsettling result. A bus timetable for the south coast.

Brighton was underlined.

It was where she lived, wasn't it? Her mother...

I got to my feet. A starting point? I really hoped it wasn't, but I couldn't ignore it.

I frowned. Time to renew acquaintance with Brighton-Not-So-Belle.

*

The next morning, the rental car delivered me to the deep south in good time, despite being the blandest vehicle I'd ever driven—a hatchback so boring I hadn't even bothered checking out the make. The MG, though, would have been a dead giveaway; Libby—should I find her—knew it far too well. And anyway, leaving it behind went some way to mitigating yesterday's jail debacle; *securely garaged* sounded so much better than *seized as evidence*.

But here I was in big bad Brighton, protectorate of the posh, wicked wonderland of the weird. I inched my way through the town centre's Monday traffic jam, absent-mindedly cataloguing the gaudy crowds and fingering the gold locket at my throat. I still hadn't asked Mike about it.

I thought about Libby. If she *had* come here, it wasn't entirely unexpected. Over the years there had been signs—the odd *I-wonder-what-she's-up-to-now* and *do-you-think-it-was-my-fault-or-my-dad's?* More, recently? Perhaps, but I was sure I'd deflected them all well enough, and I knew Mike had always tried to do the same. And there hadn't been a single phone call, or a birthday or Christmas card, never mind a present, to remind the girl of her mother's existence. So if Libby was here, *why* was she here? Rebellion after rowing with Mike? Or a motherless child's angst? Or was it down to the ever-less-predictable Ms Blossom Turl?

And if it was, had anything actually happened yet, or was it all still at the fantasy stage?

But one step at a time. I consulted the post-it I'd stuck to the dashboard—the address my trawl through the Change of Name and National Insurance databases had found. Then I turned off towards the sea, skirting a Gay Pride demo, a swarm of retro mods on scooters and a dog walker with six dalmatians. His t-

94

shirt said *Only Ninety-Five To Go*—and for the first time since the tv debut of Beth Walmsley's backside, I felt myself smile. And when I reached my destination, right on the front with a fine view of the pier, my smile widened. I'd actually found a parking space in Brighton! I sat, basking in the fact, taking in the massive white block called Bella Vista Mansions.

Twenties? Thirties? Its faded grandeur had started life as the Bella Vista Hotel, but now it was rented apartments—and, from what I'd gleaned from its snooty website, it was pretty near the top of Brighton's *des res* list, right on Marine Parade and within easy walking distance of the Pavilion. How much was the monthly screw? How well was the ex-Mrs Martin actually doing?

A preliminary reconnaissance was needed. I got out, stuck a pound coin in the meter and headed up the flagstone path between the potted palms. As I reached the double doors, two over-dressed thirty-somethings emerged in clouds of perfume. Their cut-glass voices ignored me.

"So I told him, Charlene! Don't think you're going to park yourself on me before the divorce is final, I said."

"Good for you, Jess. the bastard doesn't deserve..."

I gave a rueful smile; the great female constants, men and misery. Once they were out of sight, I searched for the name I was after.

Not Belle Martin, she was history.

And Bessie Beasley the buxom barmaid, as she'd been when Mike first clapped eyes on her, had been long buried as well.

No, Mike's ex had gone upmarket. I found her in the top row. *Third Floor Front Left 2. Ms Arabella Courteney-Smythe.*

I snorted. Pretentious, *qui, moi?*

*

Priority one was a survey of the lie of the land.

A turn round the block gave me what I needed; a telegraph pole with lots of nice spiked footholds for maintenance. The top would let me see right into what I'd calculated was Third Floor Front Left 2's living room.

New identity time. I went back to the hatchback, grabbed my

holdall, then braved the sea front's toilets. After a quick change I emerged, overalled and helmeted, tool bag over my shoulder. Generic Repairman #1, totally unmemorable. Ten minutes later, I was up the pole, mini-telescope in hand.

And yes, there she was, the diminutive Arabella, power-suited and restyled. She came in carrying a tray with coffee pot and cups. She looked better than she'd done in Cadisham, I had to admit, but even from fifty yards away, the smile looked shallow. Who was the lucky recipient? I let the scope roam the room.

And found exactly what I didn't want to.

Miss Elizabeth Martin.

Sitting on the couch, hands clasped demurely over one knee, looking absolutely butter-wouldn't-melt as she smiled back at her mother.

All the good karma of dalmatians and parking evaporated. *Why?*

*

Back in the car, still in repairman mode but with shades for insurance, I eyed the entrance and tried to work it out. One thing was obvious—from the looks they'd been giving each other, these two were not meeting for the first time. How long had this been going on?

The question was quickly shelved by mother and daughter coming through the double doors. Belle was wearing a trendy raincoat and heels so high even I would have had trouble staying upright in them. Libby, on the other hand, looked gorgeous in jeans and russet tweed jacket, her leather knapsack over one shoulder. I felt a twinge of jealousy; I'd found her that jacket in Cadisham's Oxfam shop a month ago. As she passed me, the Familiar's first instinct rose, but I suppressed it; *don't let your mind reach out, she'll feel it*. The older woman teetered across the pavement in front of my windscreen and raised an arm. A taxi pulled in to the kerb. Laughing, both of them got in. I heard Belle's voice.

"...of course they'll have your size! Hairdresser first, though. The Lanes, driver!"

I grimaced. The one thing Mike's ex hadn't managed to up-grade was Bessie Beasley's trademark *Last Orders* bark. As the cab indicated to rejoin the traffic, I started my engine.

And then, as it sped away, I switched off again.

The Lanes. I had enough Brighton geography to know what that meant.

Shopping.

Which meant the flat would be unoccupied. Probably for a fair old while...

Which meant a golden opportunity.

I reached for my lockpicks.

*

A cheery workman's whistle would have been spot-on for the next bit (I'd always had a hankering to try one), but it was an art I'd never mastered, so I didn't bother. Hard hat swapped for a woollen cap, I sauntered up the path and pressed a second floor button. An elderly male voice answered.

"Esslemont."

I mimicked the patrician tones of the aggrieved Jess. "I won-der if you'd be so kind, Mister Esslemont, I've forgotten my key."

He gave a dyspeptic grunt, then hit the buzzer. I pushed the door and strode in. Aspidistras, ferns, a desk labelled *Concierge*, stairs up to the apartments and down to the basement.

And nobody around. Fine by me. I made for the tiny lift and let its arthritic rumble carry me up to the third floor.

The corridor smelled of new paint. Eight doors, four on each wall. Two steps took me to Front Left 2. My eyebrows went up—no alarm. I shook my head; *relying on the desk downstairs... Dodgy, Belle, with the likes of me around.* I inserted my levers. The lock almost fell apart the minute they touched it, terrible quality. I donned my rubber gloves and went in.

A quick tour for the layout, then I made for the kitchen; I was ravenous. The fridge held enough loose nosh to cover larceny. I found half a packet of past-their-sell-by-date pork pies behind a pile of ready meals—she'd never been one for cooking, Belle—rearranged a couple of bottles of Moët to cover the theft, then just

97

stood, chewing, while I totted up my first impressions of the Courteney-Smythe abode.

Low-end renovation, the cheapest of fittings, badly finished party walls... *Des res* or not, the landlord of Bella Vista Mansions had his eye firmly on the quickest of upmarket bucks. Shocking, really...

But to work, Knox!

What was I going to find? I finished my stale pie and checked my watch.

Two hours, max.

*

And two and a half hours later, apart from a laminated employee ID, I'd found...

...not much of anything.

A microwaved meal was all the tiny kitchen had ever cooked, the bathroom was a beige-tiled cell with a crocheted toilet roll cover, and the boxroom beside it, where I presumed Libby was stowed, held only a single bed and a washer/drier. No luggage. Was everything Libby needed in the leather knapsack? Not impossible...

The living room—*you'd call it the lounge, Belle, wouldn't you*—was equally characterless. Expensive furniture but cheap taste, a crystal chandelier and a row of travel posters. And the bedroom was worse; other than a wall-length fitted wardrobe full of cheap designer copies, it was all peacock feathers and satin sheets, the predictable fantasy of an ageing *femme* still trying for *fatale*.

In fact, standing in the kitchen doorway munching my second pork pie, I was pretty sure the oversized TV and the well-laden drinks trolley defined most of the former Mrs Martin's current lifestyle. The only book I'd found in the place had been on her bedside table; *Refined Manners for the Single Lady*. It was very well thumbed.

Two questions remained.

Why no computer?

And who or what paid for it all? A high rent sea front flat in Brighton, full of hideous but pricey stuff... Where did the readies come from?

Because I sincerely doubted they were coming from Ms Arabella Courteney-Smythe. I looked at the plastic ID I'd found. The picture was trying for a posh come-on, but the text undercut it with brutal honesty.

Channel View Golf Club
Arabella
Bar

I found myself staring at the outmoded transparent phone on the glass coffee table. *How often does it ring, Belle, for a golf club barmaid?* And then I turned back to the window and watched the waves drenching the shingle beach with spray. If—

The phone rang. The sound was one of these irritating plastic-duck-being-garrotted-in-the-bath things. My eyes went to the translucent handset. No sign of life—and anyway, I realised, it was the wrong noise.

And it was coming from somewhere else.

I followed it. Bedroom, definitely, but the source wasn't obvious. Under the bed? I got down. A mobile, sitting in a wire supermarket basket. Why? Fallen out of her bag? As soon as my hand reached it, the duck died. I pulled out the basket, lifted the phone, sat on the bed, and pressed the green button. Immediate access, no password. Sloppiness or overconfidence? Either way, it was the same syndrome as the alarmless door. I accessed the recent call list.

None. No answerphone messages either. Newly wiped? The duck noise had been a text from someone called Rex. Four words.

Everything set for tonight?

Reply? Purloin for later examination? I decided against either option; no traces to be left if at all possible...

I put mobile and basket back exactly the way I'd found them and turned my attention to the wardrobe. Careful not to disturb the stuff on the floor, I shunted handfuls of hangers along the rail. And behind all the clothes and bags and shoes, I found two interesting things.

The first was a silver-framed black and white picture which identified waste-no-words Rex. Rex *Renaldo*, according to the florid signature. The photo was inscribed *To Darling Arabella, Till All The Seas Run Dry.* The pose was fifties film star, leaning forward in three-quarters profile with a cigarette, smoke drifting up in an artistic curl. He looked repulsive—but despite the greasy smile, he was exactly the kind of superannuated matinee idol a certain type of middle-aged woman would find irresistible. In other words, he was right up Belle's street. It came to me that I knew his face from somewhere, but I couldn't place it. I put the picture back, then turned my attention to my other discovery.

The sliding door built into the wardrobe's back wall.

Cupboard? Safe? I slid it open, then blinked away surprise.

Cold air, stale...

Neither cupboard nor safe.

A dumbwaiter—or rather, the disused shaft of one.

I peered down into the blackness; no chain, no cables, two slack and frayed pulley ropes. Hmm... What was a bit of antique thirties kitchen kit doing at the back of a bedroom wardrobe? I tried to imagine possibilities. Emergency lingerie deliveries? Puff pastry sweet nothings from a lovestruck scullion? In the end, the cheap renovation scenario was the only one which made sense—whatever this device was doing here, the renovation crew had just ignored it.

And it wasn't important now. I pulled my head back out of the space, slid the hatch shut, got out of the wardrobe and took a deep breath.

Exit time. I headed for the front door.

Just in time to hear the the barmaid bark behind it.

I made it back to the wardrobe with seconds to spare.

*

Another bloody cell—but I'd been in worse. The piles of clothes were comfy, and if I was careful to make no noise, I could even stretch my legs. Hopefully, my imprisonment wouldn't last long, but being stuck in a wardrobe only a few feet away from the two people I was investigating was definitely not ideal. I listened.

Girlish laughter. A chink of glasses, pouring sounds... Was Libs drinking? Spirits? Belle's voice walked into the bedroom.

"You get changed in the lounge, love. Don't worry, any creep trying to look in's a hundred miles away in France, and he'd need a telescope the size of Jodrell Bank to get an eyeful! Not that I wouldn't put it past some of them, mind!"

A wave of cheap perfume arrived—and suddenly, Mike Martin's ex was within touching distance. I peered through the louvred door as she took off her jacket. *Don't hang it up,* I willed her, *chuck it on the bed.* She complied, then did the same with the skirt. Stripped off to her smalls, she gave herself a quick once-over in the full-length mirror in the corner. She'd preserved her pocket Venus figure pretty well, I had to say—although when the bra came off, I saw that the boobs had begun their inevitable journey south.

But I also noticed the black underwear. Expensive...

Rex?

"Does it all fit?" she shouted.

"Like a glove!" Libby shouted, happily. "I'm just trying the shoes. Everything all right with yours?"

Belle was struggling with an olive-green skirt at least a size too small. "Sure," she yelled, breathing in.

"When are we going to talk, mum?"

A frown crossed Belle's face. "Later," she shouted. "When we get back."

Back from where?

She didn't give Libby the chance to speak again. "CD's in the big bag, love, stick it on, let's have a bit of atmosphere. Then come and show me everything."

A second's pause, then a scratchy American radio announcer's voice. *And now, live from the Hollywood Bowl, please welcome...*

I heard the clump of blocky heels, and then, as the strains of a big band filled the room, a female American army officer, forage cap perched jauntily on her blond chignon, marched into the bedroom. I didn't recognise her.

And then, open-mouthed, I did.

Coiffed and made up to forties perfection, her uniform second-skin tight, the seams of her nylons ramrod-straight.

A trio of close harmony voices multiplied my surprise.

...he's the Boogie-Woogie Bugle Boy from Company B!

The Andrews Sisters.

And Libby Martin—*my Libby!*—looked like she'd just joined them. She put an arm round her mother's shoulder.

"Reporting for duty, Captain Courteney-Smythe!"

"Carry on, Lieutenant Martin!"

As they preened themselves in front of the mirror, they both giggled.

12

IN THE MOOD.

The title was apt enough, even if the sextet wasn't half as good as the band on the CD. But it wasn't bad, either—and anyway, there was no way they'd have got the whole Glenn Miller Orchestra up on that stage. I was perched high above the dance floor, on the shelf behind the twenty-foot-tall cardboard cutout of New York's Chrysler Building, watching the Channel View Golf Club's Forties Night in full swing. A couple of hundred couples, dressed in everything from British air raid wardens' uniforms to American Rosie The Riveter overalls, were demonstrating how not to jitterbug, and having a whale of a time doing it. The noise level was uproarious. A happy thought struck me; this would be right up old Stoneyhurst's street—acres of stocking top and swinging hemline to ogle. And I was willing to bet the old bugger still had his original uniform.

But for me, the main attraction was an unhindered view of Lieutenant Elizabeth Martin, the club's new coat check girl. And that was sheer delight, not least because it was great to watch her fending off male admirers at the rate of about one every two minutes. Much to the chagrin of their partners, of course, and I could understand why—if the sheer glamour the girl was exuding had been any stronger, it would have had its own pulse. Purring, I watched lipsticked mouths purse and female knuckles whiten as they snaked round male arms, until Libby used her powers—unconsciously of course—to dole out generous doses of reassurance and comfort, just like she'd done with Blue Rinse Betty at Turl's. As the sour smiles evaporated, I felt proud of her; the creed, responsible witchcraft.

Never upset anything you don't have to.

When would I get a chance to teach her the other half?

And if you do have to upset something, rev up the broomstick to the max and make damn sure you do it properly.

But I was noticing something else as well, which brought me back to my musings in the car. Miss Elizabeth Martin was not immune to all the male attention she was provoking. I clocked a fleeting mutual smile between her and a young blond god in a flying jacket. As he was being determinedly whisked away, her eyes lingered on his backside long enough to make me wonder— had her sexual choice really been made? And if so, how definitive was it? Or was my charge shaping up to be what I'd once heard Ollie Babbage leeringly refer to as *ambisextrous*? One of the no-reasonable-offer-refused-as-long-as-you're-gorgeous brigade?

It was something I hadn't considered—but, I reminded myself, at this point it might not matter.

Because I knew that love, that oh-so-human emotion I made no claim to understanding, was a different proposition to mere attraction—a very different proposition. When Lieutenant Libby went beddy-byes in her *Bella Vista* boxroom tonight, would the beautiful view of her dreams still be Brigadier Blossom? Or would it be something more, ah, *appendaged...?* I had to get close enough to investigate—and there was other stuff, long overdue, which needed my presence. Again, the question came. *Had anything physical actually happened?*

The number stopped, the dancers applauded, the musicians leaned back, slackened their clip-on bow ties and took sly sips from their pint mugs.

"Ladies and gentlemen, take your partners please."

Moonlight Serenade.

As the smooth melody flowed languidly from the stage, most of the dancers rearranged themselves into more intimate bundles. I watched Libby watching the changed ambience. Did I detect a hint of *wistful?* A bit of *if only?*

And then I saw I wasn't the only one watching her. From behind the bar, her mother, in between slicing lemons and skewering cocktail cherries at warp speed, was eyeing her daughter.

An electric charge rippled through my fur, for the expression on Belle's face was anything but sweet now. The all-girls-together mask had slipped, and what lay beneath was chilling—cold and calculating. I felt my resolve rise. This was the woman I'd known, the one whose clutches I was determined Libby was not—*ever*—going to fall into. What, I asked myself for the tenth time, was the bitch up to?

104

My speculations were swamped by a flock of exhausted jit-terbuggers, joking and shouting, flushed with effort and fanning themselves as they took over the bar. Instantly, Belle reverted to Bessie, frenetically mixing cocktails, pulling pints with one hand while she rammed glasses up against optics with the other. Some-one's joke triggered her bark of mirth.

What, I wondered, did Libby really think of that laugh? In fact, what did my adventurous Adept think of her rediscovered mother in general? My eyes sought her out again—just in time to catch an answer.

A troubling answer. The look I'd caught on Libby's face was... ...sad.

A deflated look. A look of doubt, of disappointment.

The realisation came, slowly.

Whatever had carried Libby Martin here to her mother's side was being tempered by the reality of what she'd found. I ached for her.

And then my antennae pricked up again, but in a very differ-ent way.

Danger.

A new figure, tailored and tuxedoed, white carnation in his lapel, made his entrance. Eyes a-twinkle, tanned to perfection, not a silver hair out of place—the ageing matinee idol himself.

Rex.

He sauntered up to the bar. Automatically, the crowd parted for him. He acknowledged the consideration with an affable smile.

"Thank you. Very kind."

The voice, a sleek Belgravia purr, carried up to me effortless-ly. Belle's eyes and his never met as she put a large whisky in front of him, but only a complete fool could have missed the con-nection. He took a big swig of his drink. And then, slowly, but very deliberately, he examined his surroundings.

If I'd had any doubts about my reading of him, they died as I watched him ogle every woman in sight...

...except the most beautiful one in the room.

Whatever was going on here, Rex Renaldo was part of it, no doubt about it.

No doubt at all.

I pulled up outside Bella Vista, yanked the handbrake and tried to think.

I had to get into the flat again before the women got back, and the pick-a-name-at-random trick wouldn't work at this hour. I checked my watch. Midnight. I'd heard Belle order their taxi for one-thirty. Enough time?

I put Libby's locket in the glove compartment, pulled off my jeans and put on working trousers—black army fatigues with big leg pockets. I checked the contents; torch, screwdrivers, bendy plastic strips, pepper spray. I added the lockpicks, then the Velcroed gripper pads I'd brought on the off chance. Old dogs might balk at learning new tricks, but old cats—especially old cat burglars—weren't so stupid.

Behind the double doors, the lights in reception were still on. An actual employee, or window dressing? Too risky, I decided; the front desk had to be bypassed. I bundled my hair into my woollen cap and pulled on my jacket. Outside, I checked the street; wind and spray, nothing else, too cold even for drunks. I flashed the remote at the hatchback and headed round the side of the building.

As I'd suspected, the posh facade disappeared along with the sea view. The path wound me down a gentle slope, took me through a crumbling gateway and ended in a back yard which reeked of drains. The windows were dark, and a single dull overhead bulb illuminated the service door. I examined it. If anything in this peeling palace was going to be alarmed, this would be it. There was nothing I could see. I went to the first window. Easy. A flip of the catch with my longest plastic strip and it swung open without even a creak. I levered myself in and stood, waiting.

Still nothing.

Smells? All I knew was that I was in what had once been a kitchen, still greasily haunted by the ghosts of fry-ups past. What now?

I closed the window and explored. The room was cavernous;

tables, sinks, ancient gas cookers, kettles and hanging saucepans. There were two doors in the far corner. One was locked, the other wasn't. A back staircase? I opened it to find rows of rusting washers and wringers; the original hotel's laundry. Where was the lift? Had my bet about it been wrong? Did it come down no further than the ground floor? I turned, let the torch beam wander—and found a dingy brass door hidden under the main stairs. I walked over, pushed the call button and heard a doddery descent begin, high above. Once the cage arrived, I listened again. Silence. Good, nobody paying attention... I got in and pressed three. As the lift wheezed its way upwards, I began sorting through the lockpicks to find the ones I'd used before.

And then, as we chugged our way up, I heard a new noise.

A different electric motor. A machine. *Damn!*

I stabbed at the basement button, but the old lift ignored me. When we got to the third floor, the door rattled open. Twenty feet away a silver-haired man in a brown uniform was swishing an ancient floor polisher across the boards, whistling something I vaguely recognised.

A caretaker... Luckily, he had his back to me.

Holding my breath, I pressed the button again; *don't turn!* I shut my eyes, waiting for the greeting, the query. None came. Great whistling, I thought, absurdly. After an agonising age, the door stopped sulking and consented to close. Once the lift began its geriatric descent, I collapsed against the back wall.

My thoughts were the kind of relieved jumble which fastens on the irrelevant. Where had I last heard that tune? Hummed by the musical director of Cadisham nick, I remembered. *My Love is Like A Red, Red Rose,* that was it... Had he finally charmed his audience? As the lift inched downwards, the whistling—really skilful, really melodic—faded away.

And by the time I'd made it back to the basement, I'd worked out the only move I had left.

Not an option I was keen on, but burglars and choosers...

*

Inset into the wall beside the biggest table. I found it.

The dumbwaiter's bottom hatch.

I pulled it open, stuck my head in and shone the torch upwards. The beam followed the slack ropes into darkness. I took out the grippers and fastened them on, pulling the Velcro tight around my wrists. The next bit was tricky—installing myself. I began pushing into the hatch, wishing for once I wasn't quite so well endowed, and then, bosom safely in, I stopped.

The hatch door had a twin, on the opposite wall.

Did I have time?

*

It opened easily. A smell enveloped me. A male smell, cigarette smoke and beer and sweat. I pushed on, levering myself through and down until my hands touched cold lino. I got to my feet.

A tiny space. Bedroom? Office? The torch beam found a door. It had to be the locked one I'd tried from the other side. I stepped over and flicked the light switch beside it.

Office, bedroom, even bathroom... All crammed in tightly enough to make Knox Towers look positively spacious. I went to the cracked sink. A fearsome-looking cutthroat razor lay on it. On the wall above, a thick leather strop hung on a nail, beside a tiny circular mirror. I turned. On the other side of the narrow bedstead stood a table, buckling beneath the weight of a computer. A thick rubber-banded sheaf of letters lay beside it. They were grey with dust. I frowned. Why? As I reached for them, a door slammed somewhere near.

I froze. Heavy footsteps. Very faintly, the whistled strains of *My Love is Like A Red, Red Rose* approached.

The caretaker.

I moved fast; light switch, then exit hatch. As silently as I could, I thrust myself in, bent myself double, did a bit of leg and shoulder origami and slid the hatch cover shut. I held myself still as the key turned in the lock.

Had he heard me?

*

Levering myself up the shaft wasn't easy, but it was doable. I'd gone climbing in the Cheddar Gorge with Mike once, just for the hell of it, and while I'd hated the experience, I was grateful for it now. The dumbwaiter's shaft was exactly like the rock chimneys he'd shepherded me up.

Wedge back against wall. Right leg lift. Left leg lift.

My progress was incredibly slow, but steady. The grippers were the key, it would have been impossible without them.

Wedge back harder. Hands grip surface behind.

The last bit of the sequence was the most difficult, but as long as I kept the tension, it worked.

Bum up. Rest.

Each cycle gained about a foot, more was impossible.

Cramp and muck were the worst problems. I solved the first by building a flexing of each knee into the routine. The second was more serious; the ropes were filthy. Every time I batted them out of the way, they loosed a shower of dust and crap which had me fighting a sneeze—but I couldn't give in to it. The shaft was a natural amplifier; down in his hidden room, the caretaker would hear me.

But the modified routine worked.

Wedge back against wall. Right leg lift. Flex knee. Left leg lift. Flex knee. Wedge back harder. Hands grip surface behind. Bum up. Rest. Pinch nose against sneeze. Right leg...

How long before the women got back? I gritted my teeth. All I could do was continue my vertical crab's progress and hope.

*

By the time I pulled open the hatch and heaved myself—sweaty and filthy—into Belle's wardrobe, I was dizzy with relief. I'd had one bad experience, about halfway up, after getting the order of movements wrong. It had taken four feet of downward skid before I'd managed to stop myself. Scary.

But at least I hadn't been short of entertainment on the way. Bill and Effie on the ground floor were having a falling out over the balance of their joint account. I'd tried to see both points of view, but in the end I was with her; who could ever think two pairs of Jimmy Choos a luxury? At such a bargain price?

And then there was Tommy on floor one, who'd significantly expanded my vocabulary of Cockney imprecations by hurling them at his computer, for which I couldn't blame him—not after losing over a grand in ten minutes at internet poker.

And whatever else wasn't working in Jess's life, she was right up there in the gold medal class for stamina. The encounters I'd heard between her and Rocco and Nadine and Lance, enhanced by a fascinating array of orgasmic bleats, had lasted from the second floor almost to the third.

But now...

Stretched out behind Belle's designer knockoffs, my breathing coming in huge gulps, I waited for my heart rate to fall from Derby winner to donkey ride. I shifted position against the cramp in my knees—which brought me face to face with the portrait of repulsive Rex—and suddenly I knew where I'd seen him before. A seventies TV game show, *Celebrity* something... The cramp got worse. I had to move. I stripped off and stashed clothes and shoes in an old suit bag I found on the top shelf. And then, stark naked, I exited the wardrobe, took a deep breath, assumed the Position and Changed.

Which left me cramp-free and fresher, much. I padded into the living room—excuse me, the *lounge*—and installed myself under the sofa.

*

I didn't have long to wait. Ten minutes later I heard the latch, then Belle.

"...and once we're settled and cosy, we'll tuck in."

Sounds; garments coming off, followed in short order by boxes being opened. Then food smells—quiche, *vol-au-vents*, canapés; they'd raided the dance's buffet! *Not fair, Belle*, I thought, drooling—*I've had nothing all day except two stale pork pies!* I tried to shut out the munching. *Not bloody fair!* Then Belle's ankles appeared in my line of sight. She kicked off her heels. As she wrinkled her toes, my whiskers twitched; the smell of them had not improved with the years...

"You did great tonight, love, you really did. Nothing fazed you, not even the big rush at the end. A real pro."

"Thanks mum."

To hear Libby call her *mum* flattened my ears. My tail flicked.

"It was good of you to ask me. Fantastic experience. And I had a ball."

"That's great to hear. And this—" I heard the rustle of paper money. "—is what you've earned."

"Eighty pounds! But that's far more—"

"Not a word. You were worth it, and it's there for you again, any time there's a function. And there's always a bed for you here, you know that."

There was a pause before Libby spoke again. "Thanks, mum. This'll come in handy if I have to leave..."

The words *my dad* hung, unspoken, between them. My heart lurched. *Had it gone so far?* Then, another pause. Even from under the couch, I could feel the awkwardness. When Libby's voice came again, it sounded about nine years old.

"Why did you go, mum?"

When Belle finally answered, her voice was gentle. I almost reacted—and then the words *world-class liar* flashed before my eyes.

"Your father and me, Libby, it just didn't work. Oh, at first it was wonderful. Great-looking guy, played in a rock band—imagine! Always polite, always fun, treated me like a real lady, and— you're old enough to understand this—we just couldn't keep our hands off each other. But it wasn't enough, stars in my eyes or not. The other stuff kicked in quickly, especially after you came along. All the nights he was off doing gigs, getting up to God knows what, me left sitting at home..."

My claws came out. *True enough, but you didn't lack for company, did you? And I don't remember much sitting going on...*

"...all the times he staggered home with a skinful..."

I stifled a hiss. *Pot and kettle, love. Forgotten being nicked for D&D after the punch-up in the Red Lion?*

"...and of course, I don't suppose I was perfect either."

I was quivering with anger, now. *You can say that again. How many times did Mike bail you out for shoplifting?*

111

More silence. Libby spoke again.

"What about me?"

Belle's voice became aggrieved. "Your dad said I was a terrible mother."

Wasn't wrong there, was he? I fed your daughter more often than you did.

"By the time I left," she went on, "what with the booze and everything, he was half-mad. The truth is, Libby—"

I waited for the lie.

"—he said he'd kill me if I ever came near you again."

I felt Libby's gasp as much as I heard it. Full-blown rage came to me—*the bitch's ankles were within reach!* I began slinking forward.

"But now..."

The two words pricked my ears up. *Her voice, it was no longer steady.*

"...I've got another chance."

I felt Libby's puzzlement. Belle got up, then padded away. When she came back I saw something silver come down on the coffee table.

"Rex," Belle said. "Rex Renaldo. Handsome, isn't he? You'll have seen him tonight. Club chairman, owns this whole block, lots of other stuff in Brighton as well—boutiques, antique shops. He used to be on the telly, back in the seventies. A game show, *Celebrity Stars*, it was called." I saw her pick up the frame. "And now..."

"You mean..."

Belle's voice broke with emotion. "Yes, love! He's popped the question!"

*

Several hours later, I was still under the sofa, savouring the silence. I'd let my rage burn on, undimmed, through the hugs, the two bottles of champagne, and Libby's ever-drunker congratulations. Even through Belle—the *cow*—swearing she wouldn't take no for an answer, Libs had to be her bridesmaid. Libby had muttered something, but I wasn't sure if she'd agreed, because by then the booze had kicked in properly, and my teenage witch was very much the worse for wear. Belle—sober as a hanging judge—had packed her off to bed soon after.

But now, I thought, it was time to swap anger for analysis.

What were the chances of the mum-getting-married-again tale being true?

Possible, I decided, grudgingly—but much more likely to be part of the con. Lure Libby down to the bright lights of Brighton with the promise of some glamorous paid fun, then gild the lily with confetti and character assassination.

But the catch in Belle's voice...

Why?

And then I had it. *Fake or not, Belle wanted the wedding fantasy to be real!*

Which brought me to the enigmatic Chairman Rex. I didn't know enough to read the man properly yet, but I hadn't imagined the danger dripping from him. He was a definite threat.

But what, I wondered, was behind all this? Why had Belle enticed her daughter to Brighton? Just to spite Mike? I wouldn't have put it past her, but it didn't fit. This whole setup smacked of planning, of purpose. So why was Libby here? What made her presence advantageous to Ms Arabella Courteney-Smythe?

Somewhere, a clock chimed. Four am.

I shelved speculation. First things first; duty of care. It was time for me to be Libby Martin's Familiar.

I crept out, gave Rex's oily smile a good hiss and crossed to the boxroom door. I assumed the position, then Changed, then listened; no noise. It was chilly, but my clothes were in the wardrobe, so naked would have to do. I turned the doorknob, very quietly, and went in.

She was lying on her stomach on the bed, blonde hair everywhere. The leg peeking out from under the covers solved the lock of hair puzzle. It had become a bracelet, round her ankle. Was she far enough gone? I smiled; *a bottle of bubbly and a big shock, all on top of a strenuous night's coat wrangling...* She was completely out of it, no question.

I went to the little knapsack. Toothbrush and paste, a few changes of clothes—and in one of the side pockets...

...a small blue envelope.

Inside was a sheet of matching paper, folded round a head-and-shoulders shot of Belle.

Libby, when I saw your Facebook page, I had to get in touch.
I'm your mum.
Give me a ring. My number's on the back of the picture.

Arabella.

I examined the envelope. No stamp, no postmark. How had it been delivered?

And *when...?*

I folded it away and put it back where I'd found it. Then the sight of Libby claimed me again.

So beautiful...

And so gullible?

Because the blue note answered my biggest question—the first move had been Belle's.

I went back to my knapsack trawl. Cosmetics, a perfume bottle—Je Reviens, at least I'd taught her something—and finally, the return half of a bus ticket. For tomorrow. Leaving Brighton 1.15, arriving Cadisham 6.20. Great, I'd phone Mike. I pulled the drawstrings tight and put the bag back. Where was her laptop? I found it on the other side of the bed, lifted it, tiptoed into the kitchen, sat at the tiny table and pulled up the screen.

Emails by the dozen, most of them from her dad, ranging from frantic to pleading to apologetic and back again. Libby had answered none of them. Then there was the usual barrowload of spam, then—

Her screensaver kicked in.

I sat back. Finally... I watched the images of Blossom dissolve into each other.

Riding-breeched and laughing, leading her horse...

Tennis-skirted on a bench, impish smile, racquet on her knees...

At the wheel of the Morgan, wearing a stylish leather jacket...

I closed the computer and cocked an ear again. Still nothing. I went back into the boxroom and put the laptop back where I'd found it. Then I stood, watching Libby, letting my need for her rise, become urgent. How careful did I have to be? Very... What I had to do went right to the heart of being an Adept, and if she saw me when she didn't expect to... Without warning, she rolled over.

Now.

I got down on my knees. Gently, I lifted off the sheet. *Relax,* I told her, *be easy, let your troubles flow from you.* I lifted her right breast and found the third nipple, big and brown. Carefully, I craned forward.

And kissed it, gently but firmly.

She stirred and tried to pull herself up, but her head lolled back. I frowned. Usually, one kiss was enough. Was she so tired? Or so drunk? Or was this the stress of recent days? Try again, I decided, make it longer. My hunger for her didn't argue. I leaned down again.

This time the effect was electric. Her back arched, her mouth opened, her breasts flushed. Her nipples stiffened, all three of them. She gasped, deeply—once, twice—then sat straight up in the bed. Her eyes were wide open, but I knew she was seeing nothing.

"I *want!* I want... I, I..."

Her whole torso slackened, then she fell back. Her breath slowed, became placid.

The hair bracelet started to move, circling her ankle, slowly, sinuously, tightening and slackening.

Caressing...

Beside the bed, the laptop began to glow.

I lifted it—hot. Cautiously, I opened the lid. The Blossom sequence had speeded up, the images throbbing with life, rippling, intense with colour. Gently, I closed it again.

Between anklet and computer I had my answer. It didn't tell me whether they'd been physical, but it did tell me that what my witch felt for Blossom Turl went deep.

Very deep.

Eyes still tight shut, she frowned, then pouted.

A loud crack came from the living room—then a crash. By the time I'd worked out what had happened, I could hear Belle

115

getting out of bed, muttering and swearing. Shocked, I looked down at my charge; fast asleep, but her mouth had twisted into a savage smile.

She had smashed Rex Renaldo's silver-framed picture from fifteen feet away, through a wall.

I felt panic rise—I had to do something, fast. What? *Change?* No—*keep your nerve, Knox!*

*

By the time Belle shuffled into the living room, I was behind the TV. I heard her give an annoyed snort over the remains of Rex. When she headed into the kitchen, I crept silently to the wardrobe and got in. As I pulled the door shut, I heard the sounds of dustpan and brush. What now?

The bed's creak told me she was back. I dared a look. Her hand held the mobile. Once she'd dialled, I heard a murmured endearment, then her voice, soft.

"...anyway, she's out cold."

Ahhh, Libby's sluggishness... I understood, now—what had they used? My answer came immediately.

"...the chloral. Don't worry, I measured out the dose just like you said."

A long squawk came from the other end, punctuated by a laugh. Belle's voice changed, became concerned.

"She won't get hurt, though, will she? You promise?"

I couldn't make out the reply, but the tone reassured. Belle paused, as though the next words were hard.

"The thing is, I like her. Funny, I didn't expect to."

A longer squawk, with an edge of annoyance.

"No, love, keep your hair on, it doesn't make any difference. I'll need another pic of you, though—the framed one fell off the coffee table."

The other voice reverted to its silkier tones, Inside seconds she was hypnotised.

"Tell me about the hotel again," she said, softly. "About the honeymoon suite."

The soothing purr went into overdrive—but after a few sec-

116

onds it became sharper.

"Of course I'm ready! Sunday, pickup at eleven, Neal Street, then on to Connaught Place. Don't worry, I've got the paperwork. You're sure they'll be open?"

Back to reassurance. I made out *special appointment.*

"And we fly Sunday evening?"

I heard *of course,* then the voice at the other end asked a question. Belle gave a sigh of exasperation.

"Stop worrying, I've told you a hundred times, the tins'll be ready. You'll have them by morning."

Tins?

She ended the call. Then she got up and donned slippers and dressing gown. I chanced a peek. I saw her reach under the bed and pull out the wire basket I'd found the mobile in. She took it with her out of the bedroom.

Instant decision. Soundlessly, I came out, assumed the Position and Changed, then got myself back under the sofa. I heard the boxroom door open, then after a few minutes, close again. The cushions above me bulged as Belle flopped down. A humongous tumbler of whisky arrived on the table—

—followed by a tiny notebook computer.

It must live in her bag, go everywhere with her...

And then the wire basket came down on the floor in front of me.

It held a coil of dirty washing line. And a white plastic bag, full of...

...tins.

She took out twelve. They were small, oblong, with rounded edges, like the kind used for sardines. She stacked them up to one side. I crept close enough to watch her pull open the little computer. I could just make out the screen's top half.

A document, official-looking. Legal? She began laughing. It was a strange sound—or rather, a strange mixture of sounds, triumphant one minute, bitter the next. As she scrolled through, I read with her.

And by the time she'd got to the second page, I was quivering.

With disbelief.

It couldn't be true!

Could it...?

Still laughing her strange laugh, she took out one of the tins and prised it open. A scent reached me, one I remembered from Libby's childhood.

Plasticine.

*

It was a masterclass.

I watched in wonder. Who would ever have thought Belle Martin capable of such skill?

Front.

It was something I'd learned, half a century ago, but I'd never been as good as this. Or as fast.

Left side, right side.

Old school... None of the fancy stuff with Photoshop and bits of cut-out credit card. *Who taught you this, Belle?* Her hands were deft and assured, the silence of her concentration was fierce. Arabella Courteney-Smythe's upmarket pretensions had vanished, eclipsed by a cool criminal competence. Acquired how long ago? I watched, fascinated; nothing rushed, nothing skimped, every action executed with utter steadiness.

Three meticulous impressions of each key from Libby's key-ring. One by one, the finished products landed in the wire basket.

Then, when all the tins were done except the last three, Belle lifted the washing line and knotted one end of it tightly round the basket's handle. Understanding dawned; *the letters in the hidden room, it was why they'd been filthy...*

She leaned back, out of my sight. Above me, an exhalation came, deep, satisfied. I saw her hand reach for the whisky. A long slug was knocked back. When the glass reached the table again, it was empty.

Silence.

Broken after a few interminable moments by a sound I hadn't expected.

A lonely, timid little sound.

A sob.

Being stifled. It was followed by another, then another. The phone call came back to me.

The thing is, I like her...

And then, as though rebuking herself for sentiment, Belle Martin stopped sobbing, flexed her fingers and returned to work—this time, with even greater care.

Making three perfect Plasticine moulds of the ornate brass sword key which usually lived on a velvet ribbon around her daughter's neck.

13

"WHAT DO YOU MEAN, you *never got round to it!*"

"Well, she wasn't bothering us any more, so I suppose I just, you know, let it slide."

I suppressed a scream, but not by much. The urge to lob the mobile through the window almost won, but then I looked round the Pavilion Cafe's placid Tuesday clientele and decided I had too much breakfast left to get thrown out. I forced myself back to some semblance of calm.

"Are you seriously telling me, Mike Martin, that you are still married to the woman who made your life an absolute misery for five years? That you just couldn't be bothered to divorce her?"

"Well, I suppose when you put it like that... But you have to understand, Sammy, once she was gone..." He had the grace to let his voice become sheepish. "...what with looking after Libby and everything, it really didn't seem, you know, so important..."

I killed the call and sat there, numb. Musicians! Honestly! Feckless or what? Anything to avoid dealing with paperwork, every one I'd ever met was the same! I shovelled a rasher of bacon into my mouth, then wiped up the egg yolk with the last of my toast. And came to a decision. With a long day ahead I couldn't drown my sorrows, but I was going to have a damn good go at suffocating them. Seconds on all of it, with extra black pudding. Just as I was about to head for the counter, the phone rang. My calm evaporated. I grabbed it and pressed green.

"Well, it's about to become important, you imbecile! Because she's the one divorcing you, now—and she wants half of every-thing, cottage, business, the whole shebang! As well as spousal maintenance for every year since she legged it! So you can expect to hear from Manston, Erridge & MacSween, Brighton's finest, shysters by appointment to anyone with the readies. The papers are probably winging their way right now! So what've you got to say to that, you halfwit?"

"Not a lot," said the voice at the other end, "but I think half-wit's a bit strong. I did have evidence, and I only rang to say you could pick up the MG."

Beth? *Shit!*

An olive branch...? I settled on *hurt*, but before I could try it out, her voice came again.

"There are still details you could help us with, Ms Knox," she said, woodenly.

I plumped for *snotty/formal*. "Give me one good reason why I should, Inspector Walmsley." My pose collapsed. "After you kept me banged up for four hours longer than you needed to! Then had me chucked out in the pouring bloody rain!"

"You laughed at me."

"It was pretty damn funny." I paused to recover my poise. "But perhaps by now you'll have had time to appreciate," I said, in the most put-upon tones I could muster. "that I made a point of not sharing the joke with anyone else."

The sound which came in reply started as a full-blown snort before tailing off into a non-committal grunt. I held the phone away and allowed myself a long sigh of relief.

"What're you up to, Knox?" Beth said, finally. "Down there in Sin City, Sussex?"

How did she know I was in Brighton...?

Not important, I decided. I scoffed my last sausage and told her everything.

*

After my late breakfast and six coffees, I was beginning to feel more like a human being. How I'd feel as a cat, of course, wasn't guaranteed, but I suspected I'd better lay in some smoked salmon for Knox Towers, later. I sat back, sated, and thought about Belle Martin.

What a bloody infuriating human being she was! Had the sobs been real? Although I didn't want to believe it—for years I'd had the woman pigeonholed as a scheming slapper—I couldn't get past the fact that her emotion seemed genuine, just like her wedding fantasy. But my conclusions about what I'd overheard might, of course, be a different matter.

So which was it? A distraught mother's guilt about screwing over a long-lost daughter—or a past it old floozy's tears at knowing she'd never get the wedding she'd schemed so hard for?

And as far as the said wedding went, one other factor had come roaring into play, because there was no doubt at all what the long-lost daughter thought of her hypothetical new stepfather. The savage telekinetic smashing of Rex's picture had made that abundantly clear. I pulled out the crumpled original I'd salvaged from Belle's bin and smoothed it out as best I could. No accounting for taste, but the man really was repulsive.

But did any of it matter? Since it didn't seem to be affecting Belle's plans one whit? The memory of her fingers knotting the washing line round the wire basket's handle came back to me. It all made sense. The basket gets lowered down the dumbwaiter hatch, with the tins or letters or whatever, the caretaker delivers them to Rex, and the nefarious scheme, whatever it might be, is furthered. But why it was it necessary to keep up such a front?

I looked at the café clock. One-fifteen departure... More than enough time to see Libs off, then follow the bus to Cadisham. I should phone Mike again, I thought, no matter how pissed off I was, and let the poor man know what time his prodigal daughter would be home. I stood up.

And heard something which immediately sat me back down again.

A male voice, deep and smooth.

"I wonder if I might trouble you for two of those scrumptious looking vanilla slices. And a couple of pieces of your splendid Swiss tart. I'll take them to go."

Rex.

I turned my back, whipped out my compact and angled it round to find him over my shoulder. He was at the counter, the two teenage waitresses gazing up at him, entranced by the Belgravia purr. Too good a chance to miss, I decided. I stowed everything away, got up and slipped through the back door before he could notice me.

Because, given that Rex Renaldo was about to be the first investigation of the Knox Detective Agency's day, there was no point in letting the old letch see something he would most definitely remember.

*

I made it back to the café in time, but not by much. He emerged, Crombie-coated and homburg-hatted, beribboned pink pastry box dangling from one gloved hand, beautiful pigskin briefcase in the other, just in time for my phone's camera to catch him. He began walking along Grand Junction Road. Hair up in a careless top knot, wearing jeans and shades and the most androgynous jacket my bag could provide, I fell into step about thirty yards behind.

His pace was leisurely, punctuated with appreciative glances at the passing talent. A ladies' man to his marrow, old Rex. And successful with it; female heads turned, then went on their way, rumps swinging a little more at the attention. What does Belle think of that, I wondered. Picking up speed, he took a right up Black Lion Street, cutting a confident swathe through the crowds. I blessed the pink box for making him easy to follow. Then he did a zig-zag through a couple of alleys and came to an antique shop, *Yesterday's Treasures*, its wares spilled out over the pavement. I remembered Belle's list of his assets; did he own this? I heard hail-fellow-well-met, a jocular exchange, then the clink of silver. From the briefcase? When the voices got louder, I feigned interest in a pile of grubby crockery. *Seven quid for a chipped cup and saucer!* Rex passed behind me. A sideways glance showed me the cake box, sitting on a shaky-looking table. Why? My answer came immediately; tucking a well-stuffed envelope into the briefcase required both hands.

Once he'd picked up the box again, I followed as closely as I dared. One more turn, then it was a scruffy newsagent's. Again, he disappeared inside. I took off my jacket and slung it over my shoulder, went up to the window and started perusing the ads. *Gearbox for 1979 Vauxhall Viva... Gent's trousers, 29 waist, 32 leg, only slightly stained... Attractive Polish lady seeks generous older man with view to...*

I turned away as he came out. He began retracing his steps, but at a much slacker pace. Business done for the day?

Back to the sea front. He sat down on a bench, removed his gloves, unlocked the briefcase, brought out a napkin and spread it beside him. A vanilla slice from the cake box was laid lovingly on the linen. Then he delved into the briefcase again and brought out a newspaper, a glass and a hip flask. He took a bite of his lunch, poured himself a large one and unfolded the paper.

The Racing Post.

After a quick tally of the envelope's contents, he opened the paper at the week's meetings. Then he took out a mobile and began dialling. He was engrossed enough not to notice me snapping him again. I strolled to a bus stop and loitered. What next? An afternoon tryst with Belle?

But after half a dozen calls, a wedge of Swiss tart, a second vanilla slice and another two large ones, it was obvious the only thing Rex Renaldo wanted a tryst with was...

...a winner.

Ponies were being picked.

Bookies were being phoned.

I looked at my watch. No choice. *Tempus* had *fugited*. Frustrated, I started back to the hatchback.

And then, as I was passing behind his bench, I heard a sound I recognised.

Whistling.

Tuneful, melodic...

And good. *Really* good...

As subtly as I could, I stopped, then sneaked a look at him from the rear.

Silver hair. Tick.

Right size. Tick.

Right shape. Tick.

Well, well... I turned away and left Rex Renaldo, TV Celebrity, Golf Club Chairman and Prosperous Businessman, to his Sunday lunch and his cheery workman's whistle. And as I strode along, breathing Brighton's bracing ozone, I wondered.

Which would you prefer, Rex, your Swiss tart or your English one? Or would you rather stick with your red, red rose?

And how long have you been masquerading as the caretaker of a block of flats you're supposed to own?

14

BY TEN PM, TRAMPING through the rosebay willowherb, I was torn between self-congratulation and second thoughts. I'd been single-minded enough to turn my back on Knox Towers after a five minute gear-grabbing/knicker-changing pit stop, but the logic of what I was up to now felt dodgy. Worth the candle? I'd know soon enough...

But at least I could congratulate myself on one job well done. An hour ago, through old Baggychops Leavis's garden trellis, I'd watched father and daughter embracing fondly at the cottage's back door. Did that mean the disappearing was over? Or was a rerun still on the cards? I was pretty certain it wasn't, but it was too soon to be sure—and even if it was over for Mike and Libby, the plans of Belle and Rex, whatever they were, would still need thwarting.

Rex...

Would Beth play ball? She'd sounded guarded on the phone. Were the pictures I'd taken good enough?

I reached the edge of the splintered wall and surveyed the back of Nether Kilns House. Should I Change? Cat would be better, more perceptive... But after my exertions of the last few days I was bone-weary, and the process would leave me no energy in reserve. For now, Sammy would have to do. I catalogued my surroundings.

A sliver of moon, caught between patchy clouds...

A faint smell of approaching rain...

A gentle breeze...

And a complete absence of humanity. Excellent. Given the goodies I was carrying, the last thing I wanted was witnesses, especially of the uniformed variety. *Yes, officer, it's true I've just been released for suspected arson, but these burglary tools were my old granny's...* I sat the bag on the wall beside the empty chicken coop, donned my gloves, pulled up my hoodie and jumped over. Then I went silently on through the weeds.

Nary a sound from the lockpicks or the hinges, even easier

than Bella Vista Mansions. Seconds later I was in the kitchen. I didn't turn on the light, there was enough moon to show me the cellar door. I unzipped my bag, fished out the bolt cutters, lined them up on the padlock hasp and squeezed. With a jarring clang, it gave. I caught it before it hit the floor and listened.

Nothing.

The door creaked open. The smells were pungent; ancient air, recent rat—and the acrid residue of an old acquaintance—an old, *addictive* acquaintance. The memory paused me—*not twice*—but I got a grip on myself and reached for my torch. The steps spiralled down and ended at another door. This one opened easily.

*

It was like being inside a big round bottle—a chamber with high, sloping firebrick sides. A steel ladder curved round and up the wall to a central hole in the roof. To let out smoke or to let in light...? Below it, three doors faced me. Steel doors, I noted, new, still shiny, each with a tiny glass window. Between the two furthest ones I saw the mouth of a tunnel, about five feet high. I had no idea where it led, but it was an odds-on certainty it joined up somewhere with the sewer line. The rat reek was strongest there, as was my old friend, the lure which had almost done for me. It smelled dead—but I'd not trust myself to Change here, just the same.

What was this place? I let the torch beam examine the steel doors again. Furnace doors? I went to the nearest one and pulled it open. Wood, in neat herringbone stacks, birch upon oak... I crossed quickly to the other two.

Empty.

What they were was obvious, now; kilns—and the first one I'd inspected was ready to fire something. I let the beam scan the floor around me.

Earth.

But earth with a strange consistency. It had been trodden in.

By the rats. By their tiny rodent paws. The prints indicated hundreds of them, going round and round, as though the chamber's centre was the axis of a treadmill of muck. There were shoe

prints as well, at least three different kinds. One set was undoubtedly female. Grizelda's? I went forward, trying to disturb as little
as possible.

Near the centre I found a big circular imprint which had dug
grooves into the strange earth. Something heavy had been put
down there. What? It was about five feet across, and at one side
of the circle's edge I could see a glimpse of colour. I got down for
a closer look, and as my knees touched the strange soil I realised
there was a hard surface beneath. I began brushing away the top
layer, glad of my gloves.

Tiles. Tiny ones, a mosaic, intricate. More brushing revealed
more colours. Bright, vibrant, even in the dim light; white, black,
red, green. What was this? I went to work. And after ten minutes,
I stood up again, my heart beating faster as I looked at what I'd
uncovered.

Dark suns. Cruel-faced moons. Lightning bolts. Hydra-head-
ed serpents, horned demons, flames...

All bordered by a thin purple line, vivid in the torchlight. I
got down again and cleared away another few feet, following the
line. After the fourth sharp angle I knew what I'd found.

A pentacle.

A purple pentacle—and by my reckoning, it filled the entire
chamber.

*

Half an hour later, my back aching, I stood up.

I'd only uncovered a third of it, but it was enough. I stared at
the inscription between bearded goat and coiled serpent.

> *Three shall take strength*
> *from the vessel of clay.*
> *The four-toed bring earth*
> *that sees no light of day.*
> *The Lord of Misrule*
> *shall be swelled in His power*
> *when the maid who is chosen*
> *takes darkness for dower.*

The four-toed...

The rats I'd caught, that's why they'd tasted so strange—they'd not only trodden the earth in, they'd carried it here in their mouths. And I was sure what had made the circle in the middle, now. I let the beam examine the illustrations I'd uncovered in the three smaller circles which surrounded it.

Each was a different face, each terrifying in its own way. And evil. And triumphant. I knew them all.

Marchosias.

Camio.

Furfur.

One of hell's A-teams.

Whatever this was, it was dangerous. Could I stop it? Not without more information, that was certain—and there was only one place I could get it. Was there time? If I could—

Movement. At the tunnel's mouth. I switched off the torch.

A rat, a big one.

Then a second, and a third.

And then a whole slew of them.

I froze. They scurried over my feet, but if they were aware of me, they didn't care. They went to the area I'd cleared and spat out their earthen loads. Then they started smoothing, pushing at what they'd brought and what I'd disturbed. The pictures I'd uncovered were left bare, but nothing else was. Once the chamber had been restored to pristine foulness, they left the way they had come.

I waited in the darkness, working out exactly what I'd just witnessed.

The janitors, the cleaning crew, the set dressers...

And by uncovering the pictures, somehow I'd joined them, helped them prepare the scene.

But for what?

But now I knew, at least, what the crux of it was. I let my eyes return to the figure in the central circle.

Not the best likeness, admittedly, but it had been captured well enough. Why hadn't I recognised it the first time I'd seen it?

Wrapped round a vessel of clay—a five foot high red and

black Toby jug, on its plinth in Turl and Turl's china department.

I mean, it wasn't as though The Bad Lad and I had never met.

*

"And I must make the point again—and I do feel this is important—the lack of suitable toads has to be addressed! Surely, despite the current priorities, some ceremonial time might be given over—"

"One does not attempt, Sister, to summon one of the senior captains of His Excrescence The Prince Of Darkness, May The Breath Of His Foulness Wither All Udders, for nothing more—"

"Glory be to 'im, my dears! May the 'ooks of 'is 'orns pierce the paps o' all unbelievers! May—"

"Aptly put, Mabel, but getting back to the business in hand. One does not bring up a confidant of Belial And All His Beasts merely to rectify a toad shortage! Resources are not infinite, you know—especially as a quorum seems to have become so difficult to arrange. I remember a time when the members of this association took their duties more seriously! I don't know what things are coming to!"

"It's the bus service, Grizelda, they've cut it again. You can't blame—"

"Madam Chairperson, if you please, Sister Grimblesby! Or Madam Chair, at the very least! Small country chapter though we are, I will have the proprieties observed! And I might add, I expect to see every one of you at tonight's dance jamboree—this is, may I remind you, a full undress rehearsal for the upcoming Sabbath! Should I find anyone sneaking off, Herbert Catchpole, to phone their wife to record the Antiques Roadshow, I assure you they will be severely—"

"Oh, give it a rest, Grizelda, get down off your high goat and stop avoiding the issue! We need toads! Gladys has a point and you know it! If the milk souring programme's to be got back on track, we need at least a dozen good natterjacks, and they'd better be brighter than the ones we've got in the tank out the back—the ones, I might add, which your boyfriend palmed off on us. Took an age to train and in the end they couldn't tell semi-skimmed

129

from orange juice."

"At least Bertram is trying, Brother Pettifer, to create some genuine evil in this parish. All you've managed to contribute recently is a jackdaw which can't even identify the right head to defecate on. Vicar Leavis—"

"May the fire consume 'im! May 'is bowels shit barbed wire!"

"Quite, Mabel. But having the arch enemy walking around unscathed while his two accompanying choirboys are covered in crow droppings *simply isn't good enough*. Especially when, I might add, the young men concerned are possible recruits, already subscribers to four internet pornography services as well as readers of the Financial Times. Now, I believe we have news of our upcoming outing to Yorkshire. Sister Murgatroyd?"

"Thank you, Madam Chair. The trip, organised by our twin chapter in Mire-On-Swale, is confirmed for Saturday the 18th of December. Events include a tour of dairy herds made barren, a chance to be photographed (and pelted!) in the village stocks, a visit to the local gallows souvenir shop, followed by a sumptuous anti-Christmas Dinner in the graveyard, weather permitting. Dress optional, cloven-hooved pets catered for. Eleven pounds fifty, discount for pensioners, block bookings taken. Return the same night, bring your own cup..."

The shuffling of papers told me it was winding down, but it was another fifteen minutes before Sister Murgatroyd's squeaky voice stopped and they started the Lord's Prayer backwards.

Finally, in twos and threes, discussing soap operas and lottery tickets and complaining about the bus fares, they left.

All except Grizelda and Sister Murgatroyd.

"You can go now, Olive, I'll see you at the Manor."

Olive... She came into my sight line.

"It'd be no trouble to stay, Grizelda, I could—"

Grizelda's voice took on a long-suffering tone. "Thank you, Olive, that won't be necessary."

As the door shut on Olive's disappointment, I waited.

Grizelda switched on the lights and snuffed out the black candles, then sat down at the table. I watched her mood change. A smile crept over her features, a secret little smile. I was puzzled. The residue of power? The satisfied aftermath of ordering underlings about...?

But whatever the cause, it was tenacious, that smile of Grizelda's. It stayed in place as she tidied the chairs. It didn't budge while she gathered the leftover papers. It wasn't even dented by finding the chewing gum stuck to the underside of Councillor Catchpole's table. What was going on here?

I waited.

She placed herself before the mirror, then smoothed down her blue Margaret Thatcher two-piece.

I waited.

She went into the kitchen, came back with a can of hair spray and gave her blue rinse a restraining order with one hand, prodding it into shape with the other. The foul chemical smell wafted up to me, making my eyes water.

Still, I waited.

She rummaged in her bag, came out with a pair of nail scissors and trimmed the hairs round the awful mole. Then she took out a lipstick and leaned into the glass. When she was done, the smile became arch. And when she reached into the bag again and came out with a perfume bottle, I finally twigged what was going on.

Sex.

Grizelda was off to see the boyfriend.

A private party, or part of the night's general jollity? As the door slammed, the reek of her perfume reached me. Uggghhh... Synthetic, even worse than the hair spray, cheap, dead, vile...

In fact, probably exactly right for Bertie.

*

I gave it another ten minutes. Only when I was sure I had Buncle Church Hall entirely to myself did I pick my way down from the rafters.

I Changed, then wrinkled my nose at the mix of stenches. Unusually, it was even worse as a human. I found my clothes under the back pew, dressed, and put all thoughts of Grizelda and Bertie away as I went over what I'd heard.

A dress rehearsal for Halloween... And all this talk of senior

131

captains... That was unusual—and it smacked of the unorthodox. Perhaps even the unauthorised? What the hell—literally—were they trying to do?

But at least I'd come to the right place for enlightenment. I went into the kitchen, opened the crockery cupboard and reached up to the right. Good, my memory hadn't played me false. The secret spring was where I remembered it, from Bertha Pike's day. The shelves swung out. The Cadisham & District Coven's reference library was revealed in all its profundity. I scanned the titles.

Malleus Maleficorum... The Complete Works of Doctor John Dee... Nostradamus... Newton's Arcana... The Secret Orgies of John Knox...

My eyebrows rose. I'd no idea my ancestor had been so versatile!

...A Guide To Interesting Penile Warts, Five Hundred Practical Spells... Fond Memories Of Salem, Train Your Own Werewolf, a CD of *Aleister Crowley, The Musical...*

Finally, I found what I was after.

Pentacles And Pottery.

I settled down, stifling a yawn. I had about two hours before the 'folk dancing' was due to begin.

*

...and in honour of his devotion, the Great One bade His servant Peregrine go forth and make His image in the greatest vessel of his art, that He might have a place to dwell when He came among His disciples. And He gave unto his servant Peregrine a great secret, that the power of evil might be multiplied through His earthly domains, three times three, nine times nine, and according to the Rhyme Of Power.

And Peregrine did as he was bid by He who is immortal, The Lord Of The Air, The King Of The Senses, The Master Of Torments!

Know ye that He, in all His glory, shall be nourished on life which is death!

Well, well, fancy that. Old Perry, who'd've thought it?
Peregrine Prendergast, Perdition Perry...
A double agent.

The mausoleum, standing in pride of place outside the church door and subsiding under its own weight, was a hideous box embellished with garish Cadisham Lustreware figures. I stared at them; no one in their right mind could have mistaken them for angels. The door lock had been smashed years ago. I went in.

Crisp packets, chocolate wrappers, an empty half bottle, a burst condom—and a reek I knew only too well. I took a slow tour of inspection round the marble slab which covered old Peregrine. In the last corner I found a triangular hole. I got down and listened.

Squeaking, lots of it.

...the four-toed bring earth that sees no light of day...

I got up and brushed the dust off my jeans.

No doubt about it; Perdition Perry's remains were the source of the strange earth in the kiln chamber.

But did Grizelda and her cohorts know?

*

Even from twenty yards away, you could tell they'd started the fire with that cheap lighter fluid they sell bundled with the charcoal briquettes. The smoke was oily and unpredictable, occasionally gusting up and blotting out the Bad Lad's face on the massive jug. I watched Jocasta Pertwee's flaccid balloon of stomach rubbing itself up against it as they did their masked Ring-A-Ring-A-Rosie number.

"O Great 'Orned 'Un, you'm to come to us now! 'Elp us strike down them unbelievers!"

Never did have much of a singing voice, Mabel. Still, A for effort. The rest of them tried the answering curse, but what with the smoke, they couldn't raise much of a chorus without coughing, and by the time they reached All Fall Down and got to the serious grunting, someone had to douse the embers again, because the wood they'd used was too green. Terrible Boy Scouts they'd have made—and they'd all smell like they'd been bonking on a barbecue by morning; had to be a dead giveaway down the council offices at tea break. I slunk forward through the bushes for a better view, and felt my whiskers twitch in surprise—such an unusual use for a garlic press! Still, one was never too old to learn.

"'Elp us, O Prince o' Darkness! Reveal to us the virgin o' your choice an' we'll 'ave 'er brung 'ere this minute for the pleasurin' o' you!"

That Cotswold accent... I found myself surveying the smug jug. Would the Bad Lad understand?

And then, over the groans of worship and the squeals of orgasm, real and otherwise—how was Jess doing, back in Brighton, I wondered—something occurred to me.

Where was the bold Grizelda? Still playing hide the sausage with Bertie? Somehow I couldn't imagine either of them missing the main event—she'd laid down the law pretty firmly back in Buncle. Hardly the best form if Madam Chair didn't show for her own three line whip. Whip and chair—I grimaced at my own joke; it made her sound like a lion tamer—although tamer lions I'd never seen, I thought, watching the coaxing it was taking to get Basil Pettifer anywhere near action. Was it possible to wear out a cheese grater on a backside? But Grizelda's absence puzzled me—I'd had the woman down as a control freak. Why wasn't she striding about, dictating strokes per orifice or checking the thigh height of black stockings? And, now that I thought of it, where was the meek little acolyte, Olive?

"Once, twice, three times we be callin' to you, O Great 'Un! You'm our 'eart's desire! 'Ear the sounds of our supplication!"

Oh, lay off, Mabel, I thought. But then I chided myself. Why should she? A coveted office, orgy precentor, much sought after... Blinking away the smoke, I skirted round the action, careful to avoid the Toby's eyes while I catalogued the sights.

Andrew Morton the dentist, under his hygienist, Constance Grout. Dilys Maguire the postmistress, her huge thighs slapping pinkly at the ears of Aloysius Coyle the tobacconist. Who'd have thought the proboscis on that mask was so pliable?

And who was that with Sally Spencer? Stan Scrogg? Never!

134

A turn up for the books—the proprietress of Cadisham's toniest tea shop with a mechanic! She'd have a job getting the grease marks off her thighs, though...

And then as I rounded the next tree I was pulled up short by the sight of a pair of chubby calves bouncing against a blubbery red back.

Now that really was perverse! Effie Plumstead and her husband, Kevin the butcher! Turning up at a Satanic orgy to have it off with your own spouse! I watched the frenzied jiggling. Was it possible they didn't recognise each other in the masks? Still, if the yelping and chortling were any indication, they were getting off on it...

A pair of headlights swept down the drive, then went out. In the firelight's uneven gleam I recognised the car's shape.

A Bentley.

I peered. In between the bouncing buttocks and heaving bosoms—you couldn't say they weren't trying, bless 'em—I tried to read the number plate. Impossible. I used the cover of the hedge to slink nearer. The doors opened.

The Blues Brothers!

Still suited, shaded and hatted, they emerged quickly—but freed, for once, from their usual fearful symmetry. No 1, the driver, was holding a cocktail shaker and glasses, No 2, a platter of sandwiches. The smell cut through the bonfire's smoke.

Gravadlax.

My mouth began to water; breakfast in Brighton had been a long time ago. But as I watched them, I congratulated myself.

Minions. Somehow I'd always known they were underlings, these two. So who was the big boss?

The rear window of the Bentley descended. A hand reached out. It had nails as long as Putreficia's, but a great deal more expensive. BB1 delivered the cocktail, then scurried round to the car's other side. The repeat of the operation at the other window brought a bony claw of wrinkled skin which looked as though it could barely support the Rolex on its wrist. BB2's sandwiches were waved away. *Leave the plate,* I willed him, but it disappeared back into the Bentley. As the windows rose again, I heard the female voice, heavy with boredom.

"Elmer, honey, we've seen the floor show. Time to go."

An American accent... Who were they? BB1 appeared again, went round and opened the boot. I tensed myself. Could I make it? A quick dash, hunker down in the corner. I crouched, ready to spring. If—

The teeth in my neck were paralysing. Scrapper's voice was a fierce whisper.

"No, Changeling. We shall meet at the tall tower. Two moons from now."

The bite went deeper. As the world began to go dark, I heard him again, faintly.

"But now, do nothing. I command it. You must not meddle."

*

When I regained consciousness, stiff and painful, day was breaking. What had roused me? A sound...? I waited. It came again, a tuneless grunting. Was it meant to be singing? I forced myself into some kind of alertness.

A human.

Well, something disguised as a human... Bertie Bubb's Range Rover was parked beside the smoking embers of last night's fun. Hooked up to it was a covered trailer. The legend *Simpkins Specialist Fuels—For All Your Firewood Needs* was emblazoned in Gothic lettering on the side. Inside it I could see the red and black pottery incarnation of the Bad Lad, tied down with bungee cords.

The tuneless singing got louder but no better—*never get a gig in Cadisham nick*, I thought. Hidden by the hedge, I approached, cautiously. Bertie appeared with a bundle of coats, then struggled up on to the trailer's bed and slung it into the jug. After a careful step down, he disappeared back round the trailer.

The chance wouldn't come twice—half crippled or not, I had to take it. I tried a sprint, but the best I could do was a fast lope. The jump was agony, the climb up the trailer's side slats even worse. I felt myself go faint again. I shook my head to clear it.

One. Last. *Lunge.*

I pulled myself over the jug's rim and landed on the heap of clothes. It gave way under me and I slid down the cool porcelain

136

interior, scrabbling for a clawhold. When I came to rest I found myself perched on something cold and rubbery.

And dead. It smelled of decay and candle wax.

And cheap perfume.

And even cheaper hair spray.

Cautiously, I opened my eyes—to find myself staring at the shredded remains of a Tyrolean feather. Behind it was a mole.

A mole surrounded by hair, neatly trimmed. Instinctively, I squirmed away—to find myself facing a starred spectacle lens.

The eye behind it would never take aim through a rifle sight again.

The singing came nearer. Dizzy, I managed to heave myself out of the jug. I closed my eyes and leaped.

Ouch! Ignoring the gravel's sting, I forced myself on as far as the hedge—and when I turned I saw Bertie at the trailer's rear, pulling down the canvas flap. After he'd fastened it, he brought out one of his evil-smelling cigars, lit up and stood, surveying the grounds of Blatherwick Manor.

With a distinctly proprietorial air.

I thought, furiously. Could Blatherwick Manor have a new squire? A snout-nosed denizen of the underworld? After another few minutes, he tossed the stub away. It landed inches from me. As I flinched away from it I heard the Range Rover's smooth start.

I came out on to the path as *Simpkins Specialist Fuels* bumped away with its cargo of the dead and demonic—and as I watched it go, I made out the cheery tune Bertie had been murdering.

Another One Bites The Dust.

The bastard! The callous bastard...

And then my fury was undercut by something completely unexpected.

Libby.

The tingle was faint, but unmistakable. She was somewhere near. And she was excited. And confused. And a little afraid...

Was she in danger?

No time for clothes, no time for Changing. I turned in her direction and began limping, as fast as I could.

*

137

Breathless after two hard and hurting miles, I stopped as soon as I saw it.

The Cinquecento.

Parked behind the remains of Oxley Hill Farm, with Libby's bike propped against it. The wind brought me a female voice, shouting, hectoring. What was going on here? I hid behind a half-demolished wall, all that was left of old Charlie Oxley's barn. The voice stopped. Cautiously, I padded forward and looked.

Training...

Libby, covered in mud, was about fifty yards away, on her stomach. The rucksack strapped to her back was at least six times the size of the one she'd had in Brighton, and she was crawling up a long slope to the rusty bathtub which had once watered Charlie's Blackfaces. Stopwatch in hand, Blossom was standing beside the tub. No nice Ferragamos today, she was in landed gentry mode; tweed cap, designer wellies and Barbour jacket with an artfully torn right pocket. As I watched, she went back to haranguing my charge.

"You have to do better! If you can't beat thirty seconds, we can't use you! Up! Now! *Sprint!*"

Libby scrambled to her feet and ran flat out, then collapsed, coughing, into Blossom's arms. I scurried across to the breeze block slab which supported one end of the tub, in time to see Jonathan Turl's daughter push my witch firmly away. She consulted the stopwatch again, then, shaking her head, she extended a forefinger and tilted up Libby's mud-caked chin.

"Won't do. Another eight seconds to be shaved off."

"I can..." Libby stood, gulping in lungfuls of air. "...do that, Bloss. I know I can."

Blossom spoke again, her voice grim. "What have you been up to, Libby Martin? You were in much better shape last week. If I didn't know better I'd say you'd spent the weekend boozing."

My charge hung her head. I could barely make out her blush through all the mud. I had a flashback to glamorous Lieutenant Libby. Gone forever? It was hard to believe I was looking at the same person—but then, today's Brigadier Blossom didn't look much like the laughing girl on Libby's screensaver, either...

Blossom's voice came again, softer, now. "You're vital to this, Libs. You've got the skills we need, you've come through everything else with flying colours—but if you can't keep up physically..." Her voice relented a little more. "Rest now, ten minutes, I've got calls to make. Then we go again." She touched Libby's arm. "It's not the running that needs work, it's the crawling. Use your elbows more."

She turned abruptly, walked over to the car, sat in the driver's seat and took out her mobile. Libby sloughed off her rucksack and plonked herself down on the tub's edge. Water sloshed over and hit my ears. I shook it off and looked up. She was close to tears. Should I show myself? No, there was no need. Her exact thoughts weren't obvious, but her feelings were.

Love.

For all my bafflement at it, I've never had any trouble understanding the mayhem it brings in its wake.

Because a human being in love is sure of only one thing—that he or she is in love. The rest? An endless series of wounds and longings and insecurities, waiting to be cashed in by an answering smile.

Or not...

I tuned into my charge's mind. Pain, disappointment, frustration, whirlpools of all of them, swirling round. Through them, the questions ached.

Could she please Blossom? By being faster and better?

Could she confide in her? Tell her all about her rediscovered mum, the good bits and the bad?

Could she ask her advice?

She longed to do it all, I knew. And then, as she pulled herself to her feet, one feeling surged up through everything else, loud and clear. And swept everything else away.

Determination.

Libby Martin lifted her brute of a rucksack, heaved it on to her back, and trudged off down the hill.

15

"NOT A WORD out of her! Not one single word! About where she's been or what she's been up to. Bunked off school today and I didn't even know till one of her pals called!"

Mike was angry. *Let him get it all out,* I thought. He flung himself into his chair.

"She's up in her room now, dead to the world. Rode in a couple of hours ago, nearly fell off her bike, flung a load of clothes into the washer, then went straight to bed." Finally, he calmed down enough to look me in the eye. "And if you don't mind me saying so, Sammy Knox, you don't look much better than she did."

He was right, of course, rest could only be put on hold for so long. Feline sleep would recharge the batteries fastest—it's not called a cat nap for nothing—but it would have to wait. There were decisions to be taken. The comfort food Mike had provided would keep me going for a bit, though; beans on toast, nothing like it. After half a dozen forkfuls, I looked at him. The man was trying very hard to keep himself together. He turned, brought out a big open envelope from beneath the soup plates and laid it on the table. The courier's label told me what it was.

"Arrived this morning," he said, tonelessly.

I took out the papers. The same awful legalese as on Belle's notebook...

"Mike," I said, "with legal crap like this, staying calm is our only chance. So let's break it down. One. The divorce. There is a bright side. Even though you screwed up when Belle left, this means you get a second chance at getting shot of her properly. Not at this price, of course, the cash and land and so on, but we can make it happen. So first off, it'll have to be fought. And that means..."

I stopped at the look on his face. The only people musicians hate more than managers are lawyers. *Come back to it later,* I decided.

"Two. The house keys. They're planning to get in here, that's obvious, but we won't know why unless we catch them at it."

He blew. *"Let the buggers in!* Not on your—"

"Whoa, hold your fire! We're not done with this pair yet, still lots of shots in our locker. But we do need to know when they're going to make their move. And then we'll need people, the garden's a big perimeter."

"You honestly think they'd have a go at the garden?"

"Anything's possible."

The silence was deafening. Finally, he blurted out his fears.

"Is Libby safe, Sammy? I'd never forgive myself if anything happened to her." He closed his eyes. "Why, oh why did she have to get involved with—"

"Mike, not now."

Cutting him off felt awful, but it was necessary. His daughter running off to see his ex had hurt him, a lot. It was a downward spiral which could only end badly.

"The thing I don't understand," I said, pushing on, "is why they want the little sword key Libby always has round her neck. What does it open?"

"I've no idea."

My eyebrows rose. "Didn't you buy it? For her birthday?"

He shook his head. "The bike was Libby's present. The key was hers already."

"Explain."

His shoulders drooped as the tension left him. He got up and refilled his mug from the teapot.

"It's a long story."

*

I contemplated the photographs of Mike's Aunt Una. The first was a sepia print of a movie star who would have wowed them at the Channel View Forties Night, the second was of a chic grey-haired lady—fifty? sixty?—whose legs were still lithe enough to look great in a miniskirt. She wasn't conventionally beautiful in either picture, but she was striking, one of these women who radiate style.

"By all accounts, she was nuts till she was forty," Mike said, "but her side of the family had money, which meant she could always indulge herself, whatever the whim. They also had a reputation for starting out crazy, then sailing into calmer waters later. Una didn't get that far—hit the rocks at the upright matron by day and downright embarrassment by night stage. Grew old disgracefully, never saw her sober after teatime."

"Did you like her?"

A smile found his face. "Adored her. Great fun, wicked sense of humour. Nobody who ever met Una was indifferent to her, nobody could have been. My mum was madly jealous of everything about her and my dad nearly died of lust every time she crossed her legs. Given that neither of them could admit a word of what they felt, all that ever came out was frosty disapproval, which put the seal on old Una for me. Every Christmas, when she came to stay, she used to slip me a fiver for making sure she made it up the stairs to bed, then give me a huge slug from her hip flask."

"What was in the flask?"

"Rémy. Or Hennessy XO."

"How old were you?"

The smile broadened. "Twelve, the first time."

He got up, crossed to the window and contemplated his domain. Slowly, a serious look replaced the smile.

"Paid for my first sax, too," he said, softly. "After my old man refused to let me have one." I watched him banish reminiscence, good and painful. "Anyway, when we were still in the Notting Hill flat, not long after Libs was born, she turned up at the door one day, three parts pissed, saying she had a present for the baby. Belle wasn't there. I brought her in and took her through to Libby's cot. They got on like a house on fire, those two. Inside a minute, Una had her gurgling away, laughing and dancing—and then the bitch came back." He shrugged. "It all got very frosty."

"Why?"

"They hated each other. Oil and water. Una had seen through Belle from the start, and Belle knew it. It ended with me taking the old girl home in a cab, then having a drink or seven with her. When I got back that night, I found an envelope tucked down the side of Libby's crib. With the key and a note."

"What did the note say?"

142

He delved into the cardboard box the photos had come from, pulled out an envelope and handed it to me. I opened it.

All yours now, my darling.

Don't
Ever
Forget
Old
Una
Loves
A
Real
Dancer!

I read it twice.

And then, the Eureka moment.

I stifled a rueful laugh. No wonder the little sword spoke to me... I looked across at Mike.

"You've really no idea what this key opens?"

"No," he said. "I had a locket made with Libby's picture..."

Reflexes brought my hand to my throat—but then I remembered; in my desk drawer at Knox Towers.

"...just to say thanks. I was going to go round and give it to her, ask about the key at the same time, but before I could, she was gone. Cancer, she'd known for a year. And later, when the will was read, it turned out she'd left me—" He gestured round him. "—this. The rest of the family was livid, thought she'd done it just to stick two fingers up at them. They were probably right. To be honest, though, everything was so crazy with Belle at the time that I forgot about the key. For years, I'm ashamed to say. When I found it again, I thought it was only right that Libs should have it."

I handed him the note. "Mike," I said, gently, "examine the vertical writing. Read out the first letter of each word."

"D,E,F,O,U,L,A,R,D."

He looked at me, mystified. Totally innocent, I thought; music, computers, organic veg and his beloved daughter. I was glad

143

I hadn't laughed, it was admirable, really.

"The key's not just an ordinary sword, is it? It's a miniature sabre."

He nodded.

"A hundred and twenty years ago," I went on, "DeFoulard was probably the most famous champagne house in France. Each new year, they celebrated their latest vintage by throwing a huge high society party in Paris. On the stroke of midnight, one of the partners would start the celebrations by lopping the top off the first magnum with a ridiculously sharp sabre."

"How on earth do you know all that?"

I smiled at him. *Black satin gloves and whirling waltzes... Thierry toasting me over the top of his glass after sheathing the sword... The run up the stairs... The breathless kisses, the fumbling hands...*

"It doesn't matter, I do. Just listen. Before World War One began, being very savvy people and seeing the way the international wind was blowing, DeFoulard put the bulk of its assets into banking. In Zurich."

He looked no less clueless. I went on.

"Today, DeFoulard's Bank has very discreet branches all over the world. As well as Zurich, they're in Paris, Tokyo, Frankfurt, New York—and of course, London. In fact, DeFoulard's is probably the most exclusive and expensive private bank in the square mile."

I watched the implication of my words finally sink in.

"And I'm willing to bet Libby's little sabre will open one of its very exclusive and expensive safety deposit boxes."

*

Knox Towers, three am.

Mike's beans on toast had saved the human, and the smoked salmon from the 24 hour service station had saved the cat. But, exhausted or not, sleep remained elusive. There was too much to think about.

Rex's double life, Mike's revelations, Libby's desperate passion, Belle's intentions... Puzzles were lining up to skate around my brain. I tried to focus on the biggest ones.

Belle had never seen the key or the note, Mike was sure of that. He'd hidden it immediately, because anything given to Libby by *that stuck-up cow*, as his wife had called Una, would have sparked a fight on principle. Which left one huge question.

How did Belle know the key was valuable?

And then there was the conjunction of events which seemed to be conspiring to wreck Mike Martin's life.

An offer to buy him out.

Just a few days before a threat to effectively bankrupt him by divorce.

What were the chances of those two things being unconnected?

From below, I heard the clanging sounds of the pub being secured for the night. Nice sounds, home sounds. I looked around my cramped quarters, my tight little cocoon.

Tiny or not, I loved living here. It fitted me. I settled between two pillows, ready to drop off. And then I stopped myself.

I assumed the Position, summoned the last of my concentration and Changed, then snuggled under the covers.

The only advantage human sleep had over feline lay in the dreams.

Much more vivid.

I closed my eyes.

Thierry...

16

BY EARLY EVENING I was approaching the mediaeval ruins which overlooked the Cadisham Castle Hotel. Beth still hadn't got back to me. Should I push it? No, I decided, things between us were still delicate. Other avenues? I could try Yesterday's Treasures, I thought, the antique shop the betting cash had come from...

A rock at the side of the path claimed my attention.

I frowned. Why? A roundish rock, dark, surrounded by tufts of weeds...

Grizelda's mole.

Poor thing... I went on, threading my way between the huge sandstone blocks. Feeling sorry for her was illogical, of course— I mean, I hadn't known the woman and she must have been, by definition, a bad lot, but what had she done except run a coven and try to conjure up the Bad Lad? It was what her kind of witch was supposed to do, wasn't it? As I squeezed through the rubble at the tower's foot, I decided to forgive her the pot shots.

And anyway, the rule book was clear.

Standing order 17: In the event of termination, all employees shall receive a full solstice's notice.

Well, she hadn't had that, had she? And given that she hadn't gone at all gently into that good night, I found myself wondering exactly how ruthless Bertie's brief was—because behaviour like this was extreme, even for a hooligan like him. Was Blatherwick Manor his reward for it? Before I could come to any conclusion, the old Ministry of Works danger sign loomed up before me.

And my next problem loomed up with it.

Scrapper.

Was I ready to confront him? Why had he warned me—no, *ordered* me—not to interfere? Then the usual thought gripped me, as it did every time I got here.

How had a Norman lord's stronghold become an implacable

cat's hermitage?

I looked up. One moss-covered step in three was all that remained. And legend had it he scorned even that, ascending the wall outside, all but sheer, just to show his fearlessness.

But then, legend said a lot of things about the Fighter Of A Thousand Battles.

Slowly, careful of grip and balance, I started to pick my way upwards.

*

The top was deserted. I surveyed the uneven flagstones.

A refuge?

Or a penance...?

There was no scent of him. I padded across to the table at the centre, its concave top hollowed out by tankard and trencher, its edges worn smooth by centuries of steel elbow and mailed fist. I sprang up and sat, my haunches against the smoothness I knew so well. As I settled, the memories came.

The arabesque of two furred bodies, lit by a pale moon...

The post-coital laying, with gruff courtesy, of a vole at my forepaws...

The untamed urgency...

The thrill of being bent to his will...

The never to be equalled thrill?

Perhaps... Here, alone in the fading sunlight, I could admit it. As cat there had been couplings by the hundred since—savage and satisfying, urgent and unbridled, but I could not bring to mind a single one like those with the Fighter Of A Thousand Battles. I closed my eyes. Just because we didn't love, it didn't mean we didn't remember. Why—

"The past means nothing."

I spun round.

"Only actions which shape the future matter."

He was framed in the west window, silhouetted against the sky. After a long pause, he came forward. When he marked the boundary of his territory and mine, his scent was tainted.

With rage. With frustration. And no matter my memories, I

147

knew my own was the same.

"A hard wind to catch your eye's ire, Fighter Of A Thousand Battles."

"And a misted dawn to hide your wilful obstinacy, Changeling."

We were both angry—to the point of menace. The exchange of paw strokes was close to a mutual slap, all but an insult to the ritual. I had never seen his scars so livid.

"You were warned, Changeling, not to oppose the Cage Destroyer or his daughter. You have ignored this. Why?"

I felt my fur rise. "A warning! Does the wind in this eyrie carry so much echo? Does the great Fighter Of A Thousand Battles live so deep in it that he hears only his own voice?"

He stiffened. His ears flattened.

"I see no real reason for this warning," I went on coldly, "other than shame. A warrior's shame at being found to be no more than a pet! Who are you to order me?"

He snarled his fury. "One who has battled for you in the past! One who leads! One who thought himself worthy of being followed—but I should have known, a Changeling follows no one!"

Neck swollen, he spat his contempt.

"Mongrel!"

"Slave!"

We both charged. Claw met claw, bite met bite. The weight of him hit hard enough to send me skittering over the flags. He leaped back up to the window, ready to pounce. Last chance! I lunged upwards and felt the force of my impact match his. We toppled over. The locked thing which was the snarling pair of us flew out into the sunset—and then we hit earth and rolled down the hill, gouging, biting, yowling. It ended on the tarmac of the hotel car park. I pulled away, dancing on all four paws, so enraged I could no longer see.

And then the red mist cleared. He stood before me, braced against the front bumper of a large car. The Blatherwick Bentley, I realised, dully. The old wound of his torn ear had reopened, and his one eye was all but blinded with blood. When his voice came, it was firm.

"Cease this!" he said. "Now! You must choose, Changeling—

choose your side and your battle! Whatever your own concerns, they are nothing to what is being prepared here." His tail flicked. "The evils gathering now are beyond dangerous. To fight them I need you. *Choose!*"

And then he was gone. I peered into the dusk, searching for him. His voice came to me from high on the dark hill.

"My eyes are upon you!"

*

From the ancient oak tree outside the executive lounge window, I watched.

It was them, the two upmarket voyeurs who'd been so unimpressed by the fleshpots of the night before. Their hands told me, the skeletal claw and the lacquered talon.

The man had been tall once, but now he was an outsized stick insect, bent, dried to the point of desiccation and almost asleep, a caricature of age. The wisps of silver hair were plastered across the bony skull, the cheeks were sunken, the folds of turkey neck perched on a limp black bow tie. His Adam's apple bobbed up and down past it like the exterior lift on a sagging skyscraper, and the shoulders of his dinner jacket sat on him like a shroud stolen from a bigger man's corpse.

An apple-cheeked young waiter arrived with a bottle of red wine and poured. I watched the bony hand bring the glass up to the twisted mouth, taste, then contemptuously reject it. As the boy scurried away, the old man seemed to come alive, the bushy eyebrows crashing together like opposing thunderstorms—delivering the rebuke had pleased him. I watched him consult his Rolex. That this was the evil Scrapper wanted me to fight, I had no doubt, for malice radiated from this creature in waves. He made my skin crawl.

She, on the other hand, was ageless, a triumph of the plastic surgeon's art—exact vintage unknown, parts replaced so often everything looked new. The paint job, buffed to perfection from blonde mane downwards, would have won awards. I watched her red-nailed hand finger the diamond necklace which sat upon her chasm of cleavage. As her partner looked again at his watch,

149

she pouted. On the boy waiter's return, the pout converted itself into a fully-fanged leer, a dazzling display of raptor dentistry. Above it, the blue eyes glittered. She made no attempt to hide the hunger for young flesh. Opposite her, the old man didn't react at all, but despite the bimbo persona, I could feel that she was as dangerous as he was.

A power couple.

The question was, what kind of power? Who were they and what were they doing in Cadisham? Connected with the coven? Or the Bad Lad? It seemed likely—otherwise why observe the antics of the night before? But they were no common or garden Satanists, Scrapper's concern told me that much. A noise turned me to the doorway.

Another two arrivals... The first was a brittle-looking woman with short black hair, wearing high heels she didn't know how to walk in, an ill-chosen designer outfit and very expensive pearls.

The second was Wing Commander (Retd) J.D. Stoneyhurst.

*

The meeting was the easiest dumb show to read since the players had stitched up Claudius for Hamlet at Elsinore.

First a toast; the raptor, the thin woman and Stoneyhurst. Ms Feral Facelift's smile was full-on Hollywood, the Wingco's was at half mast, and the brittle woman's seemed close to breakdown.

Next, a passing of fat brown envelopes. As they disappeared at lighting speed, neither Stoneyhurst nor his companion could resist casting a nervous glance round the room.

Then a comparison of diaries between the two women, followed by another toast.

And through it all, the stick insect, so still he might already have been pinned to a specimen board, maintained a hunched and scowling silence.

*

Ten minutes later, I trotted across to the staircase which led up to Scrapper's lair and laid a dead pigeon on the bottom step. I prodded it with my forepaw until its drooping fan of wing was aesthetically consistent. It didn't commit me to anything—but it told him I would return. My mind went back to the snatch of conversation I'd overheard between the skinny one and Stoneyhurst as they waited for their taxi.

Her. *...on Sunday.*

Him. *...sure you can deliver?*

No, whatever this was, it wasn't over. I loped off through the undergrowth.

*

By morning I was back. I parked the MG beside the fake mediaeval inn sign and tried to ignore the monstrosity it advertised.

The Cadisham Castle Hotel.

Ivy-covered breeze block battlements and crenellated plaster turrets, topped by a long row of late baroque TV aerials and neo-Georgian satellite dishes... Completely bogus, all of it, some Victorian Gradgrind's parody of the real castle on the hill behind. Idly, I wondered; would the toff's life in Ye Olde Yngelonde ever stop producing fantasy?

I massaged my still-sore neck, put on the huge aviator shades I'd brought, adjusted the blonde wig beneath my headscarf and scanned the car park.

No Bentley.

Had they checked out? Unlikely, I thought, given what I'd gleaned from the night before. They'd return, I was sure of it—but how much time did I have? No way of knowing...

Roll the dice, I thought—and roll them *fast*.

I pulled up the collar of my trench coat and got out, checking my reflection in the windows; good, common enough to make the right impression, especially the shoes—shocking pink platforms. Along with the wig and the shades they were all anyone would remember. I pulled the yellow plastic tote on to my shoulder, barged through the double doors and clomped loudly up to the desk. The lips of the matron behind it compressed themselves into a disapproving line.

"I'm here about the Bentley, luv."

The frown deepened. "I'm sorry, I'm afraid I don't—"

I gave an exaggerated sigh. "You mean they 'aven't told you? They 'aven't left a message? They still want to sell, don't they?"

She looked blank, then realisation dawned. "Are you referring to the American gentleman and his wife?"

I nodded. "Yeah, met 'em up west. They said they'd be 'ere this week, told me they wanted to unload it before they went 'ome."

"But no one's said anything to me! They left after breakfast and I'm not sure when they'll be..."

As her dismay dribbled away I did the big sigh, then opened the tote and searched noisily for pad and pen. After scribbling a meaningless message, I lifted an envelope from the pile by the bell, folded in the nonsense note and licked it shut.

"Wot room they in?"

She hesitated, but only for a second. "402," she said, meekly.

I wrote it on the envelope, made to give it to her, then paused my hand in mid-air. Then, as theatrically as possible, I balled up the note and thrust it into the tote.

"You know wot, luv," I said, shaking my head, "I'm just not goin' to bovver. If they can't even be arsed to tell you, they're not serious. Waste o' time, innit?"

I left her, wide-mouthed with wonder, and clattered back the way I'd come.

With the room number.

*

Back in the car I changed shoes, then went in through the side door and ran up the stairs to the fourth floor. The store cupboard was unlocked. I took off the coat and the blonde wig, stowed them in the bag and hid it behind a pile of bedlinen. The new wig was long and auburn, the new glasses had plain lenses and thick black rims. I smoothed out the maid's uniform, old-fashioned except for the barely decent skirt, stuck the lace cap on my head and checked my makeup.

Just like the picture on their website; Olde Fashionede Yngelishe Service with enough leg to steam up the over-sixty specs.

That's what the Cadisham Castle Hotel offered, and that's what anyone I encountered was going to get. I perched a mound of towels on a trolley and wheeled it to the room door. The sign above the number informed me I was outside Ye Executive Suite Of His Lordshippe. I knocked. As expected, His Lordshippe's call telling me to executively bugger off never materialised.

The lock was one of these slide-in plastic jobs that's supposed to be more secure. More secure than the one in Belle's jerry-built dump in Brighton, perhaps, but that wasn't saying much. I used the catch-all entry card my B&E mate Bendy Lawson had given me. The door clicked open. I took a tentative step inside, felt carpet tickle my ankles, then pushed it shut behind me.

"Well, well, Ms Knox. Just as I was wondering if we'd ever meet."

I whirled round. Blossom Turl, in jeans and t-shirt, was sitting on a couch in the window alcove. On the wall, a picture had been removed, showing the open door of a small safe. On the coffee table before her lay a shoulder bag, a Polaroid camera, a laptop and a pile of CDs. I turned to the room's other occupant.

Who was sitting on the couch beside her, tail curled round his paws as he regarded each of us in turn.

Scrapper.

*

As a standoff it was, to say the least, intriguing. I sat down in the chair opposite, crossed my legs and watched her amused gaze catalogue my outfit. Get my retaliation in first, I decided.

"Fancy me, do you? Bit of feather duster slap and tickle? Or am I too old for your taste, Ms Turl?"

She never missed a beat. "Are you always this hypocritical, Ms Knox? I saw you checking out my dad in the supermarket. Is he too old for yours?"

Touché.

Totally unfazed, her eyes shifted to our mutual friend. When she spoke again, it was to him.

"She's so rude, isn't she? I wonder why. Worried her looks are on the slide?" She stroked his tattered ear. "Women her age

153

often are." She leaned down, let her face fall into a pretty frown. "Did you plan this, you cunning old bugger? If I'd known, I'm not sure I'd have let you come."

Calmly, Scrapper held her gaze.

She turned to me. "Straight into my lap, the minute I got in the car," she said. "Wouldn't budge. Always lets you know when he wants something, does old Scrapper." Her face became serious. "Animals, we always underestimate them, don't we?"

Old Scrapper. I felt my hackles rise. What right did she have to call him that? Never mind stroke his ear! And what right did he have to let her? The Fighter Of A Thousand Battles shrugged off her hand, descended from the couch, then sprang without warning on to my thighs. On landing, he balanced himself, then rose and let his forepaws fall against my bosom. He brought his face right up to mine. I felt the whiskers touch, the claws come out.

I waited. The claws extended, just enough to hurt.

I looked into his unblinking eyes and understood.

It was the prelude to a declaration of war—an all-out declaration, no quarter asked or given. Forever, until one of us was dead. My heart rate accelerated.

And then the claws retracted. I frowned. Not in the script. What was this? His gaze still on me, he went on holding his position. Unnerving... Then, without warning, he jumped down and sprang again, this time up to the windowsill behind Blossom. He miaaouwed and butted the catch with his forehead.

A command, an obvious command.

A puzzled frown found the girl's face. She turned to open the window. Scrapper climbed out on to the ledge. The breeze ruffled his fur as he looked back through the glass, first at her, then at me.

Again, I understood.

Not an outright declaration of war, but the threat of one.

If the Changeling didn't do exactly what the Fighter Of A Thousand Battles wanted.

And what he wanted was pretty obvious.

Co-operation.

Eyes still on me, he flicked his tail, then loped off. Blossom

Turl turned to me.

"Are you thinking the same thing I am?" she said, softly.

I kept my feelings from my face as I surveyed hers—her pretty, chameleon features; shrewd, gamine and appealing. But they could just as easily have been hard and stern, like they'd been at Charlie Oxley's farm. And I didn't doubt there were at least another dozen different personae this girl—no, this *woman*—could assume without batting an eyelid, anything from Messalina to Mother Teresa.

Did it have something to do with being the child of an Empathetic? How deep, I wondered, would I have to dig to find the real Blossom Turl?

And suddenly it didn't matter. Beneath all my anger at her, at Scrapper, at the whole situation, I forced myself to admit it.

Co-operation.

The Fighter Of A Thousand Battles was right. Mad or not, my infuriating ex usually was. I sighed. Might as well get it sorted. I pulled off the ridiculous lace cap and the auburn wig, shook out my own locks and gave Blossom a cool smile.

"I don't like you."

She returned it. "Believe me, it's mutual."

If there'd been water between us, it would have frozen over.

"Listen to me," I said, leaning across. "Very carefully. If you hurt Libby Martin—in any way, mental or physical—it will give me great pleasure to take your pretty head off at the neck. Is that understood?"

The perfectly plucked eyebrows shot up—not what she'd expected. But her composure recovered fast. Had I landed a serious punch or a glancing blow? We spent another wary minute, assessing each other. Then she pressed a button on the Polaroid. The paper curled out. Once it had developed itself, she handed it to me and indicated the pile of disks.

"These have to be wiped down and put back in the safe, exactly the way they are in the picture."

I let my chilled smile widen. "Like giving orders, don't you? Except this time, you're not giving them to a love-struck kid on her belly in a muddy field."

Again, she was good—and again, not quite good enough. I

155

read the shock on her face.

"Yes, I was there."

She decided on challenge. "I don't believe you."

"Green tweed cap with an orange check, Hunter wellies and a Barbour with a ripped right pocket. And no, Libby didn't tell me. Don't bother trying to work it out, you don't have the mental equipment."

Again I leaned over. I let irony fill my voice.

"I'd hate us to get off on the wrong foot here..." I widened the glacial smile even more. "...Bloss." I crossed my legs, ostentatiously; good as hers, any day. "It's very simple. You're not the boss, and I'm not some underling. If Scrapper wants us to work together, we do it as equals." I paused. "And there are conditions."

She made to speak, but I held up a warning hand.

"Libby's father needs a lawyer," I said. "Not you, that would be too weird, he knows about you." The phrase *and his daughter* went unsaid, but she heard it. "So you're going to find him representation. Someone good, a divorce specialist. Today. I'll tell Mike I've organised it. Libby doesn't get to know. Ever. Agreed?"

A millisecond of hesitation.

"Agreed."

"Two. At some point we're going to need manpower at Cadisham Organics. Muscle, probably at night, perhaps three or four people. Again, no word to Libby."

I waited. The cool smile reappeared.

"Done," she said. "Assuming you've no objection to womanpower, I'll be one of them."

"You promise?"

Straight faced, she made a cross-my-heart with her forefinger.

"Three. I need a look at Turl & Turl's recent CCTV, especially on Calgacus day. That also has to happen today."

The cool smile became puzzled. "Also agreed," she said. "Are we done, Ms Knox?"

She was beginning to sound annoyed. Excellent.

"Not quite. Is Stoneyhurst going to fire me?"

"Yes. Tomorrow."

I nodded. "My fee, in full. With expenses. This afternoon."

156

She nodded, slowly. "I can arrange that," she said. "I can arrange pretty much anything in the old bastard's life."

"I'll bet you can," I said, levelly.

She ignored me. "The Blicks'll be back between meetings. I know some of their schedule, but I'm not sure how much time we have. Once we're out of here we split, rendezvous later at my place."

She thrust a hand into the shoulder bag. It emerged holding a cheap mobile phone. She put it down on the table.

"Anything goes wrong, any vital communication, that's what you use. Nothing else."

I smiled. A burner phone, I'd always wanted one...

"You know where my cottage is?" she said.

"Of course."

She worked it out. I watched her blush.

"Nice stockings, Dior," I said, out of mischief.

One eyebrow came up. I picked up the pile of CDs. She handed me a Polaroid.

Scrapper had got his way, we both knew it.

The chameleon and the Changeling had pooled resources.

Or at least, I thought, some of them.

17

I WANDERED THROUGH the cottage, examining the art I'd clocked through the window on my first visit.

It wasn't just good, it was very good. Some of it was framed, some just pinned up; horses, dogs, the billy goat, pink dowsing rod well to the fore. There was a fine one of Calgacus and his groupies, and a stunning life-size adder—you could practically feel the grass parting round it. It had a line of writing beneath, in beautiful calligraphy.

Others Run, I Weave

It felt like poetry. I looked round again; all the best pictures were captioned. I went across to the biggest canvas.

Scrapper.

It was so lifelike he could have reached out and bit me again. The memory made my neck throb.

I Know Your Force, You Know Mine

My jealousy stirred; once more, evidence of a relationship...

"All yours?" I asked, keeping my voice neutral.

Blossom Turl was sitting, if you could call it that, in her old leather armchair. Her left foot was behind her neck in a seemingly effortless stretch. *How,* I wondered, and then irritation got the better of me. *And more to the point, why?* Eyes closed in concentration, she nodded.

"Slade school of art, three years, two terms at RADA, then Cambridge for law. Boring, difficult and useful. But we're not here, Ms Knox..." She scratched the ankle above her head. "...to talk about me. How much do you know?"

More than I'm going to tell you, I thought; her manner really was maddening.

"Consider me a virgin," I said, acidly.

"A challenge," she replied, "but since we're dealing in fantasy... You ask, I'll answer."

"Did you torch the warehouse?"

"No. Did you?"

I shook my head. Eyes on each other, faces blank, we let the silence simmer—and then I went for the jugular.

"Sunday," I snapped. "All of it. Right now."

True to form, she wasn't fast enough to hide her surprise. She unknotted herself and loosed a smile.

"Good at what you do, aren't you?"

Good enough to sort you out, I thought. "I'm waiting."

The smile died. "We're planning an expedition."

"That, I already know. You, Libby and Scrapper. Your dad going too?"

"If he's out. He's a whizz with the wire cutters. Feel free to join us."

"Where?"

"Hazlett Humane Laboratories, Woodstock."

Oh, shit.

I kept my face straight. I'd known it was a lab raid since the cells, but hearing it confirmed... As illegal as it gets, not to mention dangerous. And probably violent.

And my charge would be up to her neck in it.

"The old Yanks at the hotel, the monsters. Who are they?"

She held up a hand. "All in good time, it's easier in sequence."

She twisted her legs into a different pose. When she spoke again, her voice showed not the slightest sign of effort.

"Turl's is a big prize, much bigger than just the store. A long list of properties, most of the family are shareholders. There's the stuff in Cadisham, Sellingham Hall in Wiltshire, the Chambleford Park estate in Norfolk, all the gruesome grouse moors in Argyll, terraces by the dozen in Glasgow and Belfast. Banbury Vale are ambitious. They've got forty supermarkets and over two hundred smaller stores across the south and west. They want to go national. They've been scoping out sites for years, circling round Turl's in the process." She shrugged. "In come the diggers and one man's stately home is another's distribution centre."

"And the Turls will sell?"

She laughed. "Land rich, cash poor, too many mouths. The

women they choose are always too fertile, or the seed's too potent—the one thing the Turls can do is breed. Which means most of my family are either in queer street already or on nodding terms with the bailiffs. Ninety per cent of them are positively salivating at the thought of hard cash."

"And Stoneyhurst?"

"Married to one of my dad's third cousins."

"What's she like?" I asked, a thin woman hypothesis forming.

Blossom snorted. "Think sumo wrestler in drag."

I frowned. Another theory in tatters.

"He doesn't dare divorce her," she went on, "he'd be out on his ear. So he grits his teeth and goes on milking the store's profits. He'll take anything he can get his grubby hands on."

"Including you," I said.

"Easiest way to pump him for info," she said, "don't pretend you're shocked." With elastic ease, she reshaped herself yet again. "All of which brings us to that charming billionaire, Mister Elmer Blick the Third..."

Finally, *Blick*.

"...and his plastic doll of a wife, the almost entirely recycled Louise. And to ShoMe Foods."

The name on the CDs... Blossom uncoiled.

"Proprietors of acres of animal prison facilities, suppliers of chlorine-washed chicken to the struggling masses of the Americas and elsewhere, primarily through their oh-so-classy fast food empire."

I tried not to look clueless and failed. The sceptical eyebrow came again.

"Are you telling me you have never, Ms Knox, indulged your palate in the culinary delights of a ShoMe Chikkin restaurant?"

When I didn't answer, she looked out of the window at her menagerie, standing their patient guard around the cottage in the Cotswolds drizzle.

"I hate them," she said, quietly. "I hate everyone who is a purveyor of the flesh of dead animals."

Well, if you put it like that, I thought. How was I supposed to respond? I loved the stuff. Perhaps now wasn't the time to say so, though...

"What is ShoMe's stake in all this?" I asked.

She surveyed me bleakly—and then it was back to Business Blossom, *a la* Cadisham jail. "It's clever," she said, finally deigning to sit in the chair like a normal human being. "Russian dolls in reverse. Every time you open one, there's another, but it's outside, not inside. Within six months of Banbury's bid being accepted, Blick will make his move. As well as Stoneyhurst, he's already got half of Banbury's board in his pocket. Wined, dined and shackled—stick and carrot, either bribed or blackmailed. He'll be the major shareholder inside a year. And like all predators, he operates on one simple principle. Medium shark eats little shark, big shark eats medium shark. In the end, big shark gets all the protein."

"Why?"

The smile went from bleak to superior. "Corporate Sleight-Of-Hand 101, pay attention at the back. Every Banbury Vale supermarket already has a Banbury Burger Bar attached. Blick just waits till they've built more stores, hence more burger bars. Then he swallows the Banbury operation whole. The minute ShoMe has the contract signed and its name on all the storefronts, every single one of these burger bars becomes a ShoMe Chikkin joint. Classic infiltration, a ready-made business. All the legal stuff taken care of, planning permission etc., and the old bastard's hardly had to lift his nose out of Louise's silicone valley." She nodded at the laptop. "It's all in there."

"How did Jonathan find out?"

She grinned. "The Banbury Vale bit was Great Aunt Matilda in Devon. She had the first buyout offer."

She stooped forward and sucked in her cheeks. One hand extended to lean on an imaginary stick, the other rose, shakily, to an imaginary lorgnette. Her voice took on an aged Edwardian drawl, cracked and authoritative.

"Frightful people! They want to use our name to sell cheap things to the lower classes! Do stop them, dear boy!"

What talent! I almost forgot how much I disliked her.

"Mad as a production line of hatters," she said, "but the right kind of mad, like my dad." She shrugged. "We thought we could stop it, kill it with publicity. That's why we used Calgacus and did Nobbs Cross. But we were too late—far too late. It turns out Blick's been setting it up with my boss for months, promising him a fortune to convince the family to accept the Banbury offer. How much Stoneyhurst stands to make I don't know. Yet."

My smile widened. Who said co-operation couldn't be salted with a bit of *Schadenfreude?*

"How much would you reckon a king-size brown envelope can hold?"

Her eyebrows rose.

"Last night, dinner at the hotel. I never saw the denominations, but it was bulging."

The eyebrows rose even further, and then her face took on a speculative look. "You know, this might just explain something." She sprang up and headed for the bedroom. "Wait here." Her voice came over her shoulder. "There's a Gucci handbag in the dresser drawer. Get it."

Back to Brigadier Blossom, I thought, frowning. I suppressed annoyance.

"Why?" I sang out.

"He has a lunch date in Oxford. The bag has a built-in camera and photographs could be useful."

After five minutes of frenetic clothes hanger rattle she reappeared, framed in the bedroom door. Transformed. I was impressed; from head to toe she was Ms Horn Rims And High Heels again, but she'd managed to coat the image with a nicely-judged layer of the tarty—anyone watching would have to wonder whether dictation involved a pad or a paddle. She gave me enough time to digest the vision, then turned to the mirror.

"The old bastard's lunch date..." she said, tucking away an errant lock. "...is with me." She nodded out at the donkey, now giving the verge's dandelions a good chomping. "Given that he's tighter than old Dinkey there's arse about money, and that his oats are being amply laid on..." An eyebrow pencil appeared. "...he has not the slightest need to impress me. So why, Ms Knox, has he invited a poor secretary out for a bit of expense account bloodletting?" She spun round and gave me a stunning scarlet smile. "It couldn't possibly be because he wants me to hide a brown envelope full of ill-gottens, could it?"

162

Seated and napkinned, I looked round.

Symington's was an old Oxford institution, all cigar-smoke-marinaded oak panels and waiters who paused in mid-serve to let their disdain ski down their noses. The snobbery's only concession to the modern was a menu big enough to propel something in the Tall Ships Race. A peek round the side of it showed me Blossom in full all-a-flutter-at-the-boss mode, and Stoney-hurst doing his usual cold haddock number. I found myself admiring her—like the first time I'd seen them together, it looked like damn hard work.

The outfit she'd given me was fun, though—courtesy of a dressing-up box even better than my own. I was decked out in a grey wig, bunned at both ears and stuck untidily beneath an even greyer beret. The effect was completed by bushy false eyebrows and badly applied lipstick. Add a houndstooth two-piece, ugly flat shoes and a beige blouse which had probably been the pride and joy of some overweight Girl Guide, and I was the elderly upper class spinster to the life. The prosthetic buck teeth were a masterpiece. As soon as my empty soup plate (I wasn't trusting anything solid to a mouthful of rubber) was whisked away, I placed the handbag at the right angle for their table—and tried to stop salivating.

Which was a tall order, because so far I'd watched Jonathan Turl's daughter swallow her vegetarian principles and everything else in sight, from the *foie gras* to a large lump of dead cow, with the Wingco matching her bite for bite. Much more of this and I'd start drooling. As they tucked into the sticky toffee pud I hoped the money shot would come soon, otherwise I'd be down on all fours, trying for a waiter's leg.

I needn't have worried. As the coffees arrived, their heads came together. Stoneyhurst brought the brown envelope out of his satchel. Blossom gave the agreed girlish giggle get-ready signal and whispered some sweet nothing in his ear. She'd guessed right—the old fraud couldn't resist showing off the lolly. I saw the thick bundles of notes. As I listened to her oohs and aahs and

163

watched her bosom heaving against his arm, I pressed the remote, and kept on pressing it until the envelope was in her bag.

And then, as they got ready to leave, I sat back.

Again, I was impressed—RADA had not been wasted. I followed them out. He gave her his usual perfunctory peck on the cheek and watched her bum till she rounded the corner. Then, looking lugubriously pleased with himself, he headed for the red BMW.

And as he reached it, I realised I wasn't the only one keeping tabs on Wing Commander (Retd) J.D. Stoneyhurst. The pub opposite was called The Straight Arrow. From its tiled doorway, jaw jutting out like a battleship's prow, emerged a stick-thin figure wearing coke-bottle-lensed glasses.

Olive.

*

She was a ridiculously easy tail—not least because she really was the straightest of arrows. Eyes fixed (as far as I could tell through the specs) on the horizon, her progress was marching band military, a flat-footed left right left in a straight line which would have done Beau Geste proud across the Sahara. Out of the centre, up Banbury Road, through Summertown's clusters of new flats. It was unnerving—never a glance at a shop window or a poster, much less another human being, never a deviation of her head even a millimetre to either side. She could have been a determined debt collector or a Baptist banshee, but the way she radiated purpose made people give her the widest of berths. What was she up to? Was she another minion of the Blicks, like the Blues Brothers? I dodged through a crowd of cyclists, then lost sight of her behind a lorry. Where was she? I rounded a knot of gowned undergrads yelling at each other in hooray voices about Halloween parties. *Where had the woman gone?* I was about to admit defeat when I saw her at the corner, standing dead still, like a robot with a run-down battery. Was the route march over?

A beige Range Rover pulled up.

Well, well...

Olive Murgatroyd jumped undemurely into the driver's lap,

wrapped her arms round him and landed a big smacking kiss on the fat blubbery mouth of...

...the executioner of her bosom buddy Grizelda.

My old mate Bertie, Mr B.L.Z. Bubb.

*

The publicity shot of Rex went down on the bar top like an ace in a poker hand.

"Too creased, your original," Beth said, "so we had to make a copy." She emptied the last of her glass. "Rex Renaldo, aka Reginald Reynolds, born 4.3.51, Methil, Fife. Currently whiling away his days in alcoholic tax exile on the shores of Lake Geneva. Hasn't set foot in the UK since the quiz show died back in the eighties. You ever watch it? *Celebrity Stars?* My mum was addicted. Anyway, Reggie's dull as ditchwater, clean as a whistle—and on his last legs. The quacks give him six months tops."

I squinted at the image again, frowning. Now that I could see it properly, something bothered me about the face.

"Good," Beth said, watching me. "All that Brighton sunshine hasn't killed your eye."

My phone pictures arrived on the bar beside the first one. She stabbed a finger down on the one I'd taken outside the café.

"This isn't Reg, it's his identical twin, Robert, or Rab Razors as he's known on the Fife Riviera. Differs facially from his brother only in the scar above the left eyebrow. Rumour has it his mum whacked him with a frying pan when he was a kid, just so she could tell the pair of them apart. Truth is he got it in Saughton jail fifty years ago, during his first spell as a guest of Her Maj. Saughton is also where he began his extensive education."

"Explain."

"A dab hand with the slashers, our Rab started off as a pimp, then got lifted for extortion—basic dosh with menaces. Small fry; bookies and butchers, pay up or get carved up. Six years, lucky it wasn't more. But after a few months of accountancy classes in the jug, he turned out to be a dab hand with the numbers as well, could march them up to the top of the hill and back down again in any formation anyone wanted. Aced his exams, which had his

165

teachers grinning ear to ear and the trick cyclists wetting themselves. Rehabilitation works! Living proof! You get the picture. All of which raised Rab's game without altering his outlook on life in the slightest." She shared a cynical smile with me. "So, long story short, within a month of being out, Rab turned up in Wide Boy Heaven, ie the City of London. Inside a year, dodgy directorships were floating down on his mohair shoulders like manna from heaven. Surrey mansions, Spanish villas, Porsches, the lot. He started a new line, investment packages for tax exiles like his brother. The temptation was too much, especially since by then he'd developed an expensive fondness for..."

"...the geegees," I finished for her.

She nodded. "After several years of backing every three-legged nag out there, Rab finally cracked. Got caught with his hand in the till of an extremely upmarket private bank and went away for a long time. When he got out, he started specialising in shell companies for one-off cons. The fraud squad boys say that now he's just waiting for his brother to pop his clogs so he can nick the identity full time and wipe his slate clean. In the meantime, he's gone to ground. Word is he's on his uppers and looking for 'commercial opportunities' before his many and varied creditors find him and decide to call." She paused. "So it's fireworks and flowers for young Sammy," she said. "You're the first to get a line on the bugger in a year. And after you're done with him, I'll nick him, it'll look great on the CV."

I made my voice as casual as I could. "What was the name of the private bank?"

"Defoulard's."

The word slotted into place with a nice, satisfying click. I kept my face neutral. I'd half-guessed, but I didn't want Beth asking me how I knew.

"Address?"

She consulted her notebook. "The Smoke. Connaught Place, very la-di-dah." Her voice was suddenly serious. "Careful, Sammy. No scruples at all, this one, and by all accounts still a wizard with the old cut-throat."

The hanging razor...

I lifted our glasses and went to the bar, thinking.

166

Shell companies for one-off cons.

*

I lay in the bath, gripping the hot tap with my toes, listening to George's snores thundering up the stairs. Nearly five, he'd be up soon. I lifted Blossom's note again.

CCTV footage, my place, 6.30am. No time to copy the tapes, they need to be back in-house before the store opens. You can look at them here. Fee in your account.

I finally succeeded in maximising my toe-torque technique. Vibrations shook the pipe, then noises juddered up which sounded as though Calgacus was incarcerated somewhere under my landlord's bed. Eventually a trickle of brackish water spluttered out and ran down my instep; lukewarm. I awarded myself a consolation prize square of chocolate and took stock.

Two very different situations.

First up, the Rab & Belle Show. Not complicated, a story of everyday criminal folk, a tale of greed, betrayal and villainy. I still had no idea what was planned for Cadisham Organics, but the role of Libby's little sabre was obvious now; Rab Razors, ex-De-Foulard's fraudster, would have known what it was the minute he saw it. From then on, the plan was simple; Belle collects the box's contents—how the paperwork had been finessed I had no idea—and off they fly into the sunset.

Or rather, off Rab flies, I thought, waving goodbye to inconvenient impedimenta like surplus girlfriends. I had no doubt at all that Belle would be left crying into her tins of modelling clay.

But all it needed from me was legwork and a firm intervention—well within my PI job description, any kid with a magnifying glass and a deerstalker hat could do it. I treated myself to another two squares of Bournville.

The other stuff, though, was trickier, much trickier.

Turl and his daughter.

Stoneyhurst and the thin bint.

The odious Blicks.

Bertie and Grizelda and Olive.

Scrapper.

What tied all of it together?

The surface skulduggery, capitalism at its slimiest, was obvious now I'd had it explained, and a bit of probing round Ollie's drink-sodden mental database would fill in the gaps.

But the rest...

People, animals, demons and spirits, vying with each other...

Competition. That was what it felt like. The more I thought it through, the less bizarre it sounded.

But *why?*

No answer appeared from the bubbles. Which meant back to first principles—a return to the only absolutely rock-solid thing about this whole business.

What I'd found in old Perry's chamber—pentacles, mosaics of the Bad Lad and his buddies, rats delivering special earth.

To be investigated, I decided—and soon.

And then there was this Hazlett Humane nonsense...

A high profile animal liberation raid, and I had just forty-eight hours to throw a spanner in its works. Forty-eight hours to work out how to keep Elizabeth Martin—madly in love with the raid's organiser, the slipperiest customer I'd come across in centuries—away from it.

I checked Felix; 5.30. Time to be on my way.

Maison Blossom, then Libby.

18

I PUSHED MYSELF through the cottage cat flap around nine—to find Mike, dead to the world in his easy chair, still wearing the day before's work gear. A microwave dinner lay untouched on the table.

I settled down to observe him. Grey with exhaustion... How much had the last few days cost the man? The memory of his last crisis came back to me. The depression triggered by alcohol and an unscrupulous taxman had pushed Mike right to the brink, and concerted action from myself and Libby had only just saved him. Was there a risk, now, of all our good work being undone? Would my new information from the security tapes help avert that?

Because I knew now, how the first contact between Belle and Libby had been set up.

But first things first. Food. My last meal had been almost a day ago, a plate of soup ingested through rubber teeth. I eyed the fridge; no access to it without opposable thumbs, which meant Changing—and if Mike woke... Too dodgy, I decided. I hopped up on to the table and sniffed at the congealed mess in the plastic dish. Ugghh! Disgusting—I just couldn't. Upstairs, then—Libby's bikkie stash was always well stocked. I took the stairs two at a time.

The door was open. Her scent was faint, very... Where was she, on this fine autumn morning? Back at school? Out at Briggs Rare Breeds, chasing her clever chameleon? I hoped not—I had a sudden vision of my new collaborator wining and dining her somewhere with a wedge of Stoneyhurst's illicit readies, prior to the big seduction scene. Ridiculous, but still... And since my senses were telling me Libs was nowhere near, there was nothing else for it; I'd have to start quartering the town to find her. But in the meantime, the future was chocolate and digestive. I got ready to Change.

And then her little ten-inch TV, the one I'd given her the year before, switched itself on.

I stared. It had been liberated from the town hall during the renovations. When I'd got fed up with it, Libs had claimed it, declaring it classic retro, sixties kitsch at its finest. But it had always been reliable—at least until now.

I sprang up and tried to switch it off with my paw. The button wouldn't work. I flicked through the channels to see if that made any difference; game shows, a canned-laughter sitcom, a shoot-'em-up cop thing, some reality nonsense, Love Something-Or-Other—and then the channel button gave up as well. I was stuck with Beautiful People wearing too much fake tan and not enough bathing suit, sitting round a pool indulging in camera-ready flirting. I watched an aproned waiter, bald and overweight, handing round cocktails in the slowest of motion.

And then, as the waiter leaned over to peer into the camera, I saw who He was.

The Almighty. God. Jehovah.

The Headmaster.

The picture blurred. His face was replaced by another. One of the Beautiful People, a giggling bikinied blonde on his arm.

Gabriel. The Big Cheese himself, *El Jefe* of Heaven's Civil Service. Even with a sunburned nose and a pink cocktail in his hand, he looked like a bureaucrat.

"Knightsbridge Tube," he said, crossly.

He took a gulp of his drink, but it ended in a spluttering fit when the blue paper umbrella got stuck up his left nostril. The poolside crowd sniggered. After the blonde had succeeded in prising out the offending parasol, he sneezed, then scowled at the camera.

"Now," he said, even more crossly.

*

The mice in Knightsbridge underground station were definitely plumper. Under the escalator, perched on my clothes bag, I finished my third—really delicious, just the teensiest hint of *fines herbes*. Did the little darlings have access to Harrods' bins? Sated, I turned and scanned the crowds around me.

Midday beneath the swankiest part of London. I sighed. Why was everyone in such a hurry? I turned, letting the Piccadilly Line's rush of tepid slipstream ruffle my fur, and gave my at-

170

tention to an old friend, one I hadn't seen for too long.

The revamp had certainly left him looking the part, I had to say—street cred in spades. The face was still rugged, framed by the famous flowing locks. The billowing white robes of a hundred museum portraits were gone, though, swapped for a tie-dye t-shirt, dungarees and sandals. No socks. I'd have put him down as a youthful and still-up-for-it fifty—he could have been an avant-garde artist or a circus acrobat or a pirate, but whatever image he was shooting for, he'd managed to discard the beetle-browed frown the painters usually slapped on him. The new look certainly suited him—the passing ladies were casting an interested eye. And about time too, I thought, he deserved a bit of adventure. Where had he stashed his wings? I sat, wondering idly, cleaning my paws as I watched.

And watching him was great fun, for he had his shtick down to a fine art. He'd lounge against the stanchion at the foot of the escalator, smoking his roll-up (when had that started?) until a train arrived. Then, as the doors opened, he'd nip the cigarette, lift his fiddle and fix a grin to his face. As the Savile Row suits and haute couture approached, he'd start to play *If I Were A Rich Man*. The result was always the same—either a smile or a burst of self-deprecating how-nice-to-be-recognised-as-loaded laughter, usually accompanied by a bountiful rain of coin or a flutter of notes into his hat. The Oirish brogue of his *thank you, sorr* was another innovation.

But once the marks were halfway up the escalator, salivating at the approaching nirvana of Harrod's food hall, the fun would start. A cry of *Venceremos!* would come from below, and then the fiddle would burst into *The Red Flag*. The smug smiles would turn to stone, and his roar of anarchic laughter would follow them vengefully to the top. Grade A street theatre; if I'd been human, I'd have applauded. I settled down and waited till he was between trains, then sloped across. When he saw me coming he hunkered down to my level.

"Well, well, Puss," he said, eyes twinkling, "aren't you the bold one, out all on your own under the big city, eh?"

He smiled, I arched my tail; we'd always liked each other.

"I've only got a minute," he whispered. "I'm here unofficially, a favour to Himself. He's doing the rounds of the soup kitchens, can't get away. He wants you to know that, no matter how much of a go Gabe has at you, there's no harm done. And if you're not in a hurry later, I'll be up in Hammersmith. The Dove." He jingled the cash in his pocket. "My round."

He reached across and gave my rump a rub. My tail became a happy question mark.

"Next train for Cockfosters, the out-of-service one. Last carriage." He stood up. "Give the prissy bastard hell. 'Bye."

I miaaouwed. *'Bye yourself, Raphael.*

At the sound of an approaching train, he hurried back to his pitch. I headed under the stairs to Change in privacy.

Really, why couldn't all the Archangels be like him?

*

With the exception of one none too fragrant wino in the corner, loud snores escaping through the battered hat over his face, The Almighty's chief of staff had taken over the whole carriage. Computers and printers and scanners were stacked on more computers and printers and scanners—ziggurats of gear, enough to run ten heavens. The only other sentient being was the blonde from the telly, now morphed into a glum underling in an ugly brown trouser suit. As an alternative to unblocking noses, she was trying to unblock paper jams on two of the printers at the same time. I read the badge on her lapel.

Intern.

I swept past her, plumped myself down opposite my so-called superior and started doing my nails. From behind his huge hi-tech desk, Gabriel's face took on the glower I knew so well.

"Your manners haven't improved, I see," he said, in his best Old Etonian.

"Lowest form of wit," I snapped back, "and your nose is peeling."

That earned me ten minutes of busy-executive-who'll-make-you-wait-just-to-show-you. I yawned. It had been an early start, and the train's rhythm was hypnotic. Where was Libby? Finally, as we barrelled through Earl's Court, heaven's Chief Archangel leaned forward and clasped his hands together.

"Well, you've made a right mess of this one, haven't you? In all my aeons, I don't think I've ever seen a more incompetent..."

And blah, blah, blah for the next half hour. Mind you, I gave as good as I got. Where was the ancillary support? He'd doled it out often enough before, hadn't he? When Sal Dali was having trouble with his anteater, for instance? Or when that nonsense started with Diamond and the papers... Or was it only female operatives who got hung out to dry? And another thing—

"Who," he interrupted, "is Diamond?"

"Isaac Newton's Familiar, you can't have forgotten! The dog! The one who started the fire on his desk! Don't you even know your own staff?"

"You insubordinate—"

And off we went again—late reports, missing receipts, the cost of the MG... I kept hammering back at him—useless project drafting, lack of resources, outdated equipment—but eventually, I ran out of steam. I drew myself up for one final shot.

"I have to tell you, I am seriously considering making a formal complaint to FAMPOLSA."

Again, he looked clueless. A timid Welsh accent came from the other desk.

"The Familiars, Polterthingummies an' Supernaturals Association, boss."

"Thank you, Blodwyn," he said, grandly, trying to pretend he'd known all along.

I turned and let my most vitriolic smile fasten on her ink-stained digits, then rise slowly to the powdered-over pimple on her chin. My voice found its fangs.

"And exactly what kind of intern are you, Blodwyn? What exactly do you *do* for the Archangel here?"

Her mouth pursed into a defensive pout. The accent intensified.

"No need to be like that, bach. All got to start somewhere, 'aven't we? An' anyway, I bet I'll make a damn sight better Familiar than you ever 'ave, so there!"

I turned and faced Gabriel. "Tell me she's joking! She can't even say *poltergeist.*"

"I bloody can, you cow! Polterbloodyg—"

"Spell it."

Years of being yelled at by despairing teachers knitted her brows. "P-O-L-T-E-R-G-Y—"

The infuriating Eton drawl rescued her. "Leave the girl alone, Knox." He gave an exaggerated sigh. "Why are you always trouble? Your work rate's useless, you never finish anything properly, and someone's always got to clean up behind you. Depressing isn't the word."

I leaned across the desk. "Listen, you poser. I've just discovered a purple pentacle down a kiln that used to belong to a lay preacher! And there's something bloody big brewing inside it! And if you're so smart, would you mind telling me how I'm supposed to proceed?" I jerked a thumb over my shoulder at Blodwyn. "Assuming, of course, you're not too exhausted after your poolside frolic with Welsh Wonder Woman here."

"Sguthan!"

My eyebrows rose. I didn't need Welsh to understand that! Gabe pretended he hadn't heard.

"If you're referring," he said, grandly, "to the Senior Angels' fact finding mission to Key Biscayne—"

"Fact finding mission my backside—I know a jolly when I see one, mate!"

"You'll jolly yourself right out of your next re-entry review if you're not careful!"

We were both shouting, now. I was just about to let fly again when he put up a hand.

"All right, enough!" He put on his glasses. "Your current performance, abysmal though it is, is not why you've been summoned." He pulled a folder from his desk drawer and slapped it down on the desk, then gave me his best lofty scowl. "If it was up to me, you wouldn't be let near this in a month of Sundays, but He seems to think you've got some kind of special clout which might be useful."

I read the folder's title upside down, then stared at him, too surprised even to rake up another insult.

"You're kidding me!"

"Unfortunately not. We have it on the best authority, this is what the Bad Lad intends."

"You mean, like these big American chains? But creating evil isn't the same as flogging fast food—"

In the corner, the wino shook himself awake. "Food? Somebody say food?" He rubbed his bulging stomach. "*Appetite, a universal wolf!* Dead right, the Bard, as always. I could murder a bag of chips."

Gabriel's voice cut in, resigned. "Not now, Noah, go back to sleep."

He swivelled back round to face me. The Old Etonian resurfaced, at its most pompous.

"We've collated all the reports. Processed all the data. There's not the slightest doubt!"

He paused for effect. When that didn't work, he reverted to the scowl.

"Hell—" he snapped, "—is being franchised."

*

Rafe and I sat, leaning on the bar of The Dove, listening to Noah snoring in the corner as we perused the folder's contents.

Paperwork... I shook the last crumbs of the pork scratchings bag into my mouth, looked across at the staircase Charles the Second used to chase Nell Gwynne up and sighed; I'd never had to do any paperwork on that, just gather up the oranges... Rafe put down his pint.

"I know it sounds too fantastic for words," he said, "but take a step back." He gestured at the papers. "You have to admit, some of these alternative hells are pretty good. Supermarket checkout queue you never get to the front of. Multi-storey car park you never find a space in. Car wash where the foam never stops. It's inventive stuff."

I nodded. "Best one I've seen's a call centre. Can't get through, can't get off the line. Computerised Mozart, same phrase for eternity."

His eyebrows shot up. "Clever, that."

I scowled. "No respect for tradition."

He nodded his head, paused, then changed his mind and

shook it vigorously. "Privatisation," he said. "That's what I blame. Nothing's been the same since—I mean, why didn't they think it through? Couldn't they see what they were letting off the leash? It stands to reason, any teenage lowlife with a grievance and a laptop's going to go for his own startup! And if that's a given, it makes total sense for the Bad Lad—never one to let the brimstone grow under his feet—to whip them into line. Bring them all under one banner and there's a fortune to be made in the licences. He doesn't have to do a thing himself, he's got all the people— half the accountants on the planet work for him, after all."

It did make sense, grudgingly I had to admit it.

"Time, ladies 'n' gents! Drink up!"

At the barman's shout, Rafe slid off his stool and went across to Noah.

"I'll get him off."

"You'd better put some food in him on the way," I said, "a kebab or something."

Rafe shook his head. "Wouldn't hear of it. Strictly vegetarian. Says there's no point saving animals if all you're going to do is eat them afterwards."

"He has a point, I suppose."

Rafe looked down at the comatose figure. "He was brilliant in his day, you know," he said, fondly. "Hypnotize the beasts, get them on board, put them to sleep on the spot. I even saw him do it with elephants once. Out like a light, the pair of them, tusks damn near holed the hull." He took hold of an arm. "I'll do him a cheese sandwich when I get him home."

I smiled. "Where is home for the old bugger these days?"

"Houseboat in Wapping." He grinned fondly. "He keeps trying the two-by-two bit on it, nearly sank it a few weeks ago. A pair of yaks he nicked from Regents Park Zoo. Way too heavy. We had to get a squad from the RSPCA to pull them out of the river. Your mate was there."

For a second I was confused—and then I realised who he was talking about.

Glenn.

I started imagining myself in an off the shoulder blouse with an RSPCA inspector pursuing me up the stairs. Rafe spoke again.

"Is it fixed price for the licences, by the way, or bids?"

"Neither," I said, "Adjudication by an expert panel of demons after a thirty minute presentation, no appeal."

"Ripe for the fix, then. Any idea who's on the panel?"

I shook my head. Noah farted loudly. Rafe and I grimaced, then shared a last smile.

"Cheers, Sammy. Mind how you go."

Still smiling, I opened another bag of scratchings. From the corridor, Noah's voice came, declaiming its way out of the front door.

"To be served or not to be served, that is the question, to paraphrase the Bard. Shall we stroll across to this inhospitable establishment's competition, dear boy, and ask them to provide us with a nightcap?"

I stopped in mid-chew.

Competition.

Of course! I'd been right in the bath!

Franchises... The Coven vs. The Monsters!

I lifted my bag. The goings-on back in Cadisham had finally started to make sense.

*

So if I was a drowning yak, he'd save me, would he! Fat lot of use that was! My annoyance gunned the MG through the rain down the M4. I just couldn't stop thinking about it—about him, Mister Glenn Body Beautiful Barnes. Had his fiancée, brass-necked Sonja (who'd nicked him from me in the first place) been there with him? Even though she was RSPCA as well, I couldn't imagine her wrestling with damp Tibetan quadrupeds, the skinny red-haired cow—it was bad enough imagining her wrestling with him! I took the Newbury exit, went round the roundabout almost on two wheels, and forced myself to slow down.

And calm down while I was at it.

Think, Knox.

I could use the situation, couldn't I? After all, having got no guarantees of anything practical out of Gabe, a tame animal welfare inspector—if I could force my hormones to be objective about him—might be exactly what I needed.

Cameras. That's what I was thinking. Wildlife cameras; the hides he'd talked about that first day at Turl's. Yes, he'd do very nicely for that, other scenarios to follow as pouncing opportunities occurred... I twirled a strand of hair round my finger—and then my fantasy stopped in its tracks.

What about mad Jonathan?

I found myself blushing—and then I heard myself cackle.

If the Bad Lad could drum up a bit of competition, what was wrong with Sammy Knox stealing a leaf out of his book?

Grinning, I hit the accelerator again. Eighty to home.

*

By the time I turned the last corner into Cadisham's dripping marketplace, I was a danger to traffic—damn near asleep and functioning on autopilot. Even my usual get you home standby—SingAlongaSixties to the rhythm of the wipers—wasn't working. I skidded across the cobbles for the last few yards, then pulled into the kerb and switched off. Ten minutes, then I'd get on with...

...with what?

What did I have to do that was so important?

As my mind headed for the Land of Nod, I remembered.

Libby.

*

I woke with a start.

To find myself staring straight at her.

At my charge, Miss Elizabeth Martin.

Was I dreaming? I sat up and rubbed my eyes.

The soup kitchen looked as though it had begun life as a World War Two army truck, but over the years it had gathered bits and pieces of other vehicles to arrive at its current incarnation. In the middle of its serving hatch, aproned, gloved and bereted against the cold—and looking saintly and stunningly sexy at the same time—was my teenage witch. She was haloed against the rising steam from a brace of huge urns, smiling beatifically as she handed out plates to the denizens of Cadisham's small hours. Waves of contentment radiated from her. I blinked. Was she real? I sniffed, then salivated. The aroma reaching me through the drizzle was real enough—and it was mouth-watering.

Saint Libby of the Veggie Irish Stew...?

A very different figure joined her. He was small and stout, swathed in a barathea overcoat which had seen better days, his bespectacled face barely visible over knots of home-knitted mufflers. A sodden cloth cap was clamped on his head, and the outsize ladle he was brandishing cast him as Punch to her Judy. He was holding the utensil at arm's length, peering at it as though he wasn't sure whether it was a stick of rock or a Maori war club. Finally, he pulled down his spectacles and looked over the top of the misted-up lenses.

Straight at me.

No longer a cocktail waiter.

And there was no mistaking that look. I sighed, got out and started squelching through the puddles.

You didn't disobey a summons from the Headmaster.

*

He didn't let her notice me, which meant I could just enjoy her, for the first time since the golf club. And I could enjoy the stew as well; finally, some decent nosh.

I'd never seen my charge happier. Contented, I watched her, filling bowls with one hand, pouring tea with the other, laughing all the while at the joke the villainous old pavement artist was telling her. Behind him I could see the two punks who'd been in Jonathan's advance guard at Banbury Vale, still smiling their vacant smiles. In the van's light they seemed even younger than I remembered. Where was their spaniel? The Supreme Being's voice came from behind me.

"She was riding home on her bike," He said. "After visiting her friend. Her special friend. I asked if she fancied helping out." He looked at her with pride. "She's got the knack, hasn't she? The gentle touch."

179

I wasn't going to get an opening like that twice—when He was halfway lucid was always the best time to ask a favour. The problem was, you never knew how long it would last... Anyway, in for a penny.

"Her special friend. That's not a problem, is it?"

His eyebrows shot up. "Dear Me, no! In this day and age? I'm surprised you thought you had to ask." He shook His head. "As long as love is genuine..." He began, but then His brows furrowed as He forgot what He was trying to say. "...anyway, you get My drift," He finished.

"And what about the complications of Blossom and her dad, and all the stuff with Libby's mum and this Rex character?"

"Oh, that's a long way down the list," He said. "It'll all come out in the wash. And anyway, isn't that your end of things?"

No point in arguing with Him, there never was. I decided on a different tack.

"So why did You want to see me?"

"Oh, just a chinwag. Touch base and all that. Seconds on the stew? Or there's pudding—jam roly-poly."

I gave up. "Both, please."

"Ah, yes, you've had a hectic time of it, haven't you?"

To put it mildly... I took a deep breath. I had to press Him.

"Look," I said, "all this other stuff, the franchising business down below. What exactly are you expecting me to do about it?"

He thought for a long moment, then gave me a purposeful look. "I think..."

I waited, all ears.

"...I might have a Bath bun."

19

SEVEN IN THE MORNING is a hard time to witness a Moment Of Truth, even while feigning sleep on a pair of slippers.

They were both nervous. Mike was stirring his tea yet again, Libby was tying and retying her bootlaces. He cracked first.

"I'm sorry," he mumbled, looking out at the garden. "I should have told you the minute I found the damn letter." He turned and faced his daughter. "Let's have said, once and for all." He waved a hand round the kitchen. "I will never sell this. It stays ours, no matter how much money's offered. It never occurred to me that you'd think I could give it up. This is our home. This is my life—and yours, if you want it."

The lace tying stopped. The silence was deafening—and then Libby was on tiptoe, pressed up against her dad in a ferocious hug. Lochinvar started up from his basket, barking. I stretched, padded over and gave him a good hiss to shut him up; no sense of occasion, dogs. Then I threaded my way through all four human legs. Above me, Mike's voice came again, relieved.

"We OK now?"

Tears on her cheeks, Libby nodded.

"Want to tell me about your weekend?"

She hesitated, then buried her head in his chest. "Maybe later, dad," she mumbled. "I need to think a bit."

I looked up at Mike. *Play it cool, like we discussed.*

"All the time in the world, love," he replied. "Whenever you feel ready."

She planted a kiss on his cheek—and then she was off, skipping away for the back door. I galloped after and caught up as she straddled her bike. One leap landed me in the wicker basket.

"Tiddles!"

As she tore off down the lane, I felt the rush of cold air push through my whiskers—and heard the best of sounds.

A girl's loud laughter and a cat's loud miaaouwing, in fine anarchic harmony.

Later, when we were working in the garden, she was still walking on air, reciting her soup kitchen adventures.

"...and it was great, Sammy! The old chap who asked me to help was lovely. He didn't mind a bit when I told him the stew would taste better with more herbs. He came back five minutes later with a bundle of fresh flat leaf parsley and a tub of dried oregano. Which was exactly what I'd been thinking of! I asked him how he knew and he said it was a lucky guess, and we both laughed, and then I asked him how he got hold of stuff like that in the middle of the night and he said he was just good at those kinds of things, and..."

Happy yacking and serious digging. It was reassuring—but I knew we weren't out of the woods yet. My plan was shaping up, though. As she shovelled, I watched a rivulet of sweat run down past the little sabre.

"I could do something like that, couldn't I, Sammy? Start up a caff or a van with really good veggie food." Her voice became dreamy. "Food which never hurt a single animal, anywhere in the world." She dug her spade into the clay. "Food that tastes so brilliant people would forget they'd ever heard of meat!" she proclaimed.

It was a sentiment which should have been delivered to a crowd of thousands.

Instead it echoed off the garden wall.

"That would help everyone, wouldn't it? And the planet, too. And dad could be part of it as well, couldn't he? I mean..." She bestowed a golden smile on her surroundings. "...he's got the best veg around."

It was my turn to smile. A young girl's enthusiasms... How long would it take for an Adept's certainties to mould them? I lifted my spade and began digging again, putting my back into it properly this time.

She was almost ready to confide, now.

*

She tried on the lip gloss in my tiny bathroom with its six-inch sliver of mirror, examining her mouth from every angle. It looked great on her—and it would look even better if she ever reprised Lieutenant Libby. She tried a pout. *Do that at the Channel View Golf Club,* I thought, *and there'd be heart attacks on the first tee.*

"...so I was late meeting you in Turl's, you remember? The day they had the business with the bull? And I thought I'd lost my purse and when I was looking in my bag, I found it."

"Your purse?"

"No, silly. The note I told you about, from my mum. Saying she'd seen me on Facebook and I should ring her." Her voice took on a tinge of defiance. "So I did."

She eyed me in the mirror to see if I'd react. I kept my eyes on my phone. Playacting, but she wasn't to know that. She upped the ante.

"Since then we've had coffee, a couple of times."

Still, I didn't respond. Silence would make her talk, I knew.

"And then she invited me down to Brighton. That's where I was. All weekend."

Disapprove if you dare was the subtext. *So what?* was my unspoken answer.

"What's she like?" I asked, casually—as if I didn't know.

Her brows came together, but she summoned a brave face. "She's great fun, but she's weird as well." She shrugged. "And she drinks too much and she laughs like she's always got something to prove, and..."

Still I waited.

"...she's getting married again, to this old guy. He's creepy. I'd wondered, maybe..." She shrugged. "...her and dad, you know."

I'd guessed from the shattered picture. *Not a feline Familiar in hell's chance, love.*

"I haven't told him yet. My dad. That I've met her, I mean. Do you think that's wrong?"

My silence dodged the question, let it hang. In the end, there was only one thing which mattered.

"Do you want to keep seeing her?"

She hid her confusion by turning back to the mirror, but I caught the whiff of it. Libby Martin knew something wasn't quite right about her mother. *Now's not the time,* I thought. I came up beside her, dipped my pinkie in the gloss pot and daubed my bottom lip. I pursed my mouth.

"Looks better on you," I said, "so you'd better have it. You can wear it tomorrow. In London."

She spun round. "London? Why?"

"Your birthday. Covent Garden Market. A sweater, I thought, or maybe some scarves, something to go with your nice tweed jacket."

She looked thrilled—and then her face clouded over. "The main thing with my mum..." As she spoke, she let her eyes catch mine in the mirror. "...is that I'd really hate anything bad to happen to her."

Ahh... Now that put a different complexion on things. A very different complexion. I put my arm round her.

"Only natural, Libs. I'm sure nothing will. So, London?"

Her voice tried for casual. "What time do you think we'll be back, Sammy? I'm staying the night with a friend."

Long way to go before you're as good a fibber as me, Libs.

"Tea time at the latest."

When she nodded, my heart sank. Any fleeting hope I'd been harbouring that she might reconsider the raid had just died.

I kept my smile bright.

*

Cadisham, Brighton, London—twice, even, London... Too many miles stacking up, it was enough to make a girl dizzy.

But dizziness wasn't my current problem, worry was. Would this go right? There were a lot of wild cards.

My biggest fear was timing. I checked my watch; quarter to eleven... Was Libby still doing the Covent Garden stalls? I'd given her a wad of cash from my newly solvent bank account and told her I had business to do, she should take her time choosing. I was worried she'd wander off, but Rafe had promised he'd make sure she was kept well occupied. I trusted him. But still... I scanned the Sunday dawdlers emerging from the station and revisited my logic.

A Brighton train would get into London Victoria.

The fastest way from there to Belle's 11am first appointment —the pickup she'd talked about—was the Victoria Line, change at Green Park, then the Piccadilly, off here at Covent Garden.

Which meant all I had to do was wait.

The problem was, I was terrible at waiting. I checked my appearance in the window opposite; hair up in a tight bun, scuzzy leather jacket over jeans and Doc Martens. Good. I was nondescript enough for a leisurely Sunday in the Smoke. I kept my eyes on the up escalator.

And almost immediately, there she was, wearing a grey suit I remembered from the closet, and the heels she'd worn to go shopping with Libs. Over her shoulder was a big black Texier bag on a long strap; nice... I slipped into her wake and stayed twenty yards behind.

Out of the station, across Long Acre, into Neal Street, past the Crown And Anchor... *What was this pickup?* The bag was open, I noticed. I did a quick scan around; no Rab. Avoiding the security cameras? She kept up a brisk enough pace, not looking in any of the windows. Would she stop somewhere?

A racing bike flashed past me. The helmeted rider slowed just enough to drop a small packet into her bag, and then he was gone, weaving away through the bollards.

Neat, very neat.

Belle turned into Short's Gardens, zipping up the bag as she went. I let her clop along for another few minutes, then I put on a burst of speed and came up alongside.

"Ms Courteney-Smythe?" I asked, making my voice sound as official as possible. "Ms Arabella Courteney-Smythe?"

She turned, frowning.

"My name is Samantha Knox, I'm a private detective and you need to come with me."

Her mouth opened in shock—and then she spun round and swung the bag at my head, twirling it like an Olympic hammer thrower. My left hand caught it and tore it from her grip.

We stood, breathing hard, confronting each other.

And then my right hand came round...

...and delivered the king-size slap I'd been longing to give the

185

woman for damn near two decades.

She staggered back against a lamp post, then, eyes fixed on me in dazed wonder, slid down it. Rafe, pony-tailed and bulky in East End gangster pinstripe, arrived on cue and stationed himself beside her. As Belle cowered, I reached down and offered a hand.

"Don't even think of trying a runner, love," I said. "Even if you made it past my friend here..." I heaved her to her feet. "...you wouldn't get ten yards in these heels."

*

The pub at the market's edge was loud, anonymous and awful, exactly right for our meeting of minds. I watched Belle's third double go down. Like the first two, it didn't even touch the sides. Excellent, I thought, a good pickling would help soften her up. On the other side of her, Rafe was polishing his shades with a scarlet silk handkerchief.

I leaned against the bar, gauging her temper. We'd had the first blast, the *who the hell do you think you are*, followed by the *you'll regret this, I've got powerful friends*. Now we'd reached the sullen stage. The contents of the shoulder bag made a neat row on the table between us. She was trying her best to ignore them. When her voice came, it was low and vicious.

"I'm going to press charges, you know that, don't you?"

"Feel free," I said.

I brought out my last Knox Detective Agency card—slightly dog-eared, which spoiled the effect—and slid it across to her.

"Mind you get the postcode right."

She frowned at it and grunted. "How do I know this is real?"

I smiled. Then I picked up the passport which called her Elizabeth Martin.

"It's a damn sight more real than this."

She let loose a string of slurred Essex expletives which would have won her a round of applause in Cadisham nick. I lifted the paperwork which certified her as the holder of DeFoulard's Bank Safety Deposit Box 49372—grade A quality, lovely forgery—and then the contents of the package the cyclist had delivered.

A pristine little sabre key, freshly minted.

I shook my head. "Stacking up a mountain of grief, aren't you? Drugging, forgery..." I nodded at the key. "...going equipped to commit larceny." Before she could launch into another tirade, I leaned over. "The thing is, Belle, we both know you didn't come up with any of this on your own."

The arrival of the photo on the table killed the bluster. For a long, sad second, she looked at her companion in crime, custard slice in one hand, mobile in the other, smiling serenely out at the English Channel.

"Your fiancé," I said. "Calls himself Rex Renaldo, but as we both know, that's fiction too. He's Rab Reynolds, AKA Rab Razors, lowlife of Fife. Threatening with menaces, embezzlement and living off immoral earnings. And you—" I allowed myself a smile. "—are going to fill me in on exactly what variety of villainy's next on his to do list."

She scowled down at the table. When she faced me again she looked furious.

"Who're you working for?"

"Mike Martin."

She stared at me. Then, without warning, she began to cry. I felt a flash of irritation—*damn the woman!* As I watched, Libby's anxious words echoed through my brain.

I'd really hate anything bad to happen to her...

Stymied. My charge's instructions were sacred, my hands were tied, no matter how much they were itching to give Belle Martin another slap. Rafe's scarlet silk square appeared in front of her. She grabbed it and blew her nose, noisily.

"It's simple," I said, "Give me what I'm after and this goes away. When's your boyfriend planning to do the cottage?"

The tears stopped. She said nothing.

"Fine. Your daughter's round the corner, you can explain this to her yourself." I turned to Rafe. "Get Libby, would you?"

"No!" Belle shouted. *"Not that!"*

Again, floods of tears. I watched them, absolutely unmoved. I didn't recognise my own voice when it came.

"Last chance. The break-in at Cadisham Organics. And all the rest of it, everything you and the con artist who's never going to marry you were up to. *Now.*"

When she'd gone, gabbling promises not to go back to Brighton or breathe a word to Rab, I felt drained. As we walked, Rafe took my arm.

I didn't have all of it yet, but I was sure I had everything Belle knew. And the main thing was, I had the date—tomorrow night. Could Rab be lifted before then? My phone call to Beth had set it in motion, but if the cops didn't succeed...

The sound of Libby's laughter drove out all other thoughts. When we went through the gateway into the second courtyard, I saw her. She was on a raised dais, surrounded by a couple of hundred people. Two angelic-looking tousle-headed boys, with wings sewn on the backs of their t-shirts, were balancing her on their shoulders. They kept her there effortlessly while they performed a tarantella, circling round the edges of the stage. Both of them were holding out huge hats as they danced. Coins and notes were sluicing down into them. Libby, swaying from side to side, five feet up in the air, was roaring with laughter.

I stared at her.

My Libby.

The sheer life of her, filled with joy, untroubled, living entirely for the moment...

What more could I do to keep her that way?

And then I noticed something puzzling. I turned to my companion.

"Rafe, correct me if I'm wrong, but aren't these two...?"

He nodded, then gave a troubled sigh. "Difficult to hide them these days. Greeting cards, ornaments, posters, calendars—you name it, they're on it. Cocky little buggers are even talking about getting an agent. I should never have loaned them to Raphael for the damn painting—pure sentiment, just because we share a name. And when they got themselves into bother, I had to take them back."

"What kind of bother?"

"Boozing with the Bad Lad's crew after work. Ended up doing a cutpurse number round the Tiber taverns, half of Rome was ready to lynch them."

"Ah."

There was a roar of applause. Libby jumped down, then took a breathless bow with the boys.

The two mischievous Putti from one of the world's favourite paintings, Raphael's Sistine Madonna.

20

"EXACTLY HOW DODGY is what I'm aiding and abetting here, Knox?"

I tried not to drool as I watched the muscles on Glenn's right arm. They were flexing like crazy as he leaned out to fix the camera bracket to the weathervane; sexy wasn't the word. As I listened to the hammer's clang, I tried to force my mind back to the job. Finally, I let his question penetrate.

Option one, I thought. Tell the truth—that I wanted a movement-triggered camera to find out what was going on around a hidden pentacle.

Option two. Tell some kind of bland lie—that I'd been hired by a mysterious client with even more mysterious motives, involving a subterranean security setup.

Option three. Sod it, there wasn't an option three—and he'd never believe one or two anyway. Brazen it out, I decided. As he started back down the steel ladder, I eyed his perfect backside; RSPCA. *Royal Society for the Preservation of Cute Arses...* I applied a surreptitious squirt of Je Reviens and unbuttoned the top of my blouse. It had worked on Ollie... Still with his back to me, Glenn started explaining.

"Jesus, that weathervane's heavy! Getting the bracket on was tough, but it should hold. Camera in the morning, they're all up at Widgely now." He began to turn. "In the meantime, what's—"

A generous eyeful of what he'd passed on not so long ago stopped him dead. I leaned into him and went for Breathy Siren No 2.

"How would you like to be in my good books, Glenn? Permanently. I need to borrow your van tonight, back in the morning, I promise. Just let me have the keys, no questions asked about all this—" I waved up at the roof, fanning the perfume into a good waft. "—and I'll, ah, reciprocate. Any way you want."

I scanned his groin for reaction, then allowed myself a smile; sometimes, obvious really was best.

*

It took a couple of hours to get the RSPCA van parked up near Woodstock, but by seven, after a combination of geriatric bus and horrendously expensive taxi—Gabe was going to love that—I was in front of the Knox Towers mirror and still on schedule, if not by much. Was Libby? She had to be refreshed, she'd slept like a babby for most of the train journey back from London. One minute she'd been showing me her new sweater, the next she was snoring like a hibernating bear. I'd put it down to angelic company and checked my wallet.

But to business.

How to prepare for an animal liberation raid? Nothing in the PI bible about that one...

Disguise, of course, and a good slathering of black face paint, but was that all? I sniffed my wrists; the shower had scrubbed me clean of Je Reviens, good. Considering I'd be meeting Libby again in under an hour, my signature scent would have been instant giveaway. I picked up the emergency bottle of cheap scent (Cadisham Market, two quid the half pint), splashed on a bucketload, donned jacket and headgear and scanned myself; I'd do. Then I heard the rain rattling the skylight and looked up; a stormy old night—and if there's one thing I hate it's wet wool around my ears...

I pulled off the balaclava. It would have to be endured, but not yet. What else was there to do? I plonked myself down on the bed. A million things I hadn't thought of, I was sure. What was I getting into, here? The job description was insane.

Participate in an animal research laboratory raid with your teenage charge. Extricate said charge from any ensuing danger—without allowing her to recognise you.

And without the slightest idea of method—which as a guiding principle was definitely asking for it. I'd been racking my brains for hours, but so far I'd only come up with one plan, and it wasn't exactly a masterpiece of logic.

BFI. Brute Force and Ignorance.

Shanghai the girl. Come up behind her, a quick paralysis using the mindlink, then a fireman's lift and a runner. There were powers I could summon for temporary strength, enough to get us to Glenn's van, at least.

All doable, wasn't it?

I snorted at my reflection; messy hair, donkey jacket, disreputable jeans and a grime-streaked face.

My reflection snorted back at me, unimpressed.

Yes, it would be a piece of cake—Welsh Blodwyn could probably manage it in her bikini, between cocktails.

*

The transport was waiting, engine running, in one of the alleys off Fiddle Lane. I stared—a superannuated khaki Ford Thames van with near-bald tyres, a genuine antique.

A rear door opened. I hopped up; seven people, all wearing balaclavas exactly like mine. No one spoke. A quick scan of body shapes made me suspect the one opposite was Blossom, and then the wrinkle of her nose at the pong of me confirmed it. The second I was seated, a fist banged the metal partition and we were off. As my backside was all but dislocated, the thought came; where was Libs? Had Blossom succumbed to conscience?

No such luck. When we pulled up in the Shambles, the van shook as someone climbed into the cab; my teenage witch—and hyper-excited, the mindlink told me. When her laugh brought an answering upper class cackle, I realised the driver was none other than Jonathan Turl, the big chief—or rather the big mischief—himself. I found myself staring at his daughter. *Libby Martin had better come out of this well*, I thought. *Or else.*

As soon as we were out of Cadisham, Blossom opened the sack at her feet. "Anyone not got the geography down?" No one spoke. "Good. The off's 19.15, second team's creating a diversion at the front gate. There's one other decoy, but we've no way of knowing how long it'll last. Everyone got gauntlets? Padded sleeves, aniseed for the nice bow wows?" Plastic bags and bits of garment were held up. "Messrs. A & B," she went on, "perimeter fence. " She handed each of them a businesslike pair of wire cutters. "Once you've got everyone through, on to the cages. C, you next. You've got the Semtex?"

My eyebrows rose inside the balaclava; more serious than I'd thought, this bunch. The body furthest from me nodded.

"Junction box to be gone inside three minutes, that'll take out the exterior lights and the direct cop shop line." The nod turned into a shrug; another day, another detonator. "The alarm's separate," she went on, "protected mains inside the building, impossible to get at, so you keep going no matter how loud it gets." She turned. "D & E, maximum visible damage—stones through the windows, spray the doors, you know the drill. Then the cages like the others. As the most visible, you'll draw the guards first, so wits about you—rubber bullets might not kill but they hurt like hell." She let out a long breath. "Don't forget, this has to look like a normal amateur raid. Disorganised, chaotic, lots of shouting. No violence other than the minimum to stay free, retaliate only if you're forced to. Out in twenty-five, absolute tops, then rendezvous down the cart track as per the briefing. An hour to make it, then you're on your own. Remember, no one comes back to gloat, and no contact between any of us for sixty days. And if you're caught, sorry, but none of the rest of us has ever heard of you and we won't be visiting in the nick."

She turned to me. "G," she said, levelly, "My team, start to finish."

As I nodded, something occurred to me. There hadn't been any debrief on her lunch with Stoneyhurst. Why?

"L is too."

Relief surged through me—but I had no time to enjoy it.

We lurched into a layby.

The engine died.

*

Breath held, we listened.

"Can't leave it there, mate." There was an unintelligible burst of short-wave static. "I already told him, Charlie... ...blocking the gate."

Noiselessly, Blossom pushed open the back door. As a strong smell of chicken manure reached me, A and B slid past, sleek as

193

otters.

"...you got summat can tow me, then?"

Another burst of radio. Blossom nodded at C. As he went I heard the radio voices, rising.

"...telling you for the last time!"

"...oh yeah? An' where the 'eck am I goin' to get a rear tractor tyre this time o' night, eh?"

There was an answering slew of *not-our-problem-mate* and *get-it-sorted-or-we-will*. Then came swearing, then more static and a resigned shout.

"Charlie! Get on the blower, the direct line."

Blossom Turl stepped down silently from the van.

*

Before I'd gone ten yards, the explosion came, loud, followed by the acrid stench of roasting electrics. The arc lamps died, along with the lights on the fountains at the centre of the compound. The alarm began, a whoop-whoop-whoop like a diving submarine. The night air filled with yelling and yelping. Where was Libby? I recognised her rump a few yards in front of me. Never get a better chance, I thought. I put on a spurt—and then a hand shoved me down and ground my face into malodorous mud. Damn! A whispered shout bawled the word *crawl* into my ear. I did it—and then I was neck deep in foul-smelling stagnant water. I slipped. My head went under. I surfaced, gulping air. *Wet bloody wool...* Spitting out something that wriggled, I scrambled through the gap in the fence. Had they clocked us yet? A hand heaved me up; Blossom. She pointed at the tallest of the buildings, a glass-walled cube, then turned and began a crouching run. As torches lit up the advance guard's sprinting legs, I found myself balaclava to balaclava with Libby. She was carrying a bulky bag.

Now.

I improvised a heavy Scotch whisper *a la* George. "On yer knees, hen! Wait for the word!"

She did it. I came up behind her.

But as I reached out, a torch beam found us. Libs leaped up and sprinted off after Blossom.

Damn! No choice—suddenly we were both running, side by side. As we reached the building's doors, there was snarling from the direction of the main gate, then a piteous yowling. I turned. The lights had converged on the scarecrow figure of Jonathan Turl, legs wide, arms extended. I heard the strains of *Jerusalem* rising over the alarm as aniseed-maddened Alsatians cavorted round his coat tails. Diversion two, I thought; lovely singing voice... A phalanx of helmeted security guards was closing in on him at a steady—if wary—pace. His daughter gave him a brave smile, then turned back to the door. It was open. She had keys... *How?* As soon as we were in, she locked it.

"No noise," she whispered.

We took the stairs up into the darkness. Would I get another chance?

*

The fifth floor was a shin-skinning obstacle course of chairs and desks. Outside, the torches made a shifting patchwork of light which gave just enough illumination. Blossom was laying out canisters on a photocopier. Libby was at the computer on the biggest desk, her balaclava swapped for a headband with a blue light. As she turned, her light found the wall—and I saw the huge photograph. I crossed to it. The name was at the frame's bottom.

EMILY CURZON, Msc, Ph. D. MANAGING DIRECTOR

Well, well, now I knew who the skinny piece with the pearls was. I turned back to my companions—and the atmosphere of calm struck me. Cool as anything, the pair of them—it wasn't just the commando crawl which had been rehearsed. While Blossom unlocked a side door, Libby opened her bag and brought out a bolt of black cloth. She threw it over the computer, then donned a set of headphones. An oblong box with a tangle of cables came next. As she wriggled her way under the canopy she'd made, I understood. Mike's boast came back to me; *Firewalls, Libby's the ace...* The display came on, masked by the black, followed by the clacking of a keyboard. I heard Blossom's whisper.

195

"How long?"

"Twelve minutes. Don't distract me."

I found myself staring at the canisters; Mace, pepper spray, aniseed spray—and two soup tins with improvised ring pulls. Puzzled, I lifted one. Blossom's whisper was an urgent hiss.

"Put that down! Gently."

Mystified, I obeyed.

"Home-made CS gas grenades, not stable. Hands off until you have to use it."

First Semtex, now tear gas...

"What are you really up to, here?" I whispered, gesturing at the photograph on the wall. "Where does she fit in?"

She scowled. "All you need to know is that you're in the animal equivalent of Porton Down, and what comes out of here tonight will decide a large chunk of the planet's future. This is huge, more important than my life or yours." She gestured at Libby. "It's even more important than hers." She lifted one of the pepper spray cans, then consulted her watch. "Ten minutes more for the drive, another two to stow the kit, three to get clear." She thrust the can at me. "You're first line of defence. Downstairs, the main door." She paused. "If it goes wrong, you shift for yourself. The burner only in an emergency."

*

From the steps, sheltered by the entrance hall's darkness, I had a grandstand view of the scene.

Keystone Cops to the max—a bizarre cartoon of animals, guards, and intruders. Everything was chasing everything else round the fountains. What were those furry things? Mink? Ferrets? The hens were the worst—hundreds of them, brown, black, white, squawking like mad as they tried to fly through the clouds of their own feathers. All it needed was the Looney Tunes soundtrack.

And then it wasn't a cartoon any longer. A boy staggered past, trying to free his foot from a dog's jaws. Then a female body slammed into the glass. I heard her yell of pain—but she kept hold of her spray can. I read the scrawl in reverse as the bright yellow gave the door its epitaph.

CRUEL BASTARDS

No argument there... A loud thump starred the glass beside the girl's head and made me start back. A rubber bullet? I saw her turn to run and heard the hue and cry behind her. As I stood, heart thumping, pepper spray in hand, my mind could find only one thought.

Brave kids, fighting for what they believed in.

And when the chips were down, I knew I wouldn't—couldn't—be on any side but theirs.

Especially as my Libby was one of them.

Cruel bastards... The words echoed round my head, revolving slowly until they tumbled into place.

A rueful place.

I'd read the runes wrong—utterly wrong. I'd got this whole episode back to front—it wasn't my job to be my witch's *mother*, no matter how awful her real one was, it was my job to be her *Familiar*. Screw the shanghai job! How would she learn to make big decisions—dangerous decisions, even—if I stepped in every time she got close to one? I shouldn't be trying to stop Libby doing this, *I should be keeping her safe while she did it.*

And I should be proud of her at the same time—especially if what Jonathan's daughter had told me was true.

And somehow, despite my mistrust of Blossom Turl, I knew it was.

So what next? Reconnaissance, I decided, it had to be—and feline would be faster. I stripped off my wet clothes and assumed the Position.

Image. Power. Shudder.

Cat!

As I turned, I heard the door crash open, the outside cacophony multiply.

Fur electric with tension, I sprinted upwards.

*

197

The pursuit was hard on my tail.

"Out! Now!"

I heard Blossom's warning yell as I skidded through the office door. I hopped up on to the windowsill and saw Libby, resolute, thrusting the hard drive at her. She shouted.

"Run!"

Blossom shot her an agonised look. Libby's voice was iron.

"It's what we agreed! You run, I fight!"

Blossom grabbed the box and sprinted for the far door. Libby stared after her for a heartbroken second—and then she was at the photocopier. Carefully, she lifted the gas grenades, pulled the rings with her teeth, then lobbed them, one after the other. The two tins described perfect arcs, then fell with a clatter. I dived for the floor.

The smoke was yellow, thick and cloying. As it roiled its way across the room I heard Libby's coughing—and through the fog, I saw her, backing away. And then she tripped over a waste paper basket.

And fell, heavily.

And didn't move.

Libby!

As I tried to reach her, the yellow cloud reached me. Suddenly I couldn't breathe! My eyes! My paws! My fur! Weeping, giddy, I landed on my knees by her side. The lights came on, a searing brightness which rendered the gas luminous.

Two figures emerged from it.

The Blues Brothers.

My rage was an irrational scream. *"You bastards! Why are you following me?"*

I'd forgotten I was cat. The only sound I made was a hoarse miaaouw.

But it didn't matter, they never even paused. A net appeared. I raised my paws as it was cast. *I'd die fighting, first!* I watched it float down through the yellow fog.

To engulf Elizabeth Martin.

The truth dawned.

It wasn't me they were after!

It never had been!

It was my witch!

Muscles twitching, I felt consciousness fade. As I collapsed, a last thought came.

I should have been a mother to her after all.

*

Waking was agony. I was being dragged across a floor. I tried to open my eyes, but they were gummed together. I held out a burning paw to stop the progress and felt it touch another body. Human? Dog? I managed to blink away the sticky rime of my dried tears. Sight returned, but not focus. It was enough.

Scrapper.

"Be easy, Changeling," he said, "the worst is over."

"Where is she? My youngling?"

"You can stand? Alone? You can see?"

The burning...

Dizzy, I put paws to the cool marble and forced myself up. I saw the yellow paint, the hallway, the darkness beyond. How had he got me down the stairs? Pain doubled me over.

"Outside, there is water," he said. "It will cleanse. You must forget your hate."

The fountains.

"The poison which afflicts you, Changeling—I know it. It torments, it burns away fur and sight. You must cleanse eye and paw, now, before the need to scratch becomes no longer an urge, but a command."

He turned, loped across to a shattered window and hopped through. Shakily, I followed.

The courtyard was a battlefield, corpses everywhere. Dead dogs, bleeding cats... I picked my way between two throatless beagles and a monkey with a crushed skull. And everywhere, hens, desolate bundles of feathers... The mix of the chicken reek and the congealing blood was beyond evil.

Scrapper was waiting at the fountain. He steadied me from behind as my front paws found the basin's lip. I felt the heave as he shoved—and then...

...water! Hated water!

199

I battled instinct, made my eyes open and thrashed around. As I tried to get out, his paw thrust me back down. I forced myself to accept it. When I finally emerged, I shook the water from me, then looked at my saviour.

"She has been taken?"

He nodded.

"Where?"

"I do not know, Changeling. But the two creatures who took her, I have seen them leaving the Chamber of Fires."

Chamber of Fires?

"Where once you tried to follow me," Scrapper said.

The kilns, Grizelda's house...

"Old friend, I must go there. Will you help?"

"Command me, Changeling."

I turned. Where were my clothes?

And then I saw the chicken's corpse.

I frowned. Was I still groggy? Or did it really have four legs?

21

PANIC STABBED AT ME—*Why do they want you, Libs?*—but after a few miles I had it under control. I looked across at Scrapper.

The teenagers had been brave, but the calm courage he was showing now was even more impressive. He sat upright on the toolbox Glenn had left on the passenger seat, swaying with every curve, watching all the craziness a desperate high-speed night drive could bring—the oncoming lights, the thump of passing car stereos, the squealing brakes. His good eye stayed steady, refusing to blink at any of it. Where had he learned how to cope with this?

A dull certainty found me; Blossom, it had to be... I felt a stab of resentment—which I banished, immediately; the woman deserved gratitude, not jealousy, she had added significantly to his armoury. Had she made it out? Again, my panic surged. *Libby—where are you?* I gripped the wheel tighter. Scrapper turned, sensing my torment.

His gaze steadied me—it always did. But what was he feeling now, my Fighter Of A Thousand Battles? His was a life untouched by fear, that was the legend. But was it the truth? As I drove I eyed the contrary rake of fur at the nape of his neck, the only sure sign of unease in him. How much will did it take for him to go on fighting his perpetual fight? A gargantuan lorry thundering past us killed the thought. Finally, I saw him flinch, the red scars on his head become livid.

But not with fear. What I was seeing was contempt—and anger, a deep anger.

Would we speak of it? As I accelerated past an ancient Hillman Minx, as fast as Glenn's van would let me, I wondered. A blare of horn told me I hadn't executed the manoeuvre quickly enough. A futuristic sports car shot past us at insane speed, and then a desperate wail of sirens enveloped us. Oncoming police cars... I counted five. Bound for what we'd just abandoned?

Libby...

Once more I felt Scrapper's eyes upon me. I turned. The human Changeling and the feline Fighter Of A Thousand Battles had no language in common—but I knew what he was thinking.

Why do you do this?

How does this barbarity benefit the Loud Ones?

I had no answer. I put my foot down.

*

Nether Kilns House was unlocked. We waited, hardly breathing, in the kitchen. Nothing broke the silence.

The door to the kilns was open. I shone the torch down the steps, then looked at Scrapper. He understood. He would guard here, warn me of trouble.

And trouble was certainly coming.

*

The chamber had changed. The muck held a multitude of shoe prints, now. I examined them; fresh... Bertie? The Blues Brothers? I let the beam follow them to the steel doors, then went across and checked each kiln; all fully stacked now with birch and oak. I let the light travel up the wall ladder. Nothing else had changed.

And then the noise reached me.

Squealing.

Two steps took me to the ladder. I scrambled up, reached out, grabbed the weathervane's base and pulled. The roof hole was just big enough to get my bum through.

*

The Toby jug undulated through the tunnel's mouth like a carried litter, jerking and wobbling. Why? Watching it inch forward, I understood; it was being borne on the backs of the rats. Hundreds of them, trampling over each other in frenzy as the vessel neared the chamber's centre. The din was deafening—desperate, ecstatic. When their cargo reached its allotted space, they began squirming out from under it. The last one was unlucky, its back caught by the rim. A squad of its peers turned and began pulling

202

at it with their teeth. By the time they'd freed it, the beast was dead, its spine snapped. They dragged it away, leaving a red track through the clammy earth. As soon as the corpse was gone, the janitors came, scurrying round until the surface was restored.

Patience...

Outside on the roof, I willed myself to it. Once I was sure all the rats had left, I peered down into the jug's cream-coloured interior.

Empty.

Footsteps. Bertie, followed by the Blues Brothers. My anger surged. *Where's my Libby, you bastards?* Each of them held a lighted spill. I watched the steel doors being opened, the logs being lit, the doors clanging shut. Once they were gone, light began to flicker through the tiny kiln windows; the woodpiles had caught.

What was being fired?

*

I smelled the first evil before I saw it—rank, putrid, like a corpse. In one of the smaller circles, the flickering light began to coalesce into a shape. A *moving* shape.

A tail. A long serpent's tail, perpetually coiling, never still. It was followed by a man's body. A long wolf's head appeared on its shoulders. A gryphon's wings grew from its back.

Marchosias.

The mosaic portrait of him had been chilling enough, but the reality... I fought revulsion and forced myself to remember his pedigree.

A senior marquis of hell, lord of thirty legions, revealer of truth to conjurors...

A new smell added itself to the foulness of the first—brimstone. In the next circle, a different beast began to materialise. This time the wings were scaly and massive. The draught of their unfolding reached me on the roof—a dragon's wings, bright red, translucent. Suddenly they became joined to a four-legged body. Only when its head sprouted antlers did I know it as a deer.

Furfur.

An earl of hell, a habitual liar unless compelled to truth, a harbinger of destruction...

He snarled at Marchosias. His reply was a baring of teeth and a low growl.

And then came the third smell. Flesh, burning...

A hunchbacked black bird, the size of a man, appeared on the third circle, its claws gripping the mound of glowing coals beneath it.

Camio.

He threw back his head and opened his long beak. The raucous cawing doubled and redoubled the responses of the other two. I shrank back from the hole's edge. I knew what would happen next. I waited. The dying of the maelstrom of sound told me the moment had come. I put my head over the edge.

The Bad Lad.

He stood in the Toby jug which bore his likeness, but in a form I'd never seen before—a louche Victorian aristocrat, tall and elegant. The black hair, swept back from his brow, fell over his collar in a lustrous wave, the rings on his long-nailed fingers glittered. He wore an immaculate black three piece suit, his white-collared throat sporting a red cravat pinned by a massive diamond. Slowly, he turned, examining each of his lieutenants. I could see the yellow light of his gaze transform them, revitalising them, feeding them. They breathed deeply, growing as their powers were amplified. A throbbing filled the chamber—a throbbing charged with potency, with unbridled malevolence. It reached up and pulsed round me. As I struggled against it, I heard his words.

Greetings. You know why you have been summoned?

Furfur snorted.

Camio cawed.

Marchosias growled.

Good, my friends! We approach All Hallows' Eve, the time of maximum power. To be used! To be savoured!

Again the demons responded, louder now.

Our plans are near fruition, our terror is ready, waiting to be unleashed, to double and redouble this world's darkness. No more peace! No more plenty! In their place shall come pestilence! And degradation! And despair! Our first blow shall be struck in exactly...

He took a gold hunter from his waistcoat pocket.
...six minutes and thirty seconds.

His right arm shot out. Lightning leapt from his forefinger to find Marchosias. The beast's whole body lit up, the tail whipping at the air. He let fly a long, agonised wolf's howl. The Bad Lad whirled round with fluid grace. This time the bolt found Camio. Tongues of flame licked up from the coals as the bird, cawing wildly, danced on them. Then another dancer's turn, and the ragged skein of light reached Furfur. Snorting and trumpeting, the winged deer rose on his hind legs, his antlers ablaze in a fan of fire.

By now, all three kilns were glowing red hot. As I struggled against the heat, I heard the Bad Lad's laughter, low, musical, savage with satisfaction. By the time I willed myself to look again, the three demons were gone. Now the bejewelled hand was beckoning into the darkness.

A tall figure appeared.

Elmer Blick.

Naked, but no longer stooped. The stick insect had become muscular, erect. He radiated vitality. He bowed low to the Bad Lad, then stood where Furfur had been. His hands were clasped before him, his face was unreadable. The Bad Lad's words were ice cold.

The fire feeds you. You have done well, you shall sow greed and rage and pain. You are worthy of my trust. I appoint you.

Next, Louise. She ran to the circle of Marchosias. Like her husband, she was stark naked. She looked young and radiant. Her mouth opened. As her tongue ran over her lips in frank sexual need, the musk of her swam up to me. The Bad Lad's voice came again.

The fire loves you. You have fulfilled your promise. Lust and envy shall flow from you. You are also worthy. You are also appointed.

The last place, Camio's, was taken by a strange squat animal, a cross between a chicken and a frog. It was obese, with stubby clawed arms and a long-eared hare's head.

Beelzebub—in his real form. His enormous belly hung over his bulging thighs. The fur on them seemed to move, writhing down towards his taloned feet.

205

My servant, you have performed well. You are appointed adjutant to my new chieftains.

The long ears flattened themselves against the furred head. The Bad Lad gave a sigh of satisfaction—and then he began to grow. Suddenly he was naked, horned and tailed, his face red and enraged. His voice became a shout.

Go! I entrust this hell to you! Beware my wrath should you fail to make it prosper!

He gripped the jug's rim, his long red tail flicking over the side. Out of the darkness marched one of the Blues Brothers. His left hand held Grizelda's strange chequered cockerel by the neck, his right, one of the fat hens. The Bad Lad took the birds, held them apart and turned his yellow eyes on each in turn. Then he brought them together, rubbing them against each other. On the roof, I heard their excited squawking.

And then the other Blues Brother arrived. As he stepped forward, I saw the load he carried.

Libby!

My Libby! Naked!

And unconscious!

The mosaic's words burned before me.

...when the maid who is chosen takes darkness for dower...

No! Never!!

Hot tears running down my face, I pulled off my clothes and scrambled into the Position.

To Change!

A blinding jolt of pain arced my body backwards. As I fell, I managed to look at my hand.

Still human! Why...?

The cold voice answered me.

You didn't think I wouldn't know you were here, surely?

In agony, I forced myself to look down. The Toby jug was full of some kind of oil now, clear, clinging. The Bad Lad was smiling up at me. Libby was in his arms, her body writhing as he fondled her. *Was He going to—*

The yellow eyes glowed.

206

The cockerel and the hen appeared on her belly—*and began coupling!*

Roaring with rage, I pulled myself upright and grabbed the weathervane for support.

The iron stanchion fractured. As I dived, the whole thing toppled through the roof behind me.

The last thing I heard as I landed in the jug was the crash of it hitting the pentacle.

*

Oil!

Cloying, insistent!
Vile! Foul!
Filling me with pain, with lust!
With need, with madness!

I fought like a crazed thing. For good! Against evil! For sanity! The cockerel and the hen attacked me in a pecking frenzy. Screaming, sobbing, I lashed out through the feathers—to strangle, to choke the life from the Bad Lad!

But all my hands closed on was oil.

He was gone.

Wind rushed in from all sides, tearing at the pentacle's tiles, ripping them from the floor and smashing them off the walls. The chamber began to buck and whirl, then the jug, widdershins. The oil became charged with power, a vortex that gripped, sucked me down—*I was drowning!* I managed to get a hand to the rim and pull myself up. Demon cries surrounded me. All I could do was cling on.

And then it all shuddered to a stop. I heard Libby, moaning, felt her thrashing about at my side. I managed to pull her up—still breathing, thank—

Claws!

They tore at me—Beelzebub, enraged! The huge teeth lunged forward, a taloned foot raked my arm.

A black and white blur landed on the hare's head, gouging, biting. Beelzebub flailed out wildly, but Scrapper would not be dislodged. The jug began to tip over, then fell on its side and began to rock. The oil hissed away through the cracks in the floor. Beelzebub fell to the destroyed mosaic and lay still. I watched the demonic form deflate to become...

...Bertie.

Scrapper stood over him, one paw raised in readiness should he shift shape again. We both looked at the overturned jug.

Libby was still inside, sliding back and forth with its rocking. When the movement stopped, she slithered out. I gathered her shivering body to me and carried her to the steps.

And as soon as she was out of my hands, time and I lost each other.

*

When I came out of the trance, I saw the twisted remains of the weathervane. I struggled across and dragged it out of the rubble. The world swam. I was near fainting. I stood, trembling, desperately trying to summon the powers I needed.

Nothing.

I looked around me.

Libby, still unconscious.

Scrapper, by her side.

Bertie, snoring on the mosaic's remains.

Blick, a stick insect once more, his wife, a hag of unbelievable ugliness.

Suddenly I was answered. Strength surged through me. I lifted the twisted weathervane above my head and threw.

The blow shattered the Toby jug to smithereens. I fell to my knees.

Only then did I see the movement in the corner.

The cockerel and the hen were still at it.

22

"ANYTHING ELSE I can do before I go?"

I shook my head, very carefully. It didn't fall off. Glenn stood, awkward, then lifted his uniform jacket and nodded at Libby, fast asleep in my bed.

"You'll let me know how she is?"

I managed a smile. "Of course." *Lie, Knox*. "I'm sure it's nothing to worry about, she just had a rough night."

He looked doubtful. Gorgeously doubtful.

"Glenn," I said, gently. "At some point I'll explain. All of it."

Once I've concocted a version that'll make sense to you.

"Cheers, Sammy."

"Cheers, Glenn."

The door closed. I listened to his descending footsteps, dully aware of the regret I should have been feeling.

Finally, I get the man within grappling distance...

But it wasn't his fault, and he'd been good about everything else. He'd come the minute I called, collected the van at Acacia Avenue and asked no questions, despite the state of me. Then he'd driven me back to Knox Towers with an unconscious Libby in my lap, carried her up the stairs and helped me put her to bed. He was a good mate. No matter how rampant he made my hormones, it wouldn't do to forget that.

I stretched. Every joint and muscle in my body protested. How long before I felt human again? Not to mention, feline...

And then there was the question of transition between the two.

Had last night's refusal killed my Changing ability? I didn't think so—if that had really been compromised, I'd have been destroyed without trace. I knew, I'd seen it happen. But I was still wary. I'd never had a Change blocked before, not once in five centuries. Extenuating circumstances or not, I'd have to be cautious about my next attempt. Very cautious indeed. The thought scared me.

I sat down at the foot of the bed, beside my sleeping charge.

Earlier, she'd been thrashing about, boiling and freezing by turns, but now, other than the faintest rise and fall of breathing, she was completely still—which was, if anything, more disturbing. Was she dreaming? And if she was, exactly *what* was she dreaming...? The mindlink was giving me nothing, which deepened my un-ease.

And then a slim sliver of bewildered comfort came spinning up to me. The relief of it brought me to the edge of tears. I let out a long, shuddering sigh.

Whatever else I might have to contend with, I was still Libby Martin's Familiar.

But the sight of her, now... Could there be damage, perhaps even permanent damage? How much of the night would she re-member? All of it? Enough of it? Above all, would she know that she'd come within a hair's breadth of disaster, of a life bound forever to evil? That could be dangerous in the extreme... Again the signal fluttered up from her; less faint now, the comfort was growing. I was reassured—until, hidden inside it, I felt the kernel of something else.

A disturbing kernel. At the very bottom of her human self, a childlike Libby Martin wanted...

...her mother.

Once more I felt the rise of tears—and this time they were guilty tears. After everything Belle had done, how could I let that happen? I pulled myself together; what use was a weepy Fam-iliar? I took a deep breath, looked down again at the figure in the bed and projected my thoughts.

Rest. I will keep the world from you until you can deal with it.

She shifted position and settled into a more relaxed bundle.

And I will work out a way to give you what you want.

*

I ran a bath, hot this time. Once the water had begun to work on my hurts, I tried to piece together the events of the night before. The effects of what we'd come through, terrifying though they were, now had to be put to one side.

What exactly had the Bad Lad been trying to achieve?

Power, that was an odds-on certainty—it was everything to him. That his potency would have been vastly multiplied by a coupling with my virgin charge on the stroke of All Hallows' Eve, I had no doubt. But he'd been aiming the conjunction of events at something very specific, of that I was sure.

And then there was the matter of sex-crazed poultry...

What was that about? Before I'd left, I'd stowed them back in their old coop. The minute they were reunited, they'd slammed into each other again as though they were on piece work, being paid by the thrust. What did it mean? Some unleashed survival gene? Something in the awful oil? The odious roles of all the others—Furfur, Marchosias, Camio, the Blicks, Beelzebub, the Blues Brothers—were obvious, but a perpetual poultry porn show, that was beyond my ken. I let myself sink under the water and blew a stream of bubbles up to the surface.

In the end, though, Scrapper and I had beaten the lot of them, hadn't we? So why was I still wary? Why did the winning feel so hollow?

I sat up, rinsed the soap from my eyes, and pulled myself out of the bath.

The pains were bearable, now. I could function. I looked back at Libby; out for hours, yet...

I reached for the towel. Then, as I gathered my clothes and the MG's keys, I let the biggest question of all surface.

Was it over?

*

It was mid-afternoon when I reached Acacia Avenue. As I pulled up, my phone beeped. Beth, a text.

Rab still at large. Sorry. Still on it.

Another complication. A dangerous one? Had Belle blabbed after all? I'd have put money on that not happening...

But speculation dodged the main question. Had Rab done a runner, or was it still on the cards that he'd try something tonight? It couldn't be discounted. Which meant that by nightfall, whatever muscle I could round up had to be in place at the cottage.

I got out and surveyed Nether Kilns House. Logic told me to go inside, instinct told me not to. I went with the latter and began circling the place. As dingy and depressing as it had ever been... I came to the back.

The hole in the kiln chamber's roof was a jagged-edged void. Memories gripped me; my rage, the pain of refusal, the foul oil... I levered myself over the wall and went to the chicken coop.

The two Tuscaloosa Tartans were safe, at least, and they'd finally managed to uncouple. They were sitting, still as statues, on either side of a mound of straw. Or rather, a *mountain* of straw. I reached inside and cleared it away.

The egg had kept a faint impression of the strange tartan design of their plumage. Jonathan's words came back to me; *best I've ever tasted...* Would it be true of this one?

Considering it was at least three times as big as any egg I'd ever seen. I looked at the hen in sympathy, one girl to another. A noise from behind whirled me round.

Scrapper.

He jumped down from the wall, loped across, settled at my feet and looked up at me.

Instinctively, I knew what he wanted. My panic rose so fast I became breathless. Was I ready? His black and white face blurred before me. I found myself mumbling a final farewell to him.

Just in case.

Then I stripped off my clothes, assumed the Position...

...and forced myself to Change.

The last thing I felt was bone-wracking pain searing through me, first as human, then as...

*

I came to, my fur drenched in very unfeline sweat. Scrapper's calm voice came through the haze.

"May the claws of your courage always vanquish your enemies, Changeling."

"And may your scars fade in the faith of your friends, Fighter

Of A Thousand Battles."

I was so dizzy I almost didn't get the words out. His forepaw steadied me.

"Changeling, this is cruel, I know. You must rest, now, until you can once more shift shape. Then you must take these two feathered ones and their unborn from here. To the Cage Destroyer's daughter. She is at her lair."

My legs buckled. The last words I heard were filled with his concern.

"Until you are ready, I will watch over you."

*

The huge egg didn't feel fragile, but it was extremely heavy. I carried it slowly through the rosebay willowherb, holding it before me in both hands, like a priest with a sacred chalice. Behind me, the two birds cackled as they followed. I'd been worried they'd go for me when I lifted it from the coop, but they seemed content enough. Which seemed odd.

I put down my load on the straw nest I'd made in the passenger footwell and held the door open. The proud parents fluttered in, clucking with satisfaction. I watched them place themselves to either side of their offspring; good, that should keep it from moving. A loud miaaouw made me turn. Scrapper. He jumped up on to the seat and began cleaning his paws. I closed the door gently, then got in, pulled out my mobile and checked the time; not a lot of it...

I dialled the pub. George's gruff Glaswegian was sanity. Two seconds had us in agreement. I started the MG, turned her and began driving back up the hill, very slowly—this wasn't a cargo to be rushed. How long to Blossom's place? I fished out the burner she'd given me.

And as I dialled, it struck me. Did using this bit of kit make me a fully paid up Animal Liberationist? Could someone who was pretty much two animals at the same time, and who could murder a full English right this minute—

I heard a dull *whoomph* behind me and looked in the mirror. When I turned again, Scrapper's eyes found mine.

Nether Kilns House had burst into flames.

We kept looking at each other, but even if we'd been able to talk, it wouldn't have mattered. We were both thinking the same thing.

No, it wasn't over.

23

"TWENTY-ONE days for a normal fertile egg to hatch."

The hens scratching round her designer wellies clucked in agreement. Only Scrapper and the Tuscaloosa cockerel, perched opposite each other on a crossbeam, stayed silent. Jonathan Turl's daughter gave me a very old-fashioned look.

"But then, this one isn't normal, is it? Where did it come from, Ms Knox?"

"They'd made a nest about a mile from the lab."

Her brows came down; Brigadier Blossom, back on manoeuvres... "I thought I'd made it clear no one was to—"

"I had business round there," I said, sharply. "Nothing to do with last night's frolics. And given what you told me about Hazlett Humane, I thought you'd want to know." I nodded at the egg. "So do I leave it here or find it a new home?"

We stood, calmly regarding each other.

Gunfight At The OK Chicken Coop...

Mistrust... Would it always be the default between us? The thought was undercut by Scrapper's miaaouw. Blossom looked up at him. Scrapper looked down at her. After a long time, she turned back to me.

"It'll need watching. Round the clock. When—"

I cut in. "I need you at Mike Martin's, tonight."

"But—"

"You promised."

She only hesitated a second more. "I'll make some calls."

"Make one extra. I want Mike gone from Cadisham by nightfall. An extended evening consultation with his new divorce lawyer would do nicely. Somewhere far away."

Again, she nodded. I bent down to leave the henhouse. Her voice stopped me.

"She's all right?"

I turned and eyed her. Guilt? At having abandoned Libby, despite the raid's rules? She tried to keep her face blank, but she couldn't keep it up.

"Tell her..." she began.

Brusquely, I cut her off. "I will."

I tramped through the mud to the MG.

Love...

*

"Oh aye," Big George said, examining the picture of Rab as he did up the buttons of his shirt. "I mind him, right enough. Cocky bugger. Found him in my dressin' room the night I went up against Patsy O'Shaughnessy in the Kelvin Ha'. Forty-odd year ago, now. Offered me a hundred quid. When I threw him out, he told me if I didnae go doon in the fifth he'd be back wi' the auld chin chib."

He mimicked a hand holding a razor. The action could have meant either shaving or slitting.

"What did you do?" I asked.

"Told him he should see a dentist..." He cradled his enormous right fist in his left hand. "...then showed him why."

Despite my worries, I found myself smiling; that would have been something to see... As my stomach rumbled, I watched him scan the bar for custom. Then, day job taken care of, he put the picture down on the bar.

"So what's his game these days, apart frae misquotin' Burns?"

"Con artist. Lets stupid women do his dirty work and tricks people out of their money. He's got Mike and Libby in his sights."

He grunted. "Well, if tonight's the night he decides tae try it on, I hope it's me he tries it on wi'." He turned. "Rita!" he shouted.

She came up the bottom stairs from their flat, pinning up her hair. When she arrived at her husband's side, his voice became magisterial.

"Sammy'll need a mixed grill, love. Right now. She's in for a heavy night, might be rough stuff. We're no' sendin' her out tae face that on an empty stomach."

Rita answered her husband's determined look with a smile and a sigh. A satisfied sigh. *It wasn't just the Tuscaloosa Tartans,* I realised, *who'd been at it...*

"Comin' right up, big fella," she said, gently.

"Rita," I said, "the back rent. I'll be able—"

She waved my words away. "Ah, love, it's not a bother, don't you worry your head about it. This is the time o' year the taxman comes creepin', an' waitin' for the greasy knock always has me like a bag o' weasels. There'll be time enough to sort you out." She jerked a thumb upwards. "An' in the meantime, I'd wager you'll be wantin' an eye kept on your lodger?"

How did she know about Libby?

She leaned in to me. "For a wee pet lamb, she's a lion's snore on her, mind."

She crossed her arms over her chest. Acerbic joined amused in the Belfast brogue.

"When I heard it vibratin' the stairs I went up to find out who it was, seein' as how I knew you were off gallivantin'. But would you mind tellin' me, Miss Samantha Knox, what in the name o' hell you've been up to wi' the lass? The state of her bonny hair! She looks like an owl nestin' in an ivy bush!"

Before I could reply, she was off. Giddy from the verbal on-slaught, I surveyed the cosy early evening of the Angels' Arms.

In the name of hell...

Rita, I thought, *you'll never know how right you are.*

*

Would Rab show? Sitting in the MG in the cul-de-sac opposite the cottage, I wondered. He would know by now that the De-Foulard's gambit was a washout, so what would his priorities be? Sunny Switzerland, to wait for his beloved brother's demise? Or stick to the original plan? And if it was the latter, why?

No blinding flash of insight came. I shook off post-prandial mixed grill bliss and went down my mental checklist.

The egg, safe in the henhouse, mother clucking round it, father roosting on his beam, looking distinctly, ah, shagged out...

Mike, off to meet his divorce lawyer somewhere near Grantham...

George, due in twenty minutes with Bendy Lawson and the Antrim twins...

Brigadier Blossom also imminent, after recruiting someone to keep an eye on the egg...

What else could I do? Another circuit of the garden? There was no point, I had the geography down. My mind began to drift, in one definite direction.

Matters corporeal.

George and Rita, the Adult Chicken Cabaret...

I mean, how come everyone else was getting righteous doses of the old horizontal mambo and I wasn't? Now that my belly was full, the thought was making me distinctly restless. Images were forming, in glorious Randycolour; Glenn's shirt coming off, Jonathan's blue eyes boring into me... Where was the old bugger, anyway? Still in the Woodstock cop shop, charming the knickers off some cousin of Daisy Driffield's? I indulged myself in a bit of fantasy eeny-meeny. Who should come first? Hard to tell, either would do. And what would I be? Demure damsel or sinful seductress? Scenarios began flashing past in razor-sharp Legoverama.

And then the driver's door was pulled open.

The term *razor-sharp* took on new meaning. With the blade at my throat, I turned. Very slowly.

Rab.

And slumped against the wall behind him, not far from collapse...

...Libby.

*

His aftershave enveloped me from behind as we marched towards the garden's back entrance. The pigskin briefcase swung in his free hand, but the razor never wavered from my neck. Would Libby be all right? After he'd pushed her into the MG I'd managed to leave the door slightly open, hoping the cold might wake her. Would she have the sense to run?

"So Belle told you," I said, trying to keep the tremor from my voice. "Come running back, did she? As soon as I let her go?"

He was in Rex mode. "Other way round," he said, pleasantly. "Once I worked out something was wrong, I knew where to find her. She has a sister in Haringey."

The sleek purr sounded as though it had never heard of Scotland. How to get out of this? The razor's edge kept bringing me

218

back to the immediate. *Keep him talking,* I thought, trying to swallow fear, *let him enjoy the power.*

"So why pick Belle? Just easy sex?"

He snorted. "She was never much good at that, which is why all her fancy men went AWOL. But the flat was handy enough."

"As a base for Kirkcaldy Holdings?"

"Very good, you've done your homework."

I forced out the words. "So what happens now? You take care of me, then go about your business?"

He stopped. His laugh was easy, relaxed.

"Oh, no, Ms Knox."

Without warning, the voice flew back over the border. "Pretty wee thing, the young lassie." His mouth came up to my ear. "Makin' sure she stays that way depends on you, though, darlin'. Because it'll no' be me goin' aboot ma business." Again the easy laugh came. "It'll be *you.*"

*

The Cadisham Organics rear gate was a heavy slab of bolted-together railway sleepers. He handed me the key. I understood; my prints, not his... I unlocked and pushed. Still holding the razor, he surveyed the garden, then opened the briefcase and put it down between us. Two glass bottles glinted in the moonlight.

"Nae mistakes. It goes right, your pal's safe. It goes wrang..."

He brought up the blade and smiled, grimly. Then he lifted the first bottle. Inside it, long brown things wriggled.

"Dig them intae the roots in the polytunnels. The other, open it and—"

I felt a rush of air. Something bulky just missed my ear.

"Run!"

Blossom!!!

As Rab whirled round, the gas grenade hit. The dull *crump* of explosion made the world yellow. I stumbled forward—and felt the razor slice through my hair from behind.

Fear gave me wings. I hared away. *How far behind was he?* I skidded round the corner—and slammed squarely into Blossom, hard enough to bowl us both over. As we hit the gutter, Rab, coughing, face red with rage, staggered out of the fog. He looked down at me.

Everything slowed.

The feral smile...

The raised arm...

The razor's flash...

A hand shot out and wrenched the weapon from his grasp. Then Big George McArdle grabbed his countryman by the collar and swung him round—and the knuckles which had achieved twenty-two straight knockouts in their day did their work.

Rab Razors went down like a ninepin.

Silence. And then footsteps, uneven and hesitant, came from the sulphurous yellow cloud.

Libby.

She was near collapse, her mouth open, slack, her eyes, wide, glazed over. Shivering, she took in the whole scene, cataloguing us one by one. Blossom scrambled up and caught her before she could fall.

George rolled Rab over with his foot, then leaned down.

"It's till a' the seas *gang* dry, numpty."

24

"SO WHERE IS he now?"

"Cadisham nick," I said. "Being grilled by a woman you once described as having a huge arse."

Blossom's reflection suppressed a smile. "Truth will out," she said, gathering a wet handful of my hair in her comb. "Explain it again."

I sighed. "Think back to the original plan. The estate agent's letter makes Mike think about selling. Rab floods the garden with pests to bugger up his produce. The garden basically dies. What happens next?"

Our eyes met in the mirror. She shrugged. I resisted the keep-up-at-the-back line she'd thrown at me a few days ago.

"When Mike's so desperate he *has* to sell," I went on, patiently, "it's, *well, Mr Martin, the business isn't worth what we thought, this is all we can offer you now.*"

The scissors came dangerously close to my earlobe. "Ah," she said, "got you. So what about the rest? *Hold still!*"

Head rigid, I watched the black locks tumbling to my shoulders. She'd insisted on giving my hair a revamp after the depredations of Rab's razor. A simple spell would have grown it back overnight, but I couldn't tell her that. And I wouldn't have, anyway. It had been a nice gesture.

"Think about where Cadisham Organics actually is," I said. "Mike's got about twelve acres, in the middle of one of the most picturesque towns in England. The cowboy builders who prowl the Cotswolds aren't interested in organic veg—but given the chance to get their hands on that cottage, they'd have it tarted up and on the market inside a month. Even with no land, it'd fetch three-quarters of a million, easy. Next, a few well-placed incentives round the council, and before you know it, planning permission's gone through. Then—surprise, surprise!—instead of organic radishes sprouting up round the old place, there's a rash of little three-bedroom ticky-tacky boxes! What's the pitch on those rabbit hutches down by Keble's Meadow? *A prestige home for only £700,000?* They'd cram at least forty into the space. Even at four hundred grand for the land, they'd treble their dosh after flogging the first two."

"What was he going to use on the garden?"

"First bottle was wireworms, turn into beetles, the second was a bug called *Clavibacter michiganensis.* Heavy duty stuff. Mike would have been bankrupt in weeks."

"The Blicks?"

"Disappeared without trace." I smiled. "Scarpered with a nice touch, though—they stiffed the hotel for the bill."

Without warning, Blossom grabbed my head in both hands, then swivelled it left and right to examine her handiwork in the mirror. Frowning, she brought out a different pair of scissors.

"And Libby's little sabre?"

"Getting her somewhere they could knock her out and copy the keys was vital to Belle and Rab," I said. "CCTV showed them tailing her into Turl's early on Calgacus day, so her mother could slip the note into her bag and start reeling her in. Rab recognised the sabre immediately."

She lifted another handful of hair. "How much will Libby get when the dust settles?"

"No idea," I lied, quickly.

Too quickly. Blossom went back to her clipping. I felt the cold steel travel carefully along the back of my neck.

"I've got about six million in trust from my mother," Blossom said, in a measured voice. "I'd say Libby's windfall is safe enough from an animal liberation raid for the moment, wouldn't you?"

I inclined my head. "Natural reflex, Ms Turl. My apologies."

"Accepted." She lifted another handful of hair. "And please don't imagine my reflexes are any slower than yours, Ms Knox."

I saw red—until our glances connected again. My outrage died. Neither of us really knew the other; her suspicions were as justified as mine. She smiled. I realised I was doing the same.

"I do prefer snipping to sniping," she said, casually, "and given the unreliability of both our sets of reflexes, it might interest you to know that our contingency fund has recently been swelled by an anonymous donation of seventy-five thousand pounds."

It took me a second, but then I had it—*Stoneyhurst's brown envelope! Brilliant!* Who could the old charlatan complain to? Suddenly we were both laughing out loud.

The door opened on our mirth; Barnaby, the young biology lecturer she'd dragooned into monitoring the egg. Stethoscope dangling, he sat down at the table.

"Still the same?" Blossom asked.

He pushed back a long blond forelock. It came to me that I knew him, but from where...?

"Nothing cracking yet," he said, "but in the last half hour we've had a couple of kicks. Pretty hefty ones."

Blossom and I shared a look. Neither of us was smiling any more.

*

"...in a net, and then I was being carried by this skinny boy with cold hands, into a boiling hot room. He put me in something full of slimy stuff that kept dragging me down. I shut my eyes—and when I opened them again there were these weird chickens having sex on me! Ughh! It all smelled horrible! I wanted to scream, but every time I tried, the clingy stuff filled my mouth! And there was this strange guy with red skin and yellow eyes and he was..." She blushed. "...touching me, and we nearly, you know..." The blush deepened. "Then there was this crash and you were holding me and shouting and trying to hit something and everything started whirling and I fell out on to the floor." She frowned. "And then I saw the black and white cat, the one that's always with Tiddles, fighting a big rabbit." She looked across the bed at me. "It was the worst dream I've ever had in my life, Sammy, really scary. Do you think it'll come back? Dreams do, don't they?"

I smiled. "I don't think it will. When did it end, your dream?"

She shook her head. "I'm not sure. I remember being in bed up here, but I didn't wake up properly until I was in your car." She hugged herself. "It was so cold. And then I had a different dream. I was walking round our garden wall in my bare feet. In the yellow fog, like in the—"

She stopped abruptly.

"It's all right, Libs," I said, very gently. "I know about the raid.

223

I was there."

She gave me a look of pure bewilderment—and then the rest of it tumbled out in a breathless rush.

"...and I came round the corner and you and Blossom were on the ground and so was the creepy old guy my mum's marrying, and Mr McArdle was standing over him, and..."

"Libs," I said, "that part wasn't a dream."

I looked at my charge's face; anguished, confused, lost.

I had no choice, I knew.

I had to tell her.

*

Her anger came first—and of course it fastened on the wrong thing.

"You mean they've still been married *all this time?*"

"Libs," I said, "your dad never was an official kind of guy. He was just so glad your mum was gone he didn't bother with the red tape. He concentrated on you instead, on bringing you up. And despite his problems, from where I'm sitting, he did a great job."

Her bottom lip was quivering. "And now she's trying to divorce him!" She blurted the words out. "To get his money! And all the time she was being nice to me, Brighton and everything, it was just so her and this awful old man, this *Rab,* could steal what Aunt Una left me! *And I fell for it!*" She burst into tears. *"And they were trying to poison our garden!"*

The tears became sobs, big and painful. I made no attempt to check them. When they had run their course, I took her hand.

"You've nothing to be ashamed of, Libs, you were just being yourself. Like you were in a different way at Hazlett Humane."

Her head whipped up. "Why were you there? At the lab?"

I'd seen this one coming. Honesty, I thought, as much of it as I could afford.

"To look out for you." I said. "I wasn't convinced the raid was a good idea. I thought if something terrible happened, I could get you out of there."

She looked upset, then doubtful. I ploughed on.

224

"But when I saw how brave you were, and how determined, I decided it wasn't my job to rescue you, it was my job to keep you safe while you did whatever you had to. I didn't do it well enough. I'm sorry."

"How did you know about the raid in the first place? It was secret."

"I'm a detective, remember. Knowing secrets is my job."

She nodded, accepting it, then her head went down. When her voice came again, it was a miserable mumble.

"How bad a person is she, Sammy? My mum..."

The million dollar question... No ducking it.

"She's done a lot of bad things, there's no doubt. But maybe she's not all bad."

Silence. I watched her, hurting. It took a very long time for her head to come back up.

"You remember when dad was drinking, you told me I could, you know, change him?"

Easy does it now, no pressure. I nodded.

"And we did it, with the black heart and everything?"

It was what I'd been hoping for. I sat there, keeping an iron grip on my thoughts. Finally, she got the words out.

"Sammy... Do you think I could change my mum?"

*

Not all bad...

Sitting in the MG outside Woodstock police station, I thought about Libby's question.

Changing a totally bad person into a totally good one is impossible, no matter how much supernatural firepower's brought to bear. But if there's the slightest trace of good to be found, the thing can be swung. A tricky job, though, and complex—a kind of open soul surgery with moonlight instead of scalpels. A huge job for a novice.

But I would try.

Yawning, I eyed my watch. Whose idea had it been to release the old bugger at four in the morning? I looked across at the cop shop. Nothing happening. A ten minute snooze?

225

Before I could close my eyes, the door opened. Jonathan Turl waltzed out, pork pie hat and crazed smile intact, beaming as though he'd just bought the place. Then he bestowed a cheery goodbye on the two shapely policewomen who'd come to see him off and looked round for his transport. Eventually, his gaze fastened on the MG. When I got out I saw the blue eyes twinkle.

"Ah, my security consultant! How nice to see you, Ms Knox! And astride your trusty MG steed! Nearly as old as me, I'd guess, but given some encouragement, we old ones can still perform, eh?"

The next five minutes were spent folding him into the car like some lanky hinged tarantula. When I'd finally succeeded in getting the aristocratic knees up round his ears, I got in and started up.

"How was your spell in the cells?" I asked as we roared off.

"Splendid," he said. "Extremely..." He grinned. "...refreshing."

That's one word for it, I thought, watching the two WPCs waving regretfully in the rear view mirror. As we drove past the vast baroque bulk of Blenheim Palace, he turned to me, earnest.

"It would make a great sanctuary for rescued animals, that place, don't you agree, Ms Knox? Of course, we'd have to knock the old pile down—"

I cut him off. "We're headed for a different class of sanctuary, Mr Turl, one full of a very distinctive genus of wildlife. Better at knocking off than knocking down."

His eyebrows shot up. "Really? And why are we doing that?"

I smiled. "I need a second opinion on someone, the kind only a highly experienced ladies' man—" *Who's also an Emphathetic*, I added, mentally. "—can give."

I leaned across to the glove compartment, slapping his hand away from my thigh in the process. Libby's gold locket gleamed as it came out.

"It's all set up. She'll be expecting you to give her this. I'll coach you on your lines."

He took the locket and examined it. "Curiouser and curiouser," he said.

"Of course," I continued, "there'll be no *refresh*ing involved in the process. That would spoil what I've got planned."

"And what exactly do you have planned, Ms Knox?"

His hand hovered over my thigh again. The look I gave him made him think better of it.

"You'll find out later. Depending on how well you do..." I let my smile widen. "...in Haringey."

*

Cramp woke me. I uncricked my neck, turned and scanned the street, just in time to see Jonathan Turl emerge from a battered doorway twenty yards up the hill behind me. As he strode down, slaloming between the burst bin bags and rotting mattresses, I took him in.

Stained raincoat with gaffer-taped shoulders, battered pork pie hat, ancient flannels flapping in the breeze... I smiled. England's eccentrics... How comforting to know they could thrive on its mean streets as well as in its stately homes. He levered himself into the passenger seat.

"Well?" I said. "You were in there for long enough."

He sighed. "A suspicious mind is a terrible thing, Ms Knox."

"So?"

He gave me a vague smile. "As per your phone call, I was expected, but she seemed convinced I'd come to bring some kind of retribution." The smile died. "Not surprising, really."

"What do you mean?"

He said nothing.

"You gave her the locket?"

Suddenly Jonathan Turl looked sad, even sadder than when he'd been confessing to Tiddles in his cell. *Why?*

"When I put it in her hand," he said, "and told her it was a token of forgiveness from her daughter, she whispered 'I wish I hadn't' and began to cry. I'm willing to wager she's still crying now."

Behind the car, a door slammed. We both looked in the mirror.

The greasy-haired, leggings-clad woman who slouched past the MG was no longer Arabella Courteney-Smythe. She wasn't even Belle Martin. She looked twenty years older. As she turned into the churchyard and sat on a bench, I took in the green and yellow black eye, the split bottom lip, the bruised neck.

Rab...

Bessie Beasley lit up. Even from twenty yards away, I could see the tear-stained cheeks and the shaking hands. Jonathan's voice came from beside me.

"She's someone who lost her way a long time ago," he said, quietly. "If you have some way of changing the road she's on, Ms Knox, you'd better do it quickly. She hasn't much time left."

25

AFTER ALL SHE'D been subjected to, my witch was in no shape for big magic.

A week of TLC had made no difference, I finally admitted it. I sneaked a glance at her, sitting at the kitchen table, nibbling on a slice of bread like a timid mouse. Not trying to save her mother was eating Libby more every day—and that was a risky situation for an Adept to be in, particularly one who'd just been through such horrors.

It was a no-win paradox. The strength she needed was being eroded by the very thing she needed it for.

I had a workaround. On paper it looked fine, but if it failed there would be no second chances. As I stirred the pan of soup, I went over it. Clothes in the car for both of us, keys in the hands of my co-conspirators... But would my precious Midget be safe when we got to it? In such a dodgy bit of London?

I frowned. There wasn't the slightest point in worrying, there was nothing more I could do. I lifted the pan, went across and ladled mushroom soup into Libby's plate. I was on my third helping, Mike had wolfed down two before going to bed. All Libby did was stare at the plate, then look up at me.

I knew what it meant, that look.

When...?

How...?

Within the next few hours, she'd get her answer. I forced my voice to stay cheerful.

"Try to eat, Libs. Keep your strength up." I put the pan back on the stove. "Back in a minute."

*

Up in her bedroom, I lifted my t-shirt and unwound the silk scarf from my midriff.

It was special, very. Thierry had given it to me in 1900, and it had kept every one of its wild and wonderful memories. Careful

229

to keep my eyes averted, I spread it on the bed. If I looked at it now, its power would be lost.

I was proud of my work, though. I ran a finger along my new sewing—the incantation Goody Thwaite, Cadisham's last known witch, had delivered from the scaffold just before they hanged her. It had taken me the whole week. The sliver of paper with the three not to be looked at words had been the worst, folding it into the main seam had been a nightmare.

I had the text by heart.

A soul might turn from a tainted road
if a valiant heart should lift its load
and bitter winds shall cease to blow
when tainted tears no more do flow.

Eyes still closed, I frowned. Executed five hundred years ago, old Goody, for casting a spell not unlike the one we were about to try...

I refused to dwell on it. Keeping my back to the scarf, I lit the candles and opened the window. Then I went back downstairs, punching at the buttons on my mobile.

*

In the garden, the moonlight made strange shadows of the apple tree's branches. Rafe's whisper was loud in my ear.

"She's here. On the churchyard bench."

"She hasn't recognised you?"

"I haven't been close enough to let her. The two kids are doing their scouting number. She's got one hand on the locket round her neck, a half bottle in the other. She's smoking like a chimney and crying."

"And Noah?"

"Beside her on the bench, her new best boozing buddy. Latest word from him is, he'll have her out cold inside half an hour. The minute she is, I'm with you."

I pressed red and looked up at the flickering candlelight in Libby's window.

Half an hour...

*

Fifteen minutes later, I followed my charge up the stairs. At the bedroom door I stopped her.

"You have to close your eyes."

"Why?"

"It's a surprise."

She gave me a sceptical look, then did it. I shepherded her into the middle of the room.

"Why is the window open?"

I put a finger to her lips. "Take off your clothes," I whispered.

"Sammy!" she protested.

I faked a giggle. "Elizabeth Martin, How many times have I put you to bed over the years? It's part of the surprise."

She began pulling off t-shirt and jeans. When she was done I closed my own eyes and lifted the scarf from the bed.

"No peeking."

I wound the silk round her neck. As I pulled her gently to the open window, I heard her sigh of satisfaction.

"This feels wonderful. Is it another birthday present?"

"Kind of. Be still now, Libs."

Before she could respond, a beating sound echoed round us. She couldn't hear it, I knew. A shaft of light appeared from the sky and lit up the garden. A tall winged figure in billowing robes emerged from it and came to rest outside the window.

The Archangel Raphael.

With a grave smile, he reached out and touched a forefinger to the silk scarf. Libby's body stiffened.

He disappeared.

"You can look now," I said.

A puzzled look on her face, she unwound the scarf, then held it out before her in both hands. My embroidered words were gone, only the silk was left. She looked at me with tears in her eyes.

"Sammy, it's gorgeous!"

She wound me into a fierce hug, the scarf between us. I stood,

231

holding her, listening to her heart.

My witch, my lovely witch... Not strong enough to bless your talisman with your own magic...

...so the Archangel Raphael is lending you his.

I wanted to keep her in my arms forever. Instead, I readied the mindlink and forced myself to do something I hated.

I made her faint.

Raphael reappeared as I caught her. I hoisted her out into his waiting arms. As he held her, I draped the scarf back round her neck.

Then I stripped, assumed the position, Changed, and leaped out of the window to be with her.

The Archangel Raphael folded us both to him and swept us into the sky.

*

Magic... Elation... Rapture...

The headlights on a country road, the wet streets, the church spires...

The points of starlight, the black clouds, the forked tribute of the lightning...

The soft flutterings of Libby's heart, twined round the steady beat of Raphael's...

The wind, the shadow of our passing over silvered lakes and rushing rivers...

The triumphant surge of massive wings, forcing us through the night sky...

The ships in the harbours, the beasts in the byres, the laughter of the lost, the slinking foxes, the lonely lovers, the huddled homeless, the crying babes... The castles, the cornfields, the sinners, the sainted, the mothers, the madmen, the pious, the princes, the drunk, the damned, the fakers, the fearful, the orphaned, the old...

And then, a fading of ecstasy as we spiralled down into the bleak reality of a down-at-heel London churchyard.

My heart filled with revelation, I was in a daze as we landed. I was dimly aware of Noah's goodbye wave and Raphael's stately march to the bench. My focus returned as he put Libby down beside Belle and laid her head on her mother's shoulder. Within seconds the two women were breathing in the same rhythm. I stared at the tableau; both at peace, both cocooned in a deep repose far beyond sleep...

A hand stroked my fur. I turned; Rafe, once more the raffish tube station busker. He lifted me on to a broken headstone and sat beside me. The two Putti came running and squirmed their way into his lap.

He put his arms round them and looked up at the night sky. All sound—human, animal, wind, traffic—died. A rippling bubble of translucent blue light had formed high above the churchyard—the light of the moon, intensified, faceted like a diamond.

Slowly, it descended. I watched it engulf mother and daughter. The last things I saw before it became opaque were the shimmering silk scarf round Libby's neck and the shining gold locket at Belle's throat.

"Nothing to do now but wait," Rafe said.

*

Time had stopped—or paused, at least. The universe had slipped us a three-hour free pass. I realised it as I carried Libby past the kitchen clock, still chiming midnight. I half-walked, half-carried her up the stairs, then got her undressed and into bed. She was practically comatose, and I wasn't far behind her.

But bone-weary or not, I had to know. Had the spell worked? When the blue light had vanished, she and her mother had been lying apart, both ice-cold to the touch, and so still I'd feared them dead. And all the way back in the MG, Libby hadn't moved, not so much as an eyelid. Was there no sign? No signal of success?

Or failure...?

I Changed, then jumped up and claimed a space by her ankles. My eyes began to close. *Rafe would take care of Belle...* It was my last thought before the dreams took me.

My world became *wonder, flying, hope, fear, longing, worry...*

*

233

"What the hell are you doing on my bed, you filthy fleabag?"

The words shocked me awake.

Belle's voice!

Belle's accent!

Out of Libby's mouth!

"And why the hell am I here?"

Hockey stick in hand, she was standing on the carpet before me, naked, her face twisted with fury. I dodged the stick's murderous swipe and jumped for the top of the CD rack.

"You think I'd ever let myself live in a dead dump like this? Watchin' posh women flauntin' it, showin' off their money!" The voice became a shout. *"Money I should've had!"* She brandished the wooden stick. "I was a looker, I was smart! Smarter than all of them!" Her laughter came, wrapped in an evil sneer. "Poxy cows! I fucked their husbands and stole them blind! And told the whole town the dirty secrets they gave me!"

Again the stick swung round, but this time it didn't connect. The momentum brought her to her knees. She began to weep.

"Why did I never get any? Can you tell me that, cat? Why did I get stuck with a useless bloody musician who never made more than pennies! All the bastard was good for was getting me—"

Fury seized her. She threw away the stick. As I leaped again, she scrambled up, grabbed the computer with both hands and heaved. It hit the floor with a crash—and then more tears came. Tears of pure rage, a storm of them. She staggered back into the room's centre and threw back her head. Her neck muscles went rigid.

Libby! As I tried to get to her side, the whole rack of shelving crashed down around me. She fainted. As she hit the floor I heard Mike's running feet.

"Libs! What the hell—"

He stopped. Open-mouthed, he surveyed the mayhem, then swung round. When he saw me among the wreckage, his face became savage.

"No wonder you're bloody hiding, cat!"

I opened my mouth to miaaouw in protest—and then closed it. *Blame me,* I thought, *it gives Libby an alibi.* I shot past him, out of the room.

And then I turned and peeked round the door jamb.

Mike was cradling his daughter in his arms. His voice was only just loud enough to reach me.

"No big deal, love, no big deal at all, you needed a new one anyway."

She groaned. He gave a sob of relief, lifted her and laid her gently on the bed, then pulled up the covers and kissed her. Then he slumped down on the floor at her side. I padded across to him. Though I'd done nothing, the touch of his hand was forgiveness.

"It's just..." His eyes found something far away as he stroked my head. "...I could have sworn I heard a voice in here, cat, a voice that brings back the bad times. In fact, the worst times."

A third frame materialised between the images of Bacall and Monroe on Libby's wall.

The Headmaster.

His words sounded in my brain.

Her mother is purged.

I gave Mike a soft miaaouw of reassurance.

He wouldn't have to hear that voice again.

Ever.

26

SPRUCED UP in my office best, I skipped up Turl's back stairs to the Wingco's office and went into the waiting room. Something beige, the size of a battleship gun turret, blocked my path.

"Do you have an appointment, young lady?"

Blossom's description came to me; *sumo wrestler in drag.* Yes, in the absence of Ms Horn Rims And High Heels, the good Mrs Stoneyhurst had stepped into the breach. The voice was an aristocratic foghorn.

"I'm from the council," I said. I leaned in to deliver a conspiratorial whisper. "I'm here..." I paused for effect. "...about the rats."

She stepped back so fast she almost left her face powder behind. I strode round her and breezed into the Wingco's domain.

Without knocking.

*

"...And I have to say, Ms Knox, that had it not been for an inexplicable clerical error by my previous secretary, Turl's would never have paid your frankly exorbitant fee. You singularly failed to complete any of the tasks we agreed on, namely—"

I slid my rump on to his desk and unleashed my brightest smile. "Oh, Wing Commander, don't be such an old grouch! It's a lovely day, let's not spoil it with disagreements. Especially when I'm here collecting for such a deserving cause."

His brows came down, his jowls drooped like Lochinvar's. "And exactly what might this 'deserving cause' be?"

"It's called the *Symington's Next Table Revelations Fund.*"

Not the brightest candle on the cake, old J.D., but slowly the penny dropped.

"I have some brochures with me," I said, fishing an envelope out of my bag. "It does incredibly good work in so many different fields. Wealth redistribution, for instance."

The pause was long enough for me to enjoy his complexion turning from scarlet to puce.

"And how much wealth are we talking about 'redistributing', Ms Knox?" he asked, finally.

"Twenty-two thousand seven hundred pounds."

He gasped, audibly. The door opened. The foghorn was more accusatory than alarmed.

"Jeremiah! You must remember to take your pill! Remember what the doctor told you!"

I let my smile become even brighter. *Jeremiah...* What did the D stand for? *Doleful? Duplicitous?* I opened the envelope enough to let him see the top photograph.

Him and Blossom, practically welded together over the bundles of illicit readies. Puce turned pale. When his voice returned, it was through gritted teeth.

"Cynthia dear, do you think you could find us some coffee?"

The foghorn mutated into an irascible grunt before the door slammed. I kept my eyes on him as I shouted after her.

"And don't forget the Hobnobs!"

*

The bodywork needed a coat of paint, but the smell didn't. Even from fifty yards away, it lost no time permeating the MG's naturally ventilated hood.

Burgers.

Veggie burgers, done with rosemary and thyme, one of Libby's favourites. Not as good as the real thing, of course, but I had to admit they'd grown on me. I began to salivate.

The bus (second-hand, fully fitted, upstairs accommodation, six month guarantee) had been worth every penny. I'd found it online. Jonathan had offered to spring for a new one, but since Stoneyhurst had been on the point of firing me, I felt the old bugger should suffer. And, *mea* not in the slightest *culpa*, hadn't I just enjoyed our little tête-à-tête! Never did get a Hobnob, though...

Anyway, I felt vindicated. The converted 1967 Routemaster bus sat on the Lyme Regis seafront as though it had always been there, an oasis of light in the gathering dusk. The crowd round it was mostly young, chatting and laughing as they ate, enjoying the foggy view of the old harbour wall, the famous Cobb. I negotiated my way through. Where was Bessie?

I heard the bark before I saw her.

She still looked twenty years older than in her Belle or Arabella days, but it didn't matter now. The grey hair was beautifully styled, she'd lost weight, and she was in her element, aproned and smiling. I watched her setting plates down before a young couple—the Banbury Vale punks, even more pierced than before. As their spaniel's tail wagged a greeting at me, her voice cut through the noise.

"...completely veggie, of course it is! Trade Descriptions'd do us if it wasn't! That'll be eight pounds fifty, guava juice is on the house."

When she turned, she saw me. A puzzled frown creased her brows.

"Do we know each other, love?" She gave my outfit the once over. "Nice skirt," she said, "and you've got the figure for it. I did once..." She patted her tummy. "...till the cream and butter came courting." She gave me a gentle reprise of the barmaid bark, then nodded at the bus. "What d'you think of *Bessie's Burritos*, then?"

"Brilliant," I said, "you been in business long?"

She shook her head. "Friend of mine came into money, set me up."

"Lucky old you," I said. "You don't do meat? At all?"

She shook her head. "Nothing I used to love more than a sausage, but lately I've gone off it. Completely. And I found out I can cook veggie stuff pretty well."

I smiled; *Libby...*

"Truth be told," she went on, "it's been a bit of a life saver for me, this." She paused, then gave me a serious look. "I was a right old mess until it came along," she finished, quietly.

I said nothing. Within seconds, her good humour was back.

"I'll work it as long as I can, then it goes to my daughter." She brought the locket up to her lips and kissed it. "If she wants it."

Oh, she'll want it all right, I thought. No matter what her future held, Libs would find time for this.

"Anyway, can't stand here gabbing, work to do. Can I get you something, love?" she asked.

"In a bit. I'm still deciding."

238

Bessie Beasley smiled. It was a lovely smile, open and generous and contented.

"Take your time, we're open till ten."

*

As I watched Bessie thread her way back through the crowds, I found myself examining my own feelings.

Relief.

Relief that the spell had worked.

Relief that my charge was back to feasting on nut cutlets.

And finally, relief that after so many years, I could let go of my intense dislike of the woman I'd just spoken to.

But it was time, I decided, for the rest of the day's business. I smoothed out my leather skirt, took out my makeup mirror and inspected myself. Perfect. If Sammy Knox in full war paint didn't have the old bugger panting for it, I didn't know what would. Now if—

The ringing of a bell killed my musings. A hand bell, coming from the Routemaster's serving hatch. I turned. My prospective paramour, Jonathan Turl, Esq, had decided to recreate himself in town crier mode, pork pie hat swapped for a tricorne one. My eyebrows rose. This, I hadn't expected—he was only supposed to be overseeing the business side...

"Oyez, Oyez, you lovely people!"

There was ragged applause. He brandished a small blackboard with chalk writing, then put down the bell.

"Tonight's special, prepared by the dainty hands of the burrito mistress herself, Ms Bessie Beasley! Ladies and gentlemen, I give you, for your vegetarian delectation..."

He leaned out, hung the little board on two hooks beside the hatch, then flung his hands in the air and gave round two of the yell he'd delivered over a tranquillised bull in Turl & Turl's china hall.

"*...garlic butter gnocchi with crispy broccoli!!!*"

There was a collective *ooohh*. Immediately, the queue began to lengthen. Bessie, beaming, appeared at Jonathan's side. The two of them went into a no holds barred clinch, then pulled away

239

from each other, laughing. Then Jonathan Turl planted a highly unbusinesslike kiss on her lips.

My heart sank.

Love...

Bloody love!

I might never have experienced it myself, but over the centuries I'd tripped over enough of it to know the damn thing when I saw it. I felt the red mist descend—*this just wasn't bloody fair—*

And then I stopped myself.

Even if I couldn't understand it, I couldn't begrudge them it, either of them.

And I had no one but myself to blame, I thought, frowning—I should have taken my shot when the old reprobate was groping my thigh.

I sighed. Nothing else for it.

I joined the queue.

*

The wind on the Cobb was getting unruly, and the gnocchi, it had to be said, were first rate, delicious and mega-garlicky—which didn't matter one whit, given that I was no longer planning to kiss anyone any time soon. I'd started on my second helping—food being the only real antidote I know to disappointment. I heard footsteps behind me. I turned.

Glenn!

And looking more gorgeous than ever!

"I just had to come and find you," he said. "I've come to a decision, Sammy! I can't—"

Before he'd even finished the sentence I was running towards him—*darling, why the hell did it take you so long—*

And then, a millisecond before he caught me in his arms, I stopped myself.

Hell.

The air around him was cold. Freezing cold.

I took a step back. And forced myself to look at him.

"You might as well show yourself," I said.

Uniform, face and hair burned themselves away. There was

a flash of lightning, a clap of thunder and a burning smell. And then the louche Victorian aristocrat of Nether Kilns House was standing before me, an amused smile on his face.

"No need to be alarmed," he said in a silky voice. "I just felt it was time we got to know each other better."

"That's why you came disguised as someone else, is it?"

The waves crashed harder against the Cobb. He shrugged.

"I thought it might break the ice, apologies if I got it wrong. Actually, I'm here with a job offer. It really is time you came to work for me, you know. You're wasted on the Headmaster, far too good for Him—we both know He's past it. He can't last much longer, it's an open secret that Gabe's planning to take over—" He laughed. "—and I don't see you taking orders from him, do you?"

Eyes glittering, he took a step towards me. I took one back.

"Oh, please," he said, laughing. "I'm not here to *hurt* you, I'm here to *reason* with you. Okay, I was annoyed after Halloween, I admit it, but that's all behind us now. Think of what we could do together! And the rewards! Wouldn't it be nice to know you'd never want for money again? Or sex? It could be laid on night and day, any way you want it."

I looked at him, suddenly calm.

Garlic.

The Bad Lad.

It worked with vampires, didn't it? And he was their boss, after all...

I let him have it with the plate. The gnocchi hit him square in the face. He shuddered with distaste, but he didn't move.

Forcing myself to keep my nerve, I walked past him, heels clacking.

And when the sound of his mirth reached me, it was my turn to shudder.

The Bad Lad's rage, that I could have understood.

But his *laughter*...

Scarier. By far.

27

AT SOME UNEARTHLY hour of the morning, my head stuck under the pillow, I heard ringing. Was I awake? Or dreaming? I felt around under the bed till I found the phone.

Sticky... *Why was the phone sticky?* I lifted it. The bleary-eyed detective in me managed to find traces of the night before's egg salad sandwich.

"Knox Detective Agency," I croaked, licking my fingers.

It took a couple of jaw-stretching yawns before the mayhem coming down the line—a full-on barbarian onslaught of terrorised howls and frenzied hammering—registered. A long spate of high decibel crowing finally identified the call's origin.

"Ms Turl?"

After another prolonged bout of shouting and smashing—was that a *window?* —she came on the line.

"I think," she said, gulping for breath, "it might be good for you—*back, you bastard!—*"

A loud thump. Had she hit something with the handset?

"—to get yourself out here."

A blood-curdling squawk almost deafened me. It was followed by more shattering glass.

"Now," Blossom Turl said. "Bring breakfast cereal. Chocolate. Lots."

*

Winnie The Pooh would have sold up.

The place looked like a disaster movie set. Two of the cottage windows were smashed, the fences and pens looked like something from a tank training ground, the chicken coop was matchwood and the wicker lean-to was hanging in tatters. The Cinquecento stood forlornly beneath it, sporting a bent front wing and a shredded tyre.

I got out. Where were the birds? I could hear barking in the distance, and a high-pitched screeching which seemed to wax and wane, but the only actual animal presence was Dinkey the donkey's backside. His front end, busily cropping something or other, was obscured by the remains of a tomato frame. When the billy goat trotted round the corner, I was relieved. He wasted no time in showing me the pink dowsing rod. Hurrah for tradition, I thought. I gathered my seven boxes of ChokkoKrakkles—the shop's entire stock—made for the door and pushed my way in.

The art on the walls was intact, if a bit splattered, but the rest of the place...

The leather chair's stuffing was everywhere, the cupboards looked like they'd been used as dartboards, and the floor was a sticky mess; feathers, broken glass, cereal and flour, all bound together by what looked like egg yolk. Blossom was at the far window, peering through binoculars. She let them fall and beckoned me over.

"In about a minute," she said, handing me the glasses, "he'll complete his twenty-fifth circuit. When he passes, don't move."

I gave her a puzzled look and brought up the binoculars.

I heard the chickens first—a frenzied storm of clucking. Then the brown mass of them broke cover from the copse at record speed. Why? An ear-splitting screech answered me.

My jaw dropped.

A cockerel?

A *tartan* cockerel?

A four foot high tartan cockerel?

In front of the window, he launched himself. Wings whirring, he pounced on the last straggler and had his way with her, almost flattening her in the process. Business done, he dismounted. As his chosen mate staggered off, he loosed a shriek of triumph, his bright yellow comb flopping from side to side. Jerkily, he scanned his surroundings.

I must have shifted position. His mad eye fastened on me— and then he ran full tilt at the window. The crash was like a bomb going off. As glass showered over us, Blossom and I shied back, overbalancing on to the mess on the floor. I helped her up. By the time we were back at what was left of the window, he was off again. When Blossom spoke, her voice was rueful.

"I made the mistake of trying to catch him, but he's got a fair

243

turn of speed."

I lifted the binoculars again. "That might have something to do," I said, "with the six legs."

*

"Campbell." Blossom sounded certain. "I was at a tartan ball once, up in Argyll."

I shook my head. "No, it's one of the McNeill ones. Obvious when the light hits it."

We were both watching Cockzilla—Barnaby's name—on the lawn. He was happily gorging himself, completely docile now. The boy biology lecturer—*where did I know him from?*—was sitting in front of him with my compact in his hand. Every so often he'd hold it up. The bird would shake his head right, then left, flipping his bright yellow comb. We'd discovered he loved looking at himself. A vain chicken... Was it the tartan? But the diversion didn't last long. A minute at most, then it was back to the ChokkoKrakkles with gusto. Seeing the bird start on his second helping brought me out in sympathy.

Always hungry; who did that remind me of...?

"He seems to have calmed down," I said.

Blossom squeezed her mop into the bucket. "If I'd known it was so easy, all this..." She gestured at the carnage. "...might have been avoided. But it was like a hurricane, the minute he burst out of the shell. Killed off his parents and the other cockerel. Then it was scorched earth till he got what he wanted to eat. After that he started shagging anything that moved—I even thought he was going to try me at one point."

"I always thought it was just an urban myth," I said, "the fast food mob trying to maximise profits with extra legs."

She nodded, leaning on the mop handle. "It might have begun that way, but once a rumour like that starts, all it takes is one mad scientist to think *what a good idea,* and the ball starts rolling."

"A mad scientist like Emily Curzon?"

She nodded, grimly. "Hazlett Humane's been trying to create a four-legged chicken for years, the big companies have slipped them millions for research. We'd even heard rumours they were

244

experimenting on pushing the envelope further, tampering with the DNA to make the mutation's meat addictive. But the problem's always been evidence. When our contact inside said he'd finally found it in the files, there was no option but a raid."

"Did you get it? The evidence?"

Blossom shook her head, then smiled. "But what clever Libby did manage to get was a spreadsheet which proves once and for all just how much the companies have been shelling out. The papers will love that." She nodded across at the giant cockerel. "And Cockzilla there is the only other proof we need."

As I joined her in gazing out at the huge bird, now looking round for a likely recipient to satiate his other appetite, I found myself in awe at the scope and cunning of the Bad Lad's ambition.

Turbocharging the fast food industry...

Genetic engineering creates the template, hell maximises it, greed makes it unstoppable. The price of chicken falls to almost nothing, and if it's addictive...

It was a drug dealer's dream. A nation—perhaps even an entire world—of craving-driven zombies, serviced by Elmer Blick's ready-made distribution network.

Eyes still on Cockzilla, I sat back. So had we won? Had we managed to sabotage it all? Or did last night's approach to me on the Cobb mean The Bad Lad still thought there was a way to salvage his plan? I got up.

"My turn for mop duty," I said. I brought a sleeve up to my nose. "And then, if you don't mind, I'll use your shower. If I don't deglop myself soon—"

I stopped. Barnaby was standing on the step, holding his cap upside down. He came in and put it down on the table, carefully.

We looked.

Nestling in it was an egg, exactly the same shade of yellow as Cockzilla's comb.

*

Blossom's voice was incredulous. "The cockerel impregnates the hen, three days later we get a fertile egg, three weeks after that a

245

chick." She paused. "And you're telling me..."

"That's right," Barnaby replied. "Started giving them all a seeing to this morning, eggs this afternoon."

We all shared the silence. Finally, Blossom lifted the yellow egg from the cap. As she peered at it, Barnaby's voice came again.

"The good news is, it's not fertile. None of the others is either, I've checked about a dozen, now." He nodded at the cockerel. "The big boy," he went on, "would appear to be shooting blanks."

Blossom's look of relief lasted a second, then clouded over. "Do we know if that's always going to be the case?" she asked.

Again, silence. Barnaby shook his head.

"I can't say definitively," he said, "I'll keep checking. But in my opinion you might not need to worry too much about that side of things."

"Why?" I asked.

He stared out at the cockerel. "Cockzilla's scary, real science fiction, but he's also real old school, a proper throwback." Admiration crept into his voice. "A complete tyrant with his brood, but he takes care of them as well. Even killed a couple of foxes on the way round, I found the corpses. The thing is, though..."

He gave a sad smile. Somehow, I knew what was coming.

"...look at the tartan. It's already fading. I've got a feeling he's not going to be with us for long."

*

In the end, there was only one place for him.

Scrapper and I padded round the field at Briggs Rare Breeds Farm, behind Libby and Barnaby. They were pushing Cockzilla along in an old dairy handcart. I'd fibbed to Libby, told her the big cockerel had been brought in by one of the farmers over by Pigs Dangling for investigation. Cockerel and girl had become mates, which was still making me a tad uneasy, just in case it triggered some part of her 'dream'. She had, after all, been present at her new pal's conception.

"So the thing is, Libby, the human genome's a very complex phenomenon. We've only just started trying to understand it. It'll take years for us to get to the bottom..."

Libs wasn't hearing a word Barnaby was saying, but she was gazing at him as though he was the second coming. He was the blond god she'd exchanged glances with at the Golf Club dance. Poor old Blossom, I thought; what price the lock of hair now...?

Scrapper's voice came from my side. "The younglings will couple," he said. "Soon."

"I agree," I replied.

"And the Cage Destroyer's daughter?"

So he knew. Well, well... What were his thoughts on it, I wondered. A loud lowing from across the fence ended the conversation.

Calgacus. No trace of green today; he was happy. Cockzilla responded with a raucous cackle. They'd become friends as well, content in each other's company. Sweet, really...

Libby and Barnaby shared a smile. The cockerel hopped on to the fence, then flapped down to the bull's side and looked back at Libby. As she waved goodbye, I saw that his tartan plumage was now almost invisible. I felt a lump in my throat. How much longer...? Scrapper and I watched bull and bird amble off together like Laurel and Hardy.

"Strange times," he said, drily. "Farewell, Changeling. I wish you wisdom."

"Farewell, old friend. I wish you peace."

In seconds, he was gone. Tail up, I began padding back towards the main house.

And the Cage Destroyer's daughter.

*

Blossom Turl was impeccably turned out, every inch the society fashion plate, Moschinoed, Manoloed and made-up to perfection. She was standing on the balcony, orange cocktail in hand, watching Barnaby and Libby laughing as they crossed the field.

"Help yourself," she said, tonelessly.

I lifted the half empty pitcher and poured. Eyes still on the field, she broke the silence.

"I'd say I've got three choices, wouldn't you?"

The voice was more than slightly slurred. I took a sip of the drink; no wonder, ninety per cent vodka...

"I could have a real tantrum."

"Always an option," I said, remembering my exit from Cadisham police station. "Ultimately useless, but cathartic."

She nodded. "Or I could just stand here," she said, "and get totally pissed. Bladdered, I believe that's the phrase. Rat-arsed." She emptied her glass and refilled it. "Or I could just pretend she never existed." She turned to me. "What do you think?"

For once in my five-hundred-year life, I had no idea what to say. Her voice came again, curious.

"How's it going with my dad, by the way? Bedded him yet?"

I hesitated, but she would have to know sooner or later.

"It would seem," I said, grandly, "that neither of us is going to achieve bodily gratification. He's taken up with Libby's mum."

She clapped a scarlet-nailed hand over her mouth, but she couldn't stifle the giggle. Suddenly, we were both guffawing with laughter.

"Ms Turl—"

She held up a commanding hand. "I think..."

I waited. She knocked back the drink in one.

"...you may call me Blossom."

Her legs went. I caught her just before I could tell her to call me Sammy.

*

Outside the Angel's, I got out of the MG, thinking about Libby.

Unscathed?

I was pretty sure she was. In the field at Briggs Rare Breeds, I'd deliberately stopped myself from probing how deeply new love had struck; there was time enough for all that. Everything should go slowly for Libby now, for a while, at least. In a few weeks, I'd take her to see her mum and Jonathan, treat her to a proper feast of the food she loved. I'd never persuade Mike to come, I knew, but that was understandable—and there was no way I'd try to manipulate him or force him.

I checked my watch; I had just enough time to buy George and Rita a drink before Beth arrived. She was due at the end of her shift with an update on Rab. It sounded like he was going down for a very long time, and on the phone she'd sounded excited—a commendation was being talked about. No doubt a river of gin was in prospect. I'd do my bit.

And for once, the world didn't look too bad. I pulled the key from the lock, then remembered the Muscadet I'd bought for the flat. I walked round to the boot.

"Sammy."

I turned.

Glenn.

Dishevelled, unshaven, dejected... Were those tear tracks on his cheeks? What was this? I moved towards him, then stopped.

Glenn...

Calmly, I unlocked the boot. The Muscadet was lukewarm. I took the bottle out and tossed it to him.

"Catch."

He did—and looked at me, mystified.

"Sammy, what on earth—"

My eyes stayed on the bottle.

It didn't freeze or shatter.

I turned back and brought out the wheel brace. It was one of the four-armed ones, cross-shaped.

I held it up in front of him. Nothing happened, other than a deepening of his puzzled look. I lobbed it at him. He caught it in his free hand, staring at me as though I was utterly crazy.

"I just wanted to tell you," he blurted out. "Sonja's left me."

My smile came, slowly.

If I'd been cat, I'd have purred.

The Author

BRIAN McNEILL was born in 1950 in Falkirk, Scotland, and has long been acclaimed as one of the most creative forces in his homeland's traditional music. In 1989, not content with his roles as performer, composer, songwriter, music producer, teacher, musical director and band leader, he added novelist to his resumé with *The Busker*. His manic schedule in the eighties meant that most of the book was written on aeroplanes. A second novel, *To Answer The Peacock*, based on the same character, the rootless drifter and street musician Alex Fraser, appeared in 1995. *...In The Grass*, featuring shape-shifting detective Sammy Knox, arrived in 2006. The next two instalments of the Busker series, *No Easy Eden* and *The Hawk That Swoops*, are now published both as eBooks and in paperback, as is his 2020 novel about America, *The 90th Kill*. His first collection of shorter fiction, *The Horseman's Word and other stories*, also came out in 2020.

His audio visual shows, *The Back O' The North Wind*, about Scottish emigration to America, and the sequel, *The Baltic Tae Byzantium*, which explores the influence of the Scots in Europe, have won wide critical acclaim. His continuing connection with America's Lone Star State led to him being created an honorary Texan in 1998, and in 2017 he was inducted into the Scottish Traditional Music Hall Of Fame.

From 2001 to 2007 Brian was Head of Scottish Music at the Royal Scottish Academy of Music and Drama. In 2012 his home town of Falkirk honoured him by carving in stone two lines of his song, *The Lads O' The Fair*, at a viewpoint overlooking the town.

A Note from Brian

Thanks for reading ...IN A CHINA SHOP. I hope you enjoyed it and if you did, I'd love to know what you thought of it. If you wish, you can send a review to:

www.brianmcneill.co.uk

If you want to stay updated about any of my fiction—or about any of the music I make—please go to the website above and join my newsletter list. Members receive one at least four times a year.

The current list of my books is as follows.

*

THE BUSKER
Book 1 of the *Busker* Series

Alex Fraser is a rootless drifter who lives by playing Scotland's traditional music on the street. He makes his home wherever his fiddle might earn him a few coins. He's a man hiding from life, haunted by the death of his wife, which he caused. After serving his sentence in Scotland, he decides to try his luck in Europe.

In Switzerland he befriends another busker—Max, an old accordionist. Max tells him a story, a puzzle rooted in the Spanish Civil War. It's a tale of kindness and brutality, involving a German intelligence unit, a rescued child, a painting and a huge inheritance. Max, dying, charges Alex with solving the puzzle.

The maelstrom of violence and greed he uncovers is byzantine, daunting and ruthless. It pursues him across a continent, makes him confront love again, and ultimately forces him to believe in his own worth as a human being.

...a fast-moving thriller in the Hitchcock mould, sending its title character, Alex Fraser, on a desperate chase around Europe pursued by both the police and a ruthless gang of killers determined to prevent its hero uncovering a secret that goes back to the brutal Spanish Civil War incident which opens the book. Fraser, a loner with secrets of his own, makes an interesting hero, while Brian provides enough European atmosphere, intrigue and adventure, including a tense escape scene over the pre-reform East German border, to make for an exciting read. ...a fine debut novel.

Dundee Peoples' Journal.

You can buy *The Busker* either as an eBook or a paperback on Amazon.

*

TO ANSWER THE PEACOCK
Book 2 of the *Busker* Series

Alex Fraser is in Rennes, in Brittany. While busking, he's accosted by a mad beggar. The episode ends with his violin in pieces and him being worked over in a police station.

But it gets worse. Suddenly he's a target. Why? And why would anyone want to steal his clapped-out car? Or pursue him at night through the port of Concarneau?

Or plant a priceless antique violin in his battered fiddle case, in place of his own wrecked instrument?

The mysteries intensify against the web of conspiracy spun round Nathalie Gwernig, the beautiful daughter of a dead Breton nationalist hero. Torn between his growing love for her and his need to find his own fiddle, Alex finds himself unravelling the hypocrisies of an English stately home, fighting ancient rural cruelty, and being pursued by both authority and a deadly political extremist.

Finally, his quest takes him back to Scotland. It forces him to revisit his past, before ending in a bloody confrontation on a Hebridean island.

It's a breathless thriller that gives us an insight into the mind of the musician, as well as showing how a skilled writer can pace a plot... ...The novel explores the themes of Breton and Scottish nationalism, and the present state of the Gaelic language. The story is more than the fight to retrieve a lost musical instrument: it is about injustice on a wider scale and the need for cultural harmony, without the violence that sometimes attends political causes. Some of the freedom fighters in this novel are sinister characters, who have allowed their personal prejudices to become entangled with their politics... ...There are Buchanesque overtones in the way that the plot unrolls, and in the way that the principal character defends his honour.

To Answer the Peacock is an exceptionally well crafted story that holds its interest to the end.

The Herald.

You can buy *To Answer The Peacock* either as an eBook or a paperback on Amazon.

*

NO EASY EDEN

Book 3 of the *Busker* Series

In Germany, Alex is given a lift by Abigail Eve, a black US Air Force captain. They stop at a fast food restaurant in the town of Rothenburg. A few minutes later, three junkies come in. After creating a scene, the kids run off, followed by a concerned nun, and then as Alex and Abigail leave, a bomb explodes, killing her and hospitalising him. He wakes to find Gunther Klein, a reporter, at his bedside.

After Alex is discharged, Klein investigates. Who was the

nun? Why were the junkies in the restaurant? To keep Alex safe, Klein sends him to his ex-wife Sigi's family, but when Alex discovers Sigi is part of what happened—and that the US military want to arrest him—he flees. In Rothenburg railway station, trying to make the price of a ticket to anywhere with his fiddle, he meets an elderly black man. It's Abigail's father, jazz trumpeter Luther Eve, come to see where his daughter died.

With Luther's help, Alex escapes to the old East Germany, where he uncovers a plot between ex-STASI officers, a cynical American soldier and an ex-terrorist who has assumed a startling new identity.

Drugs, misplaced idealism and family betrayals come to a head in Hamburg's red light district, where Alex must make the hardest choice of his life.

You can buy *No Easy Eden* either as an eBook or a paperback on Amazon.

*

THE HAWK THAT SWOOPS
Book 4 of the *Busker* Series

Now a witness in the counterfeit drugs case which began in *No Easy Eden*, Alex is in Washington DC. He's had a letter from his father; his mother is gravely ill. Can he find an uncle he's never heard of, in Appalachia? Due to fly out in a few hours, his visa expired, Alex knows it's impossible.

A hotel bar fracas with a teenager brings him up against the girl's aunt, supermodel Rose Vannier. Then, while he's at Rose's side in a taxi rank, a boy on a scooter tries to kill her. Alex tackles him, breaking the boy's neck. No police, Rose insists. Why? What is she hiding? The idea of American authority's reaction to his criminal record panics Alex into agreeing.

At Rose's Virginia farm, he meets her entourage. They're suspicious of him. Is he in danger? When a rattlesnake is planted in his bag, he decides to run. He steals a van, only to find Lou, the girl who started the whole thing, hidden in the back.

The busker and the streetwise kid bond—but then she's abducted, and Alex's van is rigged to crash. Injured as a result, he only just escapes on a freight train.

An elderly, blind Appalachian fiddler, Jane McClintock, nurses him back to health, and her humanity gives him the strength to go on, to probe the long list of convoluted lies around Rose and Lou—and to solve the sad and terrifying mystery of his own long-lost uncle.

You can buy *The Hawk That Swoops* either as an eBook or a paperback on Amazon.

*

...IN THE GRASS

Book 1 of *The Sammy Knox* Series

In the deceptively sleepy Cotswold town of Cadisham, there's mischief afoot.

When Lady Letitia Moresby, the society stripper, finds that her python, Justin, has been stolen, she calls in Sammy Knox, glamorous private eye and witch's Familiar. Sammy, who can change with ease between cat and human, is, as usual, broke, so she takes the case with alacrity. With the help of her teenage charge Libby (a trainee witch, but she doesn't know it yet) and Scrapper, a grizzled escapee from an animal testing laboratory, she begins to investigate.

The trail, which leads her through zoos, gravel pits, scrapyards, accountants' cupboards and assorted bedrooms, involves a resolute bunch of rescued felines, a languid tiger with ambivalent motives, a venal tax inspector with an individual take on rubber stamping, and a sweet but dim bloodhound.

Who would have suspected the leafy Cotswolds of harbouring so many dark secrets...?

Sometimes we like to mention the existence of people who shouted loudly and without getting tired „over here" when talents were distributed. Ex-Battlefield Band musician Brian McNeill is one of these people, but we don't want to use up precious space by enumerating all of his talents. Suffice it to say that writing is one of them... ...In The Grass is full of speed, funny and thrilling: highly recommendable.

Folker.

Sensuous, cunning super-sleuth Sammy Knox is unmatched in the detective genre. Brian McNeill's brilliantly crafted story and fantastic cast of characters will transport you to another dimension from the very first page. Pure magic!

Carol Hird.

You can buy *...In The Grass* either as an eBook or a paperback on Amazon.

*

THE 90TH KILL

All the teenage Samuel Cadogan ever wanted to do was draw — but after the death of his father, a Pennsylvania coal miner, his family explodes in a maelstrom of child abuse and violence, and he finds himself on the wrong side of the law.

He runs. For the next six years he supports himself as a sidewalk artist in Boston — and then circumstances force him to flee even further. In the US military, under his new name of Lemuel Brecon, he discovers he has one outstanding talent. He's a world-class sniper, a natural killer.

Dishonourably discharged after serving in Iraq, burned out and barely existing on the street, he's approached by two high-ranking and high-minded ex-officers who want the re-election of a corrupt and controversial president stopped. They know Brecon's talents, and they lure him into their plot with the possibility of revenge against those responsible for his family's disintegration. Finally seduced by the promise that they will find his missing sister, he agrees to be part of their scheme. But for all their professed principles, the way these officers manipulate him is as merciless as it is cold.

This is a story about the cynicism and ruthlessness of America's elites, about the intertwined nature of its political process and its gun culture—and above all, it's about the stubborn courage of individuals and their determination to resist, to fight for their humanity as the juggernaut of American power does its pitiless best to grind them down.

You can buy *THE 90TH KILL* either as an eBook or a paperback on Amazon.

*

THE HORSEMAN'S WORD AND OTHER STORIES

A collection of shorter fiction, based mainly on the speech and dialect of Brian's Scottish lowland home town of Falkirk.

1913. Love, loss, inheritance, religion and magic; the simmering tensions not far below the surface of a lowland farm...
1958. A courageous schoolgirl's simultaneous discovery of her heroine's surprising secret and her own morality...
1966. The rough community of a working class pub coming together to protect one of their own from exposure...
1967. A teenage boy's complicated coming of age between bedroom and building site...
1972. A student whose moment of rebellion teaches him the painful difference between slogan and reality...
2016. A wronged and implacable cat taking revenge on mankind, only to discover the real depth of human cruelty...

Includes a glossary of Scottish words and phrases.

You can buy *The Horseman's Word and other stories* either as an eBook on Amazon, or as a paperback from Brian's website.

The paperback is also available from Songdog Verlag in Switzerland.

In English:

http://songdog.ch/buch-detail/the-horsemans-word-and-other-stories.html

In German:

http://songdog.ch/buch-detail/the-horsemans-word-schottische-storys.html

An audiobook, read by Brian, is also in preparation.